A STRANGER
LIES THERE

THOMAS DUNNE BOOKS
ST. MARTIN'S MINOTAUR
NEW YORK

A STRANGER
LIES THERE

STEPHEN SANTOGROSSI

THOMAS DUNNE BOOKS.
An imprint of St. Martin's Press.

A STRANGER LIES THERE. Copyright © 2007 by Stephen Santogrossi. All rights reserved. Printed in the United States of America. No part of this book may be used or reproduced in any manner whatsoever without written permission except in the case of brief quotations embodied in critical articles or reviews. For information, address St. Martin's Press, 175 Fifth Avenue, New York, N.Y. 10010.

www.thomasdunnebooks.com
www.minotaurbooks.com

Photography by Inna Kleyman

ISBN-10: 0-312-36441-5
ISBN-13: 978-0-312-36441-0

First Edition: May 2007

10 9 8 7 6 5 4 3 2 1

For Ronda, who brought this stranger to life

ACKNOWLEDGMENTS

Thanks to: Michael Murray, Ruth Cavin, Barbara L. Taylor, Melody Hampton, Sharleen Bazeghi, Reed Dinsmore, Toni Plummer, Tanisha White, Lisa Santamaria, and my family, especially my wife, Ronda Hampton, and my daughter, Allison.

A STRANGER
LIES THERE

1972

They let loose with the fire hoses around eight, two hours after it started. Somebody shot a flare gun into a tree and the dry pine needles ignited, turning the tree into a column of fire. The hard, horizontal rain suddenly stopped as the water was redirected toward the flames. They crackled and warped, licking the night sky. Glowing embers dropped like bombs onto the roof of the administration building.

I knew what it must've looked like from above: an anthill that had been disturbed, everyone scattering in all directions, eyes wild, faces lit orange and white by the flames and the floodlights over the area. I was almost to the edge of the mall, where the trampled grass ended. It was getting harder to avoid the billy clubs and the men in riot gear. The *woosh* of the water cannons couldn't drown out the blaring megaphones. A metallic screech pierced through, impossibly loud, and I turned to see the microphone stand onstage topple over. An amplified thump silenced the feedback. Then the water hit the electronic equipment, on loan from the music department, and sparks exploded, as if in slow motion, like fireworks from a great distance. Blue-white flames joined the orange ones above. The sound system began shorting out, a steady buzzing sound gaining volume. To my left, I caught sight of Turret fighting his way through the crowd before someone with a handmade sign staggered into him. The reinforced posterboard got him above the eye, drawing blood. Then the lights went out.

A half mile away, I finally reached Rowland House and started up the stairs to the second floor. The dormitory was nestled in a pine forest on the other side of a wooden footbridge spanning a small creek on the eastern edge of the UC Santa Cruz campus. Most nights you could smell pine needles and wild berries, and the ocean if the wind was right.

But not tonight. Tonight smoke was in the air, a physical manifestation of the rebellion that had taken over. A warm glow spread into the western sky, back where hundreds of students still hadn't gotten it out of their systems. It could have been a football game, except for the sirens and the mechanized voices from the megaphones, and I thought I heard glass breaking too. A helicopter suddenly streaked overhead, blades *thwacking*, heading for the vortex. I watched its spotlight recede to a point, then continued up the steps in my damp clothes.

There weren't many people around. I was one of the few that had made it back, so far. Ellen's apartment was three down, and I found the door slightly open. Joni Mitchell drifted out, tranquil and serene. As I stepped inside, the record skipped and stuttered, spewing gibberish. I walked over and lifted the needle.

"Hello?" Ellen called out from the bedroom as I drifted toward it. "I'll be right out," she said.

I stopped in front of her open door. She was lifting her damp shirt over her head. Her breasts were soft and milky white, nipples still hard from the cold water we'd been doused with. I found myself staring, unable to look away. Ellen smiled. I took a step closer, heart pounding. Still smiling, she gently closed the door.

"There are some towels in the bathroom," Ellen said from behind it.

I didn't bother. Went back into the living room, then the kitchen, where I found a beer in the fridge. It was next to some sprouts that were a little too green and a carton of chocolate milk. After opening it, I walked to the window and took a look outside. The beer made me shiver and I put it on the windowsill. Outside in the courtyard a few people had started a bonfire, but it was only to dry off. They danced around the flames in a shamanistic display, enraptured by the heat.

Ellen had come into the room behind me. "Where is everybody?" she asked.

I shrugged. "Lost 'em," I said, turning around. "Just like you."

Ellen smiled again and went into the kitchen. Picked up a glass from the counter, and after dumping what was in it into the sink, filled it from the tap. She'd changed into another T-shirt with a suede vest over it and blue jeans with butterfly patches sewn into the fabric.

"It was wild out there," she said after taking a few gulps, standing there in the kitchen. Her long silky hair shone in the overhead light. It was parted in the middle and secured with a beaded Indian headband.

I turned back to the window and watched them dance out by the fire. "It was bound to happen," I said, picking up the beer. "Probably worse up front, wasn't it?" Ellen had made her way through the crowd as it went on, drawn by the words coming from the stage. Rory and Greg and I had hung back together, taking it all in, joining in the chanting that rose up every now and then. Glenn was about to follow Ellen, but he'd glanced at me for a second and changed his mind.

"Nice to see everybody so fired up about it," Ellen said. She took a seat on the couch in the window's reflection.

Earlier today, the committee on presidential debates had denied the third party candidate, Tom Duncan, a place in the upcoming televised debate. Called him a fringe candidate with no serious stake in the campaign. He was against the war, for civil rights, and liable to shoot his mouth off at all the wrong times. But Duncan was passionate and idealistic, with a huge following among the college-age segment of the population. In other words, he was scary as hell to the political establishment.

The cops had shown up almost immediately, sparks in a tinderbox, and things had escalated quickly. Which was exactly what they'd wanted, I supposed, all for the evening news and middle-class America—youthful rebellion run amok.

Ellen got up and switched on the TV. As expected, the sounds of protest blended with what was still going on outside.

"We made the news," she said enthusiastically.

No kidding, I thought, seeing Turret appear in the courtyard alone. Passing the bonfire, he stopped and did a little dance before moving on. I could've sworn he was mocking the others, who seemed oblivious.

"Glenn's back," I said as he reached the stairs. Ellen jumped up to meet him at the door.

"Oh, what happened?" she asked when she saw the blood above his eye, reaching up to put her hand on it.

"Motherfuckers," Turret muttered, striding past her into the kitchen. Ellen followed him, found a towel, which she proceeded to wet, then started dabbing his forehead with it.

"Goddamn pigs with sticks," Turret explained. He leaned back against the sink while Ellen tended to him.

I knew he was lying about what had happened. That it wasn't the cops with their billy clubs, but a fellow protester with a cardboard sign. I kept quiet anyway.

Greg came in then, running his hand over his wet hair, those water hoses not sparing anyone.

"Any sign of Rory?" Turret immediately asked him.

"Smoking a bone with 1A," he replied, which didn't surprise me.

They always had the choice stuff down there, and Rory never could pass up an offer.

"'Cause we got some serious talking to do, you guys," Turret said, still in the kitchen with Ellen.

When she finished with him, Turret went to the refrigerator. "Anyone want a beer?" he asked, looking inside. Before anybody could answer, he took one out and closed the door. Put the bottle in the opener on the edge of the countertop and smacked his palm against it. The cap fell and rattled around on the floor. Turret ignored it. He guzzled a third of the beer and came over to sit on the couch next to Greg. Ellen sprawled in a beanbag chair, one eye on Turret, the other on the TV. I stayed standing near the window.

"Look at those fuckers," Turret said, shaking his head, referring to the authorities trying to restore order.

Greg nodded. "City statute says we have the right to assemble peacefully–"

"You think that's going to stop them?" Turret interrupted impatiently. "I been telling you guys, we gotta do it another way. All our flower-power, peace and love b.s. ain't gonna get it done, man. They just laugh at us. Right before they smash our heads against the wall."

Ellen winced but then nodded. Greg just stared at him, uncharacteristically quiet. Normally the most talkative one in the room, Greg tended to speak in a rapid-fire stream of words, like he was afraid his audience would lose interest if he didn't get it out all at once. A political science major with a short afro and almond-shaped eyes, he aspired to one day open a political consulting business. I knew him through Ellen, who'd met Greg in one of her philosophy classes.

We watched TV quietly for a few minutes. The newscaster talked about how many arrests had been made. Ellen closed her eyes, seemed satisfied that the injustice done to her candidate had inspired such outrage on campus. A petite blonde with emerald eyes and a dreamy smile, she'd roped Greg and Rory and me into running flyers and going door to door for Duncan, who had an office downtown. Ellen was drifting toward a sociology major. I'd settled on history, with no particular emphasis yet. We'd also met on campus. I'd been trying to pursue something with her since the semester started, but she'd casually brushed me off without actually saying "no." Then we'd met Turret.

This was in the student union bar near the end of last semester, right after Duncan's campaign speech in the university gymnasium. Ellen had been flushed and glowing, excited by Duncan's growing support, and the place was wall-to-wall people all talking about the address. We were in the back near the pool tables. A neon Hamm's beer sign lit Ellen's face, coloring her pale blond hair softly. She'd just convinced us to help out on the campaign, and bought us all a round in honor of our pledge. She raised her drink, a sparkle in her eyes, and said, "To victory," as we clinked glasses.

"A better world," Greg offered.

Rory was drunk. "To splitting the curl."

I'd hesitated. "To victory," I finally said.

I remembered the crack of the cue balls then, turning to see them scatter on the green felt of one of the tables. When I turned back, someone else had joined our group.

I'd never seen him before, though he stood out pretty well. A few years older than us, late twenties or so. He wore a white button-down shirt and pressed black jeans, shined patent leather boots. Medium height. Hair long on top and short on the sides, long sideburns almost reaching his jawline. Quick, intelligent eyes behind John Lennon glasses, and a forceful, confident way of speaking that made you want to listen.

He'd started by asking Ellen if she wanted a drink, correctly assuming her leadership role, then launched into a debate with her and Greg about the politics of the counterculture, whether we'd ever be accepted by the mainstream establishment. Turret thought then, and still did, that our methods were all wrong. That we should try sneaking in through the back door, right under their noses. Ellen, challenged by his viewpoints, took to him immediately and welcomed him into our circle.

Then Turret disappeared for a few weeks. Time to "check us out," he said. Later on, I wondered why we hadn't done the same for him. But we started meeting a few times a week, and continued through the summer. Always at Ellen's place, which had also been checked out. Turret was real careful, agents and listening devices everywhere. The get-togethers had to be spur of the moment. Ellen would get the word from Turret and track each of us down in person.

A few weeks ago, he'd told us his idea. Each meeting since then had been on the same subject.

Tonight would be no exception. Down below, the bonfire had been abandoned, the flames starting to die down. I heard someone coming up the steps, then stop halfway.

"That stuff is so good, it oughtta be illegal," Rory drawled in a cracked, mellow voice to his new friends in 1A. "Next one's on me." Then he appeared in the doorway, held on to the jamb to steady himself before veering toward the last spot on the couch, between Greg and Turret. He sat down heavily, bouncing the cushions.

Turret scowled and got up. Went into the kitchen and put his empty bottle on the sink.

"So what's going on?" Rory asked casually. He was a lanky surfer with sun-bleached hair that was always tangled and a permanent grin on his face. Rory knew Ellen from the beach boardwalk where she went to sketch sometimes. Laid-back and relaxed, he had off-beat political views and no visible means of support.

Turret came back with a kitchen chair, put it next to the couch and sat down. Leaned forward with his hands folded. "You guys thought any more about what I said?" he asked. I wondered if Turret had planned to bring this up tonight, or whether he was taking advantage of the situation outside. Fan the flames while they were hot.

Nobody said anything for a moment, then Greg spoke up.

"You're talking about a bank robbery. I thought we were committed to nonviolent protest. Peace, man. People could end up dead this way."

Turret put his head down, shook his head before speaking. Since meeting us, he'd let his hair get longer and shaggier, and right now it was wet and hanging in his face. "A lot of our friends have already died, fighting in a war nobody wants. How many will it take before we wake up?" He looked at each of us in turn. "And look what our peaceful protests got us today. Cops coming in and instigating, making us look bad. It's us versus them right now, and they got the power. But if we try and beat them at their own game . . ."

"And how are we supposed to do that?" Greg asked. "How does robbing a bank get us anywhere?"

"I told you. We don't keep the money. It goes directly, in small chunks, to Duncan's campaign. Give him a leg up, buy TV time, legitimize his candidacy. That's what it takes nowadays."

"You think a little cash is gonna solve everything?" Greg asked. "I seriously doubt it."

The rest of us kept quiet, watching Turret and Greg go back and forth.

"Maybe not right away," Turret answered. "But it's a process. Duncan probably won't win this time, but the more familiar he is to people, the better chance he'll have in four years. Right now, the only time anybody sees him is when those stuffed shirts on TV choose to cover him. And when is that? When there's a bunch of hippies chanting his name and burning flags. They already won't let him on the debates. But if he can get out there on his own terms, buying ads . . . that's a whole different ballgame."

"I don't know, man," Rory said. He coughed loudly, hit his chest a few times to clear it. "A Dillinger? Sounds pretty radical to me."

"Look," Turret responded, "our generation has tried a lot of different things, without much effect. Protests and marches don't do it. Blowing up draft board offices and recruiting centers just turns people against us. We wanna make real changes, we gotta do it from the inside. By getting the good guys into office, into power. Like it or not, that takes money. A lot of money. This is one way to do it."

Turret stood up, on a roll now. He paced back and forth, enumerating his points with his hands. "Think about it you guys. The bank I'm talking about finances the Rand Corporation, one of the biggest war machines in the country. Who do you think is electing the politicians, so they can continue selling guns to the very people they're putting into office? Not you and me, brother. It's companies like Rand and the bankers that finance them who are in bed with those fuckers in Washington. It's blood money, man. It deserves to be taken, to get someone like Duncan elected so he can fight for the causes we believe in."

"What about all the people who've put their savings in that bank? What do we say to them when their money is gone?" Greg asked.

"It's all insured Greg, you know that," Ellen answered. "They won't lose a dime, the government will pay it all back." She smiled and turned to Turret. "Far as I'm concerned, that's another plus to this idea. We'll be sticking our hands in big government's pockets."

Turret agreed. "That's right. This is win-win all the way. We hit the warmongers where it hurts, help get a few of our comrades into office, and make the government pay for it all at the same time! It couldn't be more perfect! All we gotta do is have the balls to get it done, to fight for what we believe in." He paused for emphasis. "You guys have what it takes? Or you gonna let others do your fighting for you?"

Things got quiet. Turret sat back down, letting us chew on everything he'd said. On TV the riot continued unabated. We watched an armored vehicle clip a protester, who, luckily, was able to get up and limp away. The newscaster said the school had made an announcement barring all future protests or campaign speeches on campus, and that all classes through the end of the semester had been canceled, as a girl on-screen was beaten bloody by a cop. The baton didn't stop even after she fell to the ground.

"Looks like Kent State all over again," Ellen said, shaking her head, then turned to Turret. "I'm in," she promised, and the admiration in her eyes when she looked at him nearly broke my heart.

"Dude," Rory said, addressing Greg. "We talk the talk, we should walk the walk." Then, to Turret: "Count me in."

Greg shook his head slowly, trying to convince himself.

"We get a free pass here in college," Ellen said to him. "You feel good about that?"

Tense silence, before Greg stood up. "I can't do it, guys. Not this way." He started for the door.

"Hey Greg," Turret said sternly. "You wouldn't sell out your friends, would you?"

"They know I wouldn't do that," Greg replied, making clear where Turret stood with him. He left without looking back, closed the door quietly.

Turret wasn't happy. "Can we trust him?" Frustration wrinkled his forehead.

"Of course," Ellen answered. "Greg's stand-up."

"He still live in the same place?" Turret asked.

"I'll talk to him, Glenn. Don't worry," Ellen said.

Turret held her gaze without blinking, went over and looked out the window. Then he turned to me and spoke, hands on his hips, voice tight. "That leaves you."

I wanted to get up and follow Greg out the door. I wished I had his courage. Ellen regarded me with a doubtful expression, like she expected me to disappoint her. The fact that she wasn't trying to convince me said a lot.

"When do we do it?" I asked, and Ellen's warm smile almost erased the doubts in my mind.

Turret came over to shake my hand. "You're doing the right thing," he said. Then he sat down next to Rory and laid out the plan.

We'd do it on Friday. The bank would have lots of cash on hand for payroll checks. Three of us would go into the bank armed, the other would wait in the car with the motor running. Pretty standard, it seemed. Except we couldn't decide who got to stay outside. We finally settled on passing a joint around and the one who killed it would do the driving.

It went around twice and got back to me. The joint was hot and short in my fingers, the smoke sweet and dense in my mouth before filling up my lungs.

Then the final burning ember fell onto my shirtfront and winked out.

"Hope you can drive fast," Turret told me with a grin.

Friday, early afternoon in downtown San Francisco. Fog just starting to lift from the city, white clouds lit by the hazy sun drifting lazily up above. The air was cool and moist, though I was sweating behind the wheel of the car, watching the entrance of the bank across the street in my rearview mirror. I looked at my watch: only a few minutes had gone by but I was starting to get nervous.

Suddenly, the pedestrians on the sidewalk in front of the bank froze, jerking their heads toward the entrance. Then they scattered in all directions, hunched over in fear, and I wasn't sure if I'd heard the muffled report of gunfire.

Moments later Turret burst through the front doors brandishing his weapon. He dashed across the street toward me, eyes blazing with adrenaline, and that's when I knew everything had gone wrong.

That morning we'd gathered once again at Ellen's place to prepare for the robbery. Everyone had a gun except me, deadly-looking automatics that Turret had acquired a little too easily from an unknown source. His ready access to them made me wonder about the type of people he was associated with. We'd never learned much about Turret's background; he'd suddenly just appeared in our lives, confident he could convince us to take such an enormous risk for a cause he professed to be loyal to. Now, far too late to say anything about it, I got a funny feeling about him.

As he went over the final details, I glanced at Ellen. Grim-faced and serious, giving Turret her full attention. Rory looked more bleary-eyed than usual, constantly rubbing his forehead and lifting his hands to his temples as if he were in pain.

Turret noticed it too and interrupted himself. "What's the matter, Rory? You didn't smoke too much last night did you? I told you we had to be on for this today. Focused. No drugs." He didn't seem happy.

Rory defended himself. "Nah man, just a little headache. I'll be fine."

"What happened?" I asked, trying to lighten the moment with levity I didn't feel. "You get smacked in the head with your board or something?"

Nobody laughed. To my surprise Rory confirmed it, shaking his head at the memory. "Wiped out pretty good this morning. But that wave was worth it. You shoulda seen it."

"You went surfing?" Turret asked, miffed. "This morning?"

Rory nodded. "Crack of dawn. Same as every morning. Something wrong with that?"

Turret opened his mouth, seemed to change his mind and closed it. Then started over. "Take a fucking aspirin or something. We gotta concentrate on this."

Ellen raised an eyebrow at Turret's sudden attitude. Rory got up without a word, went into the bathroom and came back with a bottle of aspirin. Popped two of them dry and sat back down.

Turret finished up a few minutes later, tried to be reassuring. "I got it timed out perfect, everybody. Do your jobs right and everything will be fine."

Now he was rushing toward the car alone, finger still on the trigger. He clambered in and tossed the gun in the back, kept the large canvas bag in his lap.

"Fucking go!" he yelled frantically as he slammed the door.

"What about the others?"

"They're not coming. Now step on it!"

I peeled out on the slick pavement, screeching around the corner toward a parking garage a few miles away, where we'd stashed my car–Turret had wanted to ditch the getaway car, a junker with stolen plates, as soon as possible.

"What the hell happened?" I yelled, seized with panic.

"Not right now," Turret barked, looking behind us. "And slow down for Chrissake. We're in the clear."

I eased up on the gas and glanced at Turret, feeling sick. He was still breathing hard, flush with excitement, and didn't seem too broken up that my friends weren't with us.

"What the fuck happened back there, goddamnit!" I persisted.

He wouldn't meet my eyes, evading the question. "It doesn't matter now. Just drive."

I did as I was told. A few minutes later we pulled into the parking garage, a five-story structure that Turret had picked out carefully. The entrances were served by automatic ticket machines with an all-day flat rate, and the exits were unmanned, perfect for our purposes. It never filled up, according to Turret, and the top two floors were invariably empty. As a precaution, my car was on the fifth floor, away from the elevator to avoid company when we returned.

"Fuck!" Turret said under his breath when we reached level five, and I wouldn't know how lucky I'd gotten until later.

There was one other car in addition to mine up here, a VW bug parked a few spaces down with a man and woman inside. They were making out. They'd obviously wanted some privacy and watched with annoyance as we approached.

"What should I do?" I asked.

"Act normal. Gimme your keys and drop me off at your car. I'll meet you right below."

I looked at him dumbly, scared out of my mind, and he explained impatiently, "It'll look weird if we both get out and switch cars. Just do it!"

I stopped behind my car and handed him the keys. I could feel the two lovers watching us, waiting for us to leave. Turret got out nonchalantly, duffel bag in hand, and leaned back in after closing the door. "Better make it the third floor. I don't want these idiots noticing this one parked all by itself on their way down. Got it?"

"Yeah." I crept away unhurriedly, drove down two floors, and parked in a crowd of other vehicles. Turret pulled up behind me moments later. I got out and dashed to my car, making the mistake then that saved my life.

"Come on, come on!" Turret urged impatiently, as I climbed in beside him and slammed the door. It echoed loudly in the enclosed garage, along with the screech of rubber on concrete as we sped off.

When we reached the street, Turret shook his head and muttered, "That stupid ass Rory, man."

"What? What the hell happened? Are my friends dead?"

"Maybe. They both went down. That's all I know."

"Shit! How? What went wrong?"

"Fucking Rory. He lost it, man!"

"What the hell does that mean?"

"It was going beautifully. We had everybody on the floor except the vault manager, and she was handing over the cash like her life depended on it. I mean, it was perfect! No one got hysterical, none of those guards tried to be a hero, and I'm watching all that bread going into the bag with one eye and my watch with the other. Next thing I know, Rory's lettin' loose with the bullets, man! All hell broke loose after that. I don't know how I made it out of there alive. But thanks to Rory, that bag is only halfway full."

Two of my friends were probably dead and he was worried about the money. I looked at him with new fear, suddenly wanting to get far away from him.

"When he started shooting, the guards pulled their own weapons. Ellen was, like, frozen. The rent-a-cops might've gotten her, I'm not sure. Rory was already on the floor."

"And you just left them there?" I asked hysterically. "How could you?"

"You weren't there, man. It was like a war zone," he said, getting on the highway toward Santa Cruz. "If I'd stopped to help them none of us would have made it. Including you." He looked at me, frowned. "And it didn't take much coaxing to get you to step on the gas back there."

He was right about that, and I felt like a coward and a traitor for leaving my friends behind. Please God, I thought, let them be alive.

Alone with those dark thoughts, sick with worry and regret, I didn't notice that Turret had pulled off the freeway into a deserted rest area. When he stopped in front of the restrooms I came back to myself.

"What the hell are we doing?" I asked, confused.

Turret didn't respond. Just leaned over the seat and reached for something in back, pushing the bag of money aside impatiently. He stopped suddenly in surprise and our eyes met, and that's when I realized that he'd been going for the gun. The gun that we'd left in the other car in all the confusion.

I was a split second faster than he was and turned to throw open the door, getting one foot on the pavement before he grabbed me and tried to wrestle me back into the car. Cramped by the steering wheel in front of him, he couldn't get a grip on me with both hands. I used my leverage against the doorjamb and the edge of the seat to tear myself away, scraping one side against the open door before landing on the other shoulder on the ground outside. I got up and took off the way we'd come, toward the highway to flag someone down. I looked back. Turret had started around the back of the car, then stopped and pounded his fist angrily on the trunk before scrambling back behind the wheel and screeching away in the opposite direction. When I reached the freeway he was already gone, blending in with the traffic down the road.

I sprinted back to the restroom for the pay phone, frantically searching my pockets for change. Then I realized I didn't need it for an emergency call and hit "0."

My breath was loud in the earpiece before the connection went through. A disinterested voice said, "Operator," and a few seconds later I was talking to the police. I gave them a description of Turret and the car, as well as my own location and a rundown of the crime.

It wasn't until much later the following day, after I'd been arrested, that I found out exactly what had happened. By that time, the robbery was all over the news and a tape from the bank's security cameras had been released. It showed a grainy, black and white view of the lobby and teller counter, but the carnage it depicted was all too clear. Everybody was on the floor. Rory was near the entrance guarding the door. Ellen stood in the opposite corner. Their guns covered the room. A second angle from a different camera showed Turret near the vault urging the attendant to fill the bag quickly. He brandished his weapon threateningly. Suddenly, for no apparent reason, Rory toppled to the floor. His gun went off, spraying the ceiling with automatic weapon-fire, the rounds bursting from the barrel in white flashes before he hit the floor. The guards came up firing, pointing toward Ellen, who seemed to be in shock. Somehow, they both missed her. Turret came rushing forward, gun blazing. One of the guards dove behind a desk and the other one got hit and folded to the floor, blood staining his shirt-front. On his way out Turret leveled his weapon at Ellen and blew her over the desk she'd been standing in front of.

A few seconds later Turret disappeared out the front door. Rory tried to stand, shaking his head dazedly. The guard that dove for cover shot him twice in the chest. Rory didn't move after that.

I told the police that Rory had probably fainted as a result of his surfing mishap earlier that morning.

DESERT

CHAPTER ONE

"Hope you can drive fast."

The dream always ended with those words, reaching through the years in that half-state between sleeping and waking, when my defenses were down. I was used to it, though; had been for quite some time. It brought guilt and an empty feeling in the pit of my stomach, but that Sunday morning, it became more than just a reminder of the mistake I'd made in my youth.

I woke up early, six sharp as usual. No alarm clock from years of regimented wakeup calls. Deirdre had been tossing and turning the last few nights, so I let her sleep. In the kitchen I made some coffee, the special blend I saved for weekends, and while it was brewing, wiped down the counter and rinsed out the mug that I kept on the hook next to the microwave. After checking on Deirdre–still knocked out–I put on some pants and a shirt, then went to get my coffee. I took it out to the front porch, but my first sip stalled halfway to my lips when I realized what I was seeing. Flies don't circle like that around anything that's alive.

My coffee cup dropped from my hand and shattered on the concrete. I stepped over it onto the lawn. Dry grass crackled under my feet, the sound of the insects, like high-tension wires, getting louder as I approached. I stopped. Squatted tentatively. Reached out my hand. But I knew it was no use and pulled it back. Then

Deirdre was there kneeling beside me, nightgown fluttering in the hot morning breeze, cinnamon hair kissing her soft, bare shoulders.

"He looks like you," she said quietly.

My neighbor's timed sprinklers suddenly switched on. The spray misted in the morning sunlight. Rainbows danced like shimmering ghosts.

"Call the cops," I said, standing. Deirdre backed away slowly, hand over her mouth. A wet sob hiccupped out before she turned around and hurried inside. I felt dizzy for a second, and had to steady myself. The sprinklers were a soft counterpoint to the hammering in my ears. I wiped the sweat from my forehead, which felt cold and clammy despite the temperature, like the TB patients that used to come out here to die. At funerals, I never wanted to view the body, laid out and posed in a casket, with too much makeup on. At least the eyes were always closed.

He was lying face up near the edge of the grass, gazing into the clear blue sky. He'd been shot in the side of the head near the temple, a small hole that was slightly elongated, like the bullet entered from an angle. Early twenties or so, wearing a concert T-shirt and faded jeans. Arms in the grass at his sides. Spent dandelions poked from between his fingers.

Deirdre didn't say much when she came back out. "They're coming. They said not to touch anything." She wiped a tear from her cheek roughly, another one replaced it.

"How long?"

A resigned shrug. "Few minutes."

I nodded, looking up and down the street. Still early, nobody around yet. Sirens wavered in the distance, getting closer. Deirdre grabbed my hand and squeezed. She was shivering in the sweltering heat. The flies were buzzing angrily, darting in and out over the body. One of them crawled back and forth over an eyeball. *He's really dead*, I thought, as the sirens reached a fever pitch. Then two patrol cars rounded the corner, shot up the block and made a hard stop behind my car.

Moments later we were in the house with two of the officers.

"You made the call?" Things were moving fast now.

"Yeah. My wife did, actually." The living room seemed small and unbearably hot. They both wore the black, short-sleeved uniforms of the Palm Springs PD, their black leather gunbelts shiny and dangerous. The officer who'd addressed me had his notebook and pen out while the other one was moving slowly about the room, looking around. The bookcase with its collection of counseling and psychology texts stopped him before he moved on. Deirdre watched him, her hands shaking; she could have been one of her strung-out clients.

"Are you okay?" the cop with the notebook, whose nameplate said Tyler, asked her.

Deirdre gave him a look: *there's a dead body on my front lawn*, but didn't voice anything.

"Why don't we sit down," he suggested.

Deirdre took a seat on the couch, switched on the table lamp next to the old photograph of her sister. I sat next to her on the edge of the cushions, leaning forward with my elbows on my knees. I rubbed my hands together nervously.

Tyler didn't move. "Mind if my partner looks around?"

"Looks around? Why? We're the ones that called it in," I pointed out.

"Just routine."

"Routine? I don't understand."

"Look, we just have to cover all the bases. You can say no."

"Go ahead," Deirdre told him, putting a hand on my leg. "I don't mind."

"Well I mind," I said, "but just get it over with. One of us can go with you, right?"

"If you think that's necessary," Tyler answered.

I nodded to Deirdre and she got up to follow the second officer. A worried glance over her shoulder as she left. Maybe this wasn't a good idea. But before I could say anything Tyler started in with me, and I let it go. I told him everything, starting with getting up this morning and making coffee. How I'd dropped it on the front porch in surprise. That Deirdre thought the boy looked like me. Tyler scribbled in his notebook. He took me back to last night.

I shrugged. "Worked in the shop till around ten. Then watched some TV and went to bed a little after eleven."

"Shop?"

"Yeah. My garage. Power tools."

"They loud?"

"In there? Yeah. Not so much from outside."

"Probably why you didn't hear anything," Tyler said, writing some more. "What time you start?"

"Must have been around eight. I was in there a couple hours."

He asked about Deirdre. I told him she was asleep by the time I got in bed. No, we hadn't seen anything unusual in the neighborhood recently. No unfamiliar cars parked on the street or strange people hanging around, at least that I could remember. When we were done, Tyler glanced out the front window.

"At least you found him early. Must be ninety out there already."

I checked the indoor-outdoor thermometer by the front door. Eighty-eight.

"Detective Branson is here," Tyler said. "Let's go outside."

The white coroner's van had backed up to the driveway and yellow crime scene tape had already been strung up. Lots of uniforms; one guy in street clothes, carrying a toolbox and wearing a vest and baseball cap identifying him as PSPD. Some of my neighbors were gathered in the street, talking quietly, trying to process it all. We pushed through them to a patrol car, where the detective was speaking with one of the deputies. When he turned to us Tyler introduced me.

Branson was dressed in slacks and a sport coat, his tie pulled down to allow the top button of his shirt to be open. Tall and well built. Late forties, with a brown crew cut that was going gray at the top. He had a military man's air about him and an arrogance that a lot of cops seem to adopt. I decided I didn't like him.

He pulled off his sunglasses and addressed Tyler and the other uniform. "Start talking to the neighbors. See if anybody saw anything." To me he said, "Let's go over here," as both officers hurried off. We crossed the street and went up a few houses to where his sedan was parked. He sat against the front side of the car, put his sunglasses in his shirt pocket and pulled out a pack of cigarettes. Lit one and stuffed the pack and lighter back in his pocket.

"Tell me what happened."

He took a hard pull on the cigarette, his small, dark eyes appraising me. Blew smoke into the warm breeze. I'd read somewhere that a lot of homicide detectives smoked to mask the smell of death.

"There's not much to tell. I woke up this morning about six, made some coffee and went out to the front porch with it. The body was lying there. There was nobody around. We called you guys—my wife did—and that's it. We already told the deputies all this."

Branson tapped his cigarette and I watched the wind carry the ash into the gutter.

"Uh-huh. Tell me about yourself."

"What do you mean?"

"How long you've lived here. What you do. Like that."

Another pull, another tap, more drifting ash. Seemed to accelerate as it neared the ground. I couldn't help thinking of the boy's life in the same way—a fragile thing carried off by a killing wind. Figured what happened was just starting to hit me.

"Well . . . we've lived here about three years, been married for two. I do carpentry, woodworking, furniture refinishing and repairing. Most of it here at home in my garage. My wife works in a clinic–"

"What kind of clinic?"

"Drug rehab."

He raised an eyebrow at that. "Young people?"

I shrugged. "Sure, I guess. You think this is drug related?"

"She know him?"

"No, of course not." Silence. *You sure?* "Look, we have nothing to do with it. Neither of us has ever seen him before. I'm sure he could have ended up next door just as easy."

Branson frowned. "That's entirely possible. Either way, we'll need you and your wife to make an official statement down at the station. Tomorrow morning? We'll say eight o'clock." He pulled a business card out of his shirt pocket and held it out for me. "Ask for me."

I took the card. Branson started walking toward the crime scene.

"Do you know who the victim is yet?" I said to his back.

Branson stopped, turned around and told me, "That kind of information will be released at the appropriate time. See you tomorrow morning." Then he continued towards the blinking red and blue lights, the uniforms, the milling spectators, and the news van that had just pulled up.

I followed him back to the house. Snatches of conversation billowed out: official talk, questions from reporters, cops interviewing the neighbors, conjecture about the crime. Across the street, a TV reporter live on camera. My house was dwarfed by the San Jacintos rising behind it–if it were an animal, it would have been trembling, ready to bolt. I wanted to go inside, lock the door, and never come out. But first I had to get through the rabble on my front lawn. A deputy cleared a path, and I stopped a moment before going inside.

The body was being lifted onto a stretcher. Someone hadn't zipped the body bag all the way closed. They wheeled it over to the back of the white van and slid it inside. Just before the doors were slammed shut, one of his hands slipped out. Gloved with a brown paper bag and a rubber band, it dangled over the edge of the pallet, a parting gesture that only I seemed to notice. Then the van was gone and the space it had occupied was quickly filled with people, some of them here to investigate, some to keep order, and others to package the event and sell it.

I turned away. Deirdre had cleaned up the mess on the front porch and was sitting alone in the living room. *Face the Nation* on TV with the sound too low. I closed the curtains and sat beside her on the couch. We didn't speak for a long while.

"What are you thinking about?" Deirdre finally said.

I shook my head slowly.

"I mean, I know what you're thinking about, but . . ."

"How much we could get for the house. Where I would put my tools."

She put down the remote she'd been holding for the last twenty minutes. "Why?"

"Been too long in the desert," I answered, half to myself.

"You want to move."

Ten years here, three of them with Deirdre. So the desert was only outside.

"No."

That night was a night of release, desperate and life-affirming. We slid against each other, salty and slippery, our pores joining through a feverish sheen of sweat. Deirdre's breath was hot in my ear, her heart thumping against mine, and the end made us forget for a while what had happened that morning.

Afterwards, we lay on top of the damp sheets and listened to the night outside our open window: the clicking of the palm fronds in the warm night wind, the intermittent chirping of the crickets, and the electronic buzz of our neighbor's halogen security lamp in the backyard next door.

Deirdre spoke first, her voice small and hesitant in the dark bedroom. "I saw a dead body once, a long time ago."

I could feel her head turn toward me on the pillow, and I let her take her time.

"It was in a tenement off St. Mark's Place in New York City. I was looking for one of my friends in the basement of the building. She'd had a fight with her boyfriend and I hadn't seen her in a couple days. Somebody told me she might be there." She paused and went on. "Terrible place. You had to get past the drug dealers and gang members out front, and inside was even worse. Piss all over the floors, graffiti covering the walls. I stepped over a few drunks passed out in the hall before getting downstairs. It was another world down there, like an anteroom to hell. Rats scratching around in the shadows, their eyes shining red in the flickering candlelight. People sprawled all over the floor, lying in filth. I started looking around, hoping to find her quick and get out of there, but I didn't see her. I could hear someone sobbing a few feet away and I went in that direction, trying not to trip over anybody. Some of them hardly looked human, Tim. Teeth rotting out. Hair and beards like wild animals. One guy had just fixed and his eyelids were fluttering like . . . like dying moths. And the stench was unbelievable. The smell of disease, hopelessness. And then I saw him, over in a dark corner. Separated from the rest, like they were afraid of catching something. I got closer and saw that his eyes were wide open, just staring at the ceiling. Young guy, like today. Not as far gone as some of the others in the room. Except not one part of him moved, Tim. Not one. His body was so still, it seemed to suck the life from the room."

Silence, then the breeze came in and lifted the curtain in the window.

"How come you never told me that story before?"

"I don't know. Maybe I felt like talking about it would rob him of whatever dignity he had left."

"What about your friend?"

"I didn't find her. And I never went back there."

CHAPTER TWO

The Palm Springs Police Department is just south of downtown near the airport. The sprinklers were on when we arrived, feeding lush green grass and spraying the walkway at our feet. Two enormous palm trees flanked the entrance. Golf carts and tennis rackets wouldn't have looked out of place. The heavy plate glass doors were spotless, the lobby a good fifteen degrees cooler than outside. Not even May yet, and I wondered how much hotter it could get before summer.

Deirdre and I hadn't spoken much on the drive over, still avoiding the particulars of yesterday's murder. As if by not talking about it, it would just go away. Now we had no choice.

We were greeted at the front desk by a young officer. I told her why we were there, and she led us around the counter into a short corridor. On one side was a heavy steel door with reinforced glass that probably let into the jail; we took a right into a large room under fluorescent lights. Ten or twelve battered metal desks paired off with each other. A low hum of conversation, phone-work and form-filing, some rolled-up sleeves and loosened ties even at this early hour. A few desks were unmanned, with sport jackets slung over the chair backs. One had a purse sitting on the desktop. Around the perimeter of the room were several windowed offices with room for coatracks and trophy cases. In the far corner, a coffee machine with

three detectives gathered around it. An empty conference room behind glass contained a large table and chairs, and a TV and VCR on
a stand.

Branson was sitting at one of the middle desks, opposite another detective who was on the phone. Branson looked up when
we entered, then approached, hand extended.

"Good morning. Thanks for coming in. My partner should be
done in a second," he said, shaking our hands. The words were
friendly, but the manner was all business. He introduced himself to
Deirdre as his partner finished his call and our escort left. "This is
Detective Tidwell," Branson said, leaving it at that.

Tidwell was about my height and slim. Late thirties, with short,
curly brown hair that was slicked back from his forehead. He wore
glasses and an open expression that felt reassuring. A sharp contrast with his partner. Tidwell shook both our hands, apologizing
for the inconvenience. Led us out of the squad room to a series of
small, windowless rooms with straight-backed chairs and a table
visible in each.

"This shouldn't take long," he assured Deirdre as they entered
the room on the right.

Branson seated me in the one next to it. Shut the door and sat
down across from me in front of a large mirror on the back wall.
After switching on a small tape recorder that sat in the middle of
the table, he recited both our names, the date and time, and the
case number. Then he began the interview.

We started with the night before I found the body. I repeated
the same things I'd told the officer that morning about working in
the shop and then going to bed.

"Why do you think your neighbors didn't hear anything?"

You kidding? I wanted to say. People in their homes with the AC
blasting and the TV on, you could scream your ass off and nobody'd hear. And a small gun wouldn't make much noise.

"I don't know. You'll have to ask them."

"Your tools aren't that loud are they?"

"No, they're not. And my shop is pretty well sealed up."

Branson glanced at his notepad. "Where are the Hagstroms?"

Neighbors next door. "They're retired. Clear out every year before the spring breakers arrive. Not to mention the heat."

A skeptical look.

"You always park your car in the street?"

I wondered where that came from, until I realized it had shielded the body from the street. "Mostly. Deirdre takes the driveway. Garage is occupied."

He nodded. "Let's go to the next morning."

I didn't get too far before Branson interrupted. "You brought your coffee out to the front porch?"

"Yeah."

Branson didn't say anything for a while, just tapped his pencil against his cheek. I waited.

"Here we are in the middle of a heatwave, and you're bringing hot coffee outside?"

Now it was my turn to pause. "So what?"

"Seems a little strange to me. Why would you drink it outside in the heat when you could relax with it inside, in the air-conditioning?"

"I don't use the air conditioner. I like the heat."

"You seem pretty comfortable in here."

"I prefer the heat."

"Okay," he said, shaking his head. "Go on."

"Where was I?"

"Tell me about the body."

"He was just lying there."

"You touch him?"

"No."

"Check for a pulse?"

I just said I didn't touch him. "No."

"How did you know he was dead?"

"There were flies all over him."

"You didn't think you should make sure?"

He was making a simple story very complicated. "They were crawling on his eyeballs, for Chrissake. That seemed like a pretty good sign."

"Just answer the questions, Mr. Ryder."

"What's the problem, detective? Somebody just got killed and you're hassling me about nothing."

"I have to pursue whatever doesn't sound right to me."

"Do I need a lawyer?"

"That's up to you."

I tried to read him and didn't get anywhere. "We almost done here?"

"You know he's out, don't you?"

For a second I wasn't sure I'd heard him correctly. Then my mind made the connection, the blood rushing to my face, and I could tell Branson knew he'd scored a direct hit. "Who's out?" I managed.

He leaned forward, zeroing in on me. "Turret."

"You checked me out?" I croaked, trying to recover and not doing a very good job of it.

Branson sat back, not blinking. "Somebody shows up dead on a guy's front lawn, it tends to pique my curiosity about that guy. Yeah, I checked you out. So what about Turret?"

"Sounds like you know more about him than I do right now," I answered. "When was he released?"

"Last Monday, a week ago. Have you had any contact with him since the trial?"

"None whatsoever. Not in thirty years. I'd like to wipe him from my memory completely." That would never happen. I'd gotten involved in what was supposed to have been an anti-Vietnam War action back in the early '70s. Several people died.

Turret was the ringleader. He and I survived, and both of us went to prison.

Branson pushed on. "No letters, no phone calls, no contact with friends of friends?"

"Nothing. And he wasn't a friend."

A hard stare.

"You think he's mixed up in this?" I asked.

"Does seem kind of coincidental. Turret gets out of prison and not a week goes by before this happens right on your doorstep." He paused. "What I really think, though," he said while reaching over to shut off the tape recorder, "is that you and your friends and everybody like you fucked everything up back then. What do you think of that?"

I sat there speechless, not believing this was happening. "I think you have a serious chip on your shoulder," I finally answered.

Branson leaned forward, his voice lowered. "My father died in a helicopter at Ap Bac, before anybody in this country could even find Vietnam on a map. He didn't question the integrity or motives of the country he grew up in, just did his duty like a man in that piss-poor jungle halfway around the globe. And then people like you, too cowardly to do the right thing, come along and crap all over their memories. Bunch of over-educated, protest-marching, flag-burning, pot-smoking, free-loving little pricks. Spoiled brats going to college on Daddy's dime, who didn't even know how damn lucky you were. You should have been grateful, but instead, all you did was divide this country and mock the hardworking Americans who took their responsibilities to this nation seriously."

"Are you finished?" I asked at the first sign of a pause.

Branson sat back in his chair and folded his arms. "You can leave the same way you came in. We're done. For now."

I'd heard viewpoints like his over and over, and it pissed me off that I'd had to listen to it again. Screw it, I thought, and turned back to him as I opened the door. "Did you know that cops and serial killers have the same psychological profile?"

Branson put his pencil down and watched me leave.

CHAPTER THREE

"You look spooked, Tim. What happened in there?"

We were walking to the car outside, where only a few small puddles remained from the early-morning watering.

"He asked about Turret."

"Turret. Why?" Deirdre asked, perplexed. "That's ancient history."

"He was released last week."

Deirdre gave me a long look before speaking. "Do they know where he is?"

We reached the car at that point, and I unlocked the door and held it open for Deirdre. When she got in I squatted on the sidewalk next to her as she rolled the window down. I rested my arms on the door. It was hot, the metal baking in the sun. Across the street, the bank thermometer clicked from ninety to ninety-one.

"So where is he?" Deirdre repeated.

"We never got to that. Branson started working me over pretty good right about then."

"What do you mean?"

"His dad got killed in Vietnam. Made it real clear how much he despises people like me."

"What did he say?"

I recounted the conversation with Branson.

"What's his problem?" Deirdre asked when I was finished.

"I think it's obvious what his problem is," I said. "His father was military, and he's a cop. He's got that mentality." That sounded harsh. "I guess he's got a reason," I admitted.

"He's being a jerk," Deirdre said, miffed. "And unprofessional. Why don't you get in the car."

I circled around to the driver's side and slid in next to her. We sat for a moment.

"So they think Turret's after you?" Deirdre asked. "For testifying against him?"

"Apparently."

Deirdre frowned, shook her head. I waited while she turned it over in her mind. "It doesn't make sense. Why would he kill somebody we don't even know?"

I thought about the first thing Deirdre had said yesterday morning after seeing the body. *He looks like you.* She was right, to a certain extent. What if Turret had been there for me, chanced upon the boy outside and mistaken him for a son I didn't have? What if Deirdre was next?

"What are you thinking?" Deirdre prodded.

I told her. Deirdre nodded in mute agreement, a silent surrender, as if she'd been expecting something like this for a long time. A final domino falling into place.

"There was this guy I used to hear about," she finally said. "Back in New York. A bookie." Someone walked by on the sidewalk, and Deirdre let him pass before continuing. "Never bothered with the welshers. He'd go after their friends or family instead. Started with pictures of their kids at school or something like that." She paused. "He always got his money."

Across the street the bank guard, an overweight rent-a-cop, paced back and forth in front of the building. I told myself Turret had nothing to do with it. Wasn't convincing. Maybe I'd always suspected that I'd gotten off too easy for what I'd done.

I turned to Deirdre. "How'd it go with you in there?"

"My clients came up."

"What do you mean?"

"Tidwell asked if I knew of any drug activity that could've led to this."

"There's nothing, right?"

"Not that I know about."

"What else?"

"I told him everything. Why I came out here."

"And?"

"Tidwell wanted to know about Triumph."

"It's a work camp in the middle of the desert. What does that have to do with anything?"

"They're ex-cons, Tim."

"Shoulda guessed," I said, shaking my head. "They let you out, but you get a knock on your door every time something goes wrong."

"You know how it works."

"Doesn't mean I have to like it."

We sat a little bit more. A patrol car left the parking lot in front of us, the driver giving us a quick glance before heading up the street. I adjusted the rearview mirror that didn't need adjusting and turned to Deirdre. "I don't want to be thinking about this all day," I told her. "You should take the day off. We could–"

Deirdre stopped me with a hand on my arm. "I can't. I have to–"

"Yeah, okay," I interrupted. "No problem." Thought about it a second. "Probably Patrick again, isn't it?" A new client of hers. They'd found him splashing around in the City Hall fountain a few weeks ago, all his clothes piled on the sidewalk next to it. Apparently, in a drug-induced schizophrenic frenzy, he'd been trying to wash off the bugs he thought the CIA had attached to his skin.

Deirdre got defensive. "So?"

"He's not done spilling his guts to you yet?" I said before I could stop myself.

Deirdre's mouth dropped open; probably the same look I'd

given Branson earlier. "I can't believe you just said that." She huffed, shook her head. "The one time I tell you anything about one of my clients and you shovel it back at me?"

I couldn't answer. Truth was, I didn't know what had gotten into me—I was used to people needing Deirdre. All the late night phone calls from desperate clients. Leaving the house in the middle of the night to help a wavering addict. Deirdre never talked about the people she served; a privacy thing. But Patrick was different. Deirdre seemed to have formed a special attachment to him. And now, when *I* needed her ...

"I'm sorry. I'll drop you off at work."

"No. Not like this. What's going on with you?"

I felt like a kid demanding more attention. But Deirdre deserved an answer. "It's just ... maybe enough is enough." This client had been homeless for a while, according to Deirdre. He'd gotten raped one night in an abandoned building in L.A., a few months before the fountain episode. "All that stuff he's told you ... I mean, is that really necessary?"

"Yeah, Tim, it is. I would think you'd know that better than anybody."

"Okay," I said, rubbing the back of my neck against an oncoming headache. "Talk about shoveling it back."

"Hey. I didn't start this ... whatever this is."

I was about to respond but thought better of it. Started the car instead, and Deirdre let it go.

The clinic was just a few minutes away, a small storefront closer to downtown. I drove slowly, tried not to think about how stupid I'd just been. We got to Palm Canyon Drive, the city's main drag. The fashionable boutiques and umbrella-tabled eateries drifted past, the looming San Jacintos advancing in slow motion above the city to our left. Here and there, pockets of spring breakers caroused. Fewer and fewer every year as the college kids discovered new hot spots. Still, some residents got out of town before the yearly ritual began.

Deirdre remained quiet, her hands in her lap. I wanted to ask about her friends at Triumph Outreach, if she'd had any recent contact with them. Instead, I turned on the radio.

"–highly volatile chemicals caused a massive explosion on a remote ranch in Yucca Valley this morning, at what turned out to be an illegal methamphetamine lab. Two bodies were found when the fire was put out, burned beyond recognition. Last week, sheriff's deputies, acting on an anonymous tip, arrested four people in Brawley operating a similar lab. The two events are most likely related, police say, though a connection to the unidentified body found yesterday morning in North Palm Springs, on the property of a local substance abuse counselor, has not been established. Coming up–"

Deirdre switched off the radio, a cloud crossing her features. The sun reflected blindingly off the shop windows and the cars parked along the street, and I wondered again what had drawn us both here. You could barely catch your breath when the sun flamed full in the white-hot sky. Reptiles and rodents made for the desert ducked under rocks, burrowed deep.

In her teens, Deirdre helped care for her younger sister, who'd eventually died of leukemia, and the instinct never left. She loved working at the clinic; her coworkers and clients were like a second family. Deirdre was that hand in the darkness when everything else had failed. Turning people around, literally saving their lives sometimes, satisfied some deep part of her in a way she could never describe. I suppose it was the closest she could get to bringing her sister back.

As for me, maybe deep down I believed all the Old Testament stories about the desert I'd been taught growing up.

Traffic was light but slow through the shopping district, and my attention wandered. Up on the mountainside, I found the Desert Angel, a geological accident shaped like an angel in flight. Some days it was brighter than others, depending on the light. Today it was barely visible, or maybe it was just the angle from where I was.

It brought back the day I'd proposed to Deirdre. Sitting out there near Windy Point, the car rocking and shaking in the wind. Gazing up at that landmark, praying she'd say yes.

I made a right and stopped at the curb in front of Jericho Health. Deirdre opened her door and left it there, making no move to get out of the car.

"All I meant was that if you really trust someone, you should be able to tell them anything," she said, by way of apology. A searching look in her eyes, as if she were trying to read something not quite in focus. Was she beginning to wonder if I'd given her the whole story about my past?

"Yeah. I know." I watched a few cars pass by in the street, the people inside them ignoring us. "You never told me about seeing a dead body before," I said turning back to Deirdre, just as she opened her mouth to say something. She held whatever it was, pursing her lips, and I tried to clean it up. "I didn't fault you for that."

"That was big of you," Deirdre retorted before getting out of the car and shutting the door. "I'll call you when you can come pick me up," she told me, leaning in. "It'll be late." Then she went into the clinic without looking back. I wanted to follow her inside, tell her I was sorry. Instead, I hit the steering wheel in frustration and pulled away.

Thirty minutes later I was in Beaumont, where I spent the day looking at antiques, trying to get some ideas for a project I was working on. But questions about the murder kept circling around in my head.

Mid-day I stopped at a fast food joint. Sat there and barely ate, going over it all again and again. A young woman came in with two young boys, her son and his friend from the look of them. They were giggling and teasing each other, while the mother admonished them to hurry up and order. But you could tell they were all having a good time.

Moments like those were few and far between when I was growing up. That's what happened when you had a mother who threw in the towel before you hit puberty and a father who became distant and short-tempered trying to raise you alone. Mom wasn't cut out for marriage or motherhood. She didn't have the dedication or stamina that my friends' mothers had. As a kid I didn't realize all this, I just knew she was different. A "free spirit," Dad said. One day towards the end, Mom forgot to pick me up from school. This was in second grade. She'd spent the day with her single friends and lost track of time. I broke into a donation box in my parochial school church for bus fare. I was caught immediately by one of the parish priests and driven home. My parents argued deep into the night about that. Dad cursing my mother's irresponsibility. Mom responding that he shouldn't have knocked her up so young. When she left a few weeks later Dad told me it wasn't my fault and that maybe she'd come back someday. But I knew better. Even without the note from my mother saying she loved me but didn't deserve to have me, and I was better off without her. A note I never showed my father because he lived on his hope.

That hope faded over the years, along with my dad's interest in me—I was a daily reminder of the woman who'd left him. Yearly fishing trips were the only time we ever spent together. With no one to really talk to, no family except an aunt and uncle on my mother's side I'd only met once, I retreated inward. By high school I was a loner. I found it difficult to connect with anybody. At graduation, I heard one of my classmates ask who I was when my name was called. He didn't recognize me even after I stood up to get my diploma.

College was different. The war and all the unrest brought my generation together. It felt good to finally be a part of something. I was tired of being dismissed, overlooked. I wanted to do something that mattered, show my dad and all the rest of them that I could be reckoned with. Turret offered a way to do that. A robbery to help finance the political campaigns we believed in. Something to effect real change, not just symbolic destruction, he said. Which made sense. Except everything went to hell, and it turned out that Turret was just using me and the others–college students who thought we could change the world. The Symbionese Liberation Army, the radical militant group founded by an escaped convict and several ex-Berkeley students, pulled the same thing–three times in fact–a few years later. Ours had the dubious distinction of being the first. A prison psychologist had gone on and on about social conformity theory, and how I'd been caught up in something bigger than me. But I wasn't interested in excuses. No second visit with that shrink.

Back in the here and now, I'd suddenly lost my appetite. Food only half-finished and cold. I threw it away and tried again doing what I'd come here to do. I wandered from shop to shop, unable to shut down, the fog I was in getting thicker and thicker. Finally gave up when I almost knocked over a Tiffany lamp in one of the stores. I got in the car and drove home, watched TV until Deirdre called a few hours later. She was standing outside the clinic when I arrived. Her hair was shining under the streetlamps just starting to come on, and she smiled when she got in.

CHAPTER FOUR

I could go for days on that smile.

So I kept my mouth shut; words would only diminish the feeling I had inside. We drove for a few minutes in peaceful silence.

"I was wrong this morning," Deirdre said suddenly.

I looked at her looking out the window. The sky was purpling in the east, the wind out of the west a bellows for the emerging stars. "No you weren't. I was just being selfish. Wanted you all to myself."

We passed an old mobile home park, then a salvage yard, its odd-shaped cast-offs just shadows in the dusk.

"I'm the one that was being selfish," Deirdre said. "I can get so wrapped up in my clients' problems I forget I have someone more important to me at home. Guess you need to remind me of that sometimes." She turned to me and smiled. "Maybe not in the way that you did. But . . ."

I smiled back. "Not one of my prouder moments."

We reached the barren outlie north of Palm Springs, where the streetlights were few and far between. Here, the desert reclaimed the night, a reminder that we were just visitors on this ancient land. Made me feel small and fragile, and put me back in the emergency room the night I met Deirdre. I'd sliced my hand open on a table saw, and the meat of my palm pumped out blood into a towel. As I sat there alone, holding a towel that was getting heavier by the minute, everything seemed brighter, but less real at the same time. Until Deirdre sat down a few chairs away, waiting, I came to find out, for word on one of her clients who'd just OD'd. Tonight, I looked down at that scar on my palm and knew it was my real lifeline.

"Wasn't much good at work today anyway," Deirdre said. "Couldn't seem to concentrate. Or bring myself to give much of a shit about everyone else's problems."

"You're entitled. I was in a fog all day myself," I admitted, as we crossed over the interstate into North Palm Springs. A large traveler's complex squatted next to the highway under bright white floodlights.

"I did have a new client, though," Deirdre continued. "A walk-in at the end of the day. I think he could sense my distraction. Didn't stay too long."

"Will he come back?"

"I think so. Set him up for something later this week."

I made a few turns to get to our street. It looked like it always did when the heat of the day lingered past sunset: lonesome and empty, but filled with movement. Tree branches waved to no one, stirred by the wind snaking through the pass. Living room windows closed to the heat, TV-light flickering in the curtains. Air conditioners hummed steadily in the animated dark, imparting a static charge to the night I could feel as we pulled up in front of the house. Faintly outlined by the mountains in the distance, it looked forlorn and unsettled, still not recovered from yesterday's chaos.

It was close to nine as we approached the front door. The porch light was a hot yellow glow that attracted fluttering moths. It also illuminated a man slumped against the door. He was sitting on the dust mat, head down on his knees.

Just as Deirdre and I noticed him he looked up, rousing himself quickly. "Mr. Ryder? Are you Tim Ryder?"

Something in his hand glinted in the shadows as he moved. Instinctively, I sprang forward and threw him back against the door before he had a chance to get up. I trapped his wrist against the doorframe, pinned his neck with my other forearm, and pressed my knee against his chest so he couldn't move. Whatever it was dropped from his hand, hit the pavement and broke apart. Not a gun, I saw, looking down at a small handheld tape recorder with the battery cover and batteries scattered around it.

The man struggled against me, legs scissoring. His free hand clutched at my arm on his throat as he tried to breathe.

I gave him a little air. "Who the hell are you?"

When he didn't answer, Deirdre came up and roughly turned him sideways, then reached around his backside.

He took his hand off me and grabbed her hair, jerking her head forward sharply, but let her go when I drove my arm back into his throat. She kicked him once in the ribs, angry, and he grunted in pain. Deirdre reached behind him again to pull out his wallet.

She opened it, squinted at the ID displayed inside.

"He's a reporter," she said, tossing the wallet at him as I grabbed his collar and picked him up.

I let him go once he was on his feet. He staggered a few steps away and leaned face-first against the wall, one arm pillowing his forehead, the other hand massaging his neck. He was panting pretty hard.

"Shit!" he got out between breaths. "What the fuck . . . is your . . . problem?"

I picked up his wallet and had a look for myself. One slot held his driver's license. John Sheehan. 4-23-64. The other had a press ID for the *Desert Sun*.

Sheehan turned around to face me, muttering angrily under his breath as he dusted himself off. "I'm just a reporter, for Chrissake!" he finally said, then looked down. "Where's my gear?"

He saw the tape recorder lying in pieces by the door and took a step toward it.

"Not so fast," I cautioned, stopping him with a firm hand on his chest. I handed him back his wallet. "What do you want?"

"Take a wild guess," he answered, stuffing the wallet in his pocket. I pushed him hard against the wall, and the back of his head cracked against the concrete. He put his hands up in a "stop" gesture, a scared look in his eyes replacing the hostility he'd shown moments earlier. Again my hand was clamped under his chin, holding his face high.

"Listen asshole, we just had a murder go down on our property, maybe you heard about it. So we're a little nervous about strangers waiting in the dark on our front doorstep. Now cut the bullshit and tell us what you want." I loosened my grip on his neck. "Okay?"

He nodded as well as he could, eyes bouncing nervously between me and Deirdre. I let him go.

Sheehan cleared his throat and rubbed the front of his neck, as if he were checking the closeness of a shave. He straightened the collar of his polo shirt and jerked his shoulders forward to readjust the fit. He reminded me of someone trying to save face after losing a bar fight.

"I'm a reporter for the *Sun*," Sheehan finally said. "I wanted to talk to you about what happened yesterday." He turned to Deirdre and asked if we could talk inside. Maybe he thought she'd be more hospitable, despite the kick in the ribs.

He was wrong. "I don't think this conversation is going to be long enough to bother," Deirdre told him.

"We don't know anything more than you do," I said. "And we've got enough problems without talking to a reporter about it."

"Well then perhaps I can enlighten you with some information I've run across," he offered hopefully, seeing an opening. "Then you can give me your comments, maybe shed some light on a few things."

"Who have you been talking to?" I asked. "Do the cops know who that boy was?"

Deirdre took a step toward Sheehan.

"Who was he?" she demanded, her eyes big and dark in the faint porchlight.

Sheehan nodded toward our front door. "You have something cold to drink?" he asked, wiping the sweat from his brow. "It's hot out here."

"It's going to get hotter if you don't start talking," I said through clenched teeth. "You're beginning to piss me off."

"Tell us what you know or leave," Deirdre said. "We're not gonna play any games with you."

Sheehan finally relented, shaking his head with frustration. "Fine. Whatever." He turned his attention toward me, suddenly all business. "I plugged your name into Lexis and got a hit. You had quite a little escapade thirty-odd years ago, didn't you?"

"So what?" I replied. "It's never been a secret. You think you're Woodward and Bernstein, coming up with that?"

"Well how 'bout this, then? Your old bunk-buddy and his unfortunate demise."

"What are you two talking about?" Deirdre demanded.

"Oh, you didn't know about that?" he asked Deirdre, then addressed me. "Keeping secrets from the old lady, huh?"

Silence for a moment, Sheehan and I regarding each other coolly, before Deirdre cut in. "You don't know what the hell you're talking about," she told him with a kind of desperation, then turned to me. "This is getting old. Maybe he should leave."

"Look, I'm sorry," Sheehan said. "I guess I went about this the wrong way—"

"You sure did," I interrupted, picking up the tape recorder and returning it in pieces. "You heard my wife. Scram."

Fuming, Sheehan backpedaled toward the street. "You want me to dredge your whole story up again in the newspaper? I will, you know."

"And if you didn't, somebody else would," I replied. "Unless you're the only reporter with access to a computer archive."

"But wouldn't it be better if the first story to come out with this angle put you in a positive light?" Sheehan responded, stopping on the lawn. "I can slant it any way I want. And I *will* be first with it."

"I don't really give a damn," I said, raising my voice. "I hope you win the fucking Pulitzer for it. You can take your story and shove it up your ass. Just do it off my property."

By this time Deirdre had unlocked the front door and was pulling me inside.

"You know Turret's out don't you?" And when that didn't get a response: "I should have you two arrested for assault! See how you like jail again after all this time."

Deirdre slammed the door, turned on the living room lights, and looked me up and down. "You okay?"

"Yeah, I'm all right. That was a pretty good kick you gave him, though."

"I had a feeling he was a reporter even before I saw his ID," she said, moving into the kitchen.

It was stiflingly hot in the house. Deirdre opened the sliding glass door and stood a few moments in front of the screen, breathing in the night air. Our backyard was dusted with a silvery light from our neighbor's security lamp. It outlined Deirdre in a faint aurora, as though she was lit from within.

The illusion lasted only half a moment in her stillness, then she spoke.

"I knew he'd dug up your past. I don't think I would have kicked him if he hadn't grabbed me. But I might have."

I didn't respond.

"So. Your cell-mate," Deirdre said without turning around.

No reason not to tell her. "He was a Hell's Angel. Don't remember his name. I found him dead one morning. My first year, when I was on laundry detail." Deirdre turned to face me. "They had those big, industrial, stainless steel machines. He was floating in one. Just him and all that soapy water." I paused. "That wasn't what killed him, though." Deirdre raised an eyebrow. "Sticky fingers are a no-no when you're part of a prison drug ring. Got him a bleach cocktail. Followed by the hot bath."

"And you?" Deirdre asked.

"I just shared a box with him."

I switched on the overhead fluorescents. They flickered to life, bathing the room in a blue-white glow. Deirdre went to the cabinet and took down two glasses, then got a pitcher of iced tea from the refrigerator. She sat down at the table, which had a slight wobble that I hadn't gotten around to fixing yet, and poured us both a glass.

When I sat down across from her, she took a sip of her tea and said, "So I guess your story will be all over the newspaper tomorrow."

Just then the telephone rang, startling us. It seemed blaring and strident in our small kitchen and I hesitated before getting up to answer it. Deirdre looked at me expectantly as I picked up on the third ring, just before the answering machine would have taken it. I wished I'd let it.

"Hello?"

"Is this Mr. Ryder?"

"Who wants to know?" I asked, shaking my head with disgust. It had to be another reporter, I thought. They'd be coming out of the woodwork now. Deirdre got up from her chair and approached inquisitively. Our eyes locked as the man on the other end continued.

"I'm James Parker from the *Pilot*, hoping to get some comments about the murder that happened out there yesterday." Out there. Like North Palm Springs was alien territory from where this guy was calling from.

"This *is* Tim Ryder, isn't it?"

"How did you get this number? It's supposed to be unlisted. And don't you guys go home at night?"

"I'm just a working man trying to get ahead, sir. Putting in a few extra hours to get some background, some human interest on the story."

"The fact that he was murdered in cold blood isn't human interest enough for you? You gotta bother me at home, use a kid's death to get ahead?" I asked, getting irritated.

Who is it? Deirdre mouthed.

"I understand how you feel sir. You've probably been getting calls from reporters all day."

I looked at the answering machine. Its single red digit blinked a flashing "9," signifying the number of messages went into the double digits.

"But if you'll just answer a few brief questions about the crime I won't bother you again," Parker continued. "Promise." He paused in my silence. Then: "Only about what happened. Nothing personal." Which sounded like Sheehan's threat to expose my past.

"Look, we just had one of your competitors from the other paper show up unannounced. Kinda ticked us off, so we're a little press-shy right now. We don't know anything anyway."

"Who was it? Sheehan, I bet. What did he have to say?"

"Same thing as you, Parker. Sticking his nose where it doesn't belong. We got nothing beyond what we told the police. Talk to them."

"I did. Which reminds me. Did you and Branson have some sort of run-in? I don't think he likes you much."

"Why? What did he tell you?"

"Nothing specific. But there was something there. Care to talk about it?"

I wondered why Branson hadn't spilled the beans on me just for the fun of it. Maybe he thought it would be more amusing to drop a few hints and see what the press came up with.

"There's nothing to talk about. You must've misread him."

"Maybe," Parker admitted, then pushed on. "So what were your first thoughts when you saw the body? Ever seen something like that before?"

"This conversation is over, Parker."

"Take my number in case you feel like talking."

"I know where to find you, but it's not going to happen," I assured him. "Good night. And you can lose my number." I hung up the phone. "Damnit."

"This is going to be bad," Deirdre said. "Maybe if we give them just a little, they'll back off."

"You know that's not true, Deirdre. It'll just make it worse. If they know they're not getting anything they'll eventually give up."

Deirdre didn't reply. I reached for the answering machine and pressed the "play" button.

"Yeah, this is Chris Anders from KMIR-TV in Palm Springs," a voice announced.

I cut it off and hit "delete," then ran through the rest. Nothing but reporters, Parker and Sheehan among them. Bloodhounds locked on a scent. I deleted them one by one, getting more steamed as I did so. When the phone rang again I yanked it out of the cradle and hurled it against the opposite wall. Deirdre jumped, then recovered. Gave me a look like a disappointed mother at a misbehaving child. I felt like one, embarrassed at my loss of control.

"Beautiful, Tim," she said. "Feel better?"

"Sorry. I shouldn't have done that."

Deirdre glanced at the damaged wall. "You done redecorating? Or you want to try the bedroom next?"

We could hear the phone in the bedroom ringing, and since the handset I'd demolished was a cordless model, the base with its built-in answering machine was still intact. It answered a moment later. After the beep we heard yet another journalist pleading for an interview. I let it go, resigned to the intrusion. Tried to ignore it as I sat back down at the table. My blood was boiling but the iced tea was cool and refreshing, the glass slippery with moisture.

Deirdre sat down and sighed, studying me as the reporter hung up.

"I said I was sorry," I repeated defensively.

Deirdre shook her head and looked down at her iced tea. She was making sweat rings on the table with the glass and joined two of the circles together. Then she absently wiped them away, leaving a smeared puddle, and lifted her eyes to mine.

"We gotta try and relax," she said. "We can't let this get to us. They'll find the killer and then it'll be over. We just have to keep it together until then."

"I don't think I'll get that scene out of my head any time soon," I answered.

"You mean . . . when you found him?"

I nodded, my eyes sliding away from her.

"Fucking Branson," she muttered. "He had no right—"

"I would have gotten to this point whether he'd unloaded on me or not. This is what happens when you screw up as bad as I did. It just keeps coming back. In different ways. Under different circumstances. Doesn't matter if Turret's been in prison all this time. In my mind he's right here."

"He doesn't have anything to do with it, Tim."

"I know. I just wish my heart—and my gut—agreed."

Deirdre reached out and ran her hand through my hair, her voice close to a whisper. "There's no way you can undo the mistake you made. I thought you'd come to terms with that."

"I thought so too. Maybe I was just fooling myself."

"But it was so long ago. Why do you keep going back?"

Because I haven't found a way to fix it yet.

Deirdre studied me for a moment. Then a look of defeat spread over her features. Maybe she recognized in me the same determination she drew on to guide her clients through their pain.

"Please leave it alone," she said, knowing it wouldn't change my mind.

"I'm already involved, Deirdre. Whether I like it or not. At the very least, he died on our property. I can't just let it go."

"Why not?"

I flashed on the image of the boy's hand falling out of the body bag just before the door of the coroner's van had shut, hanging over the stretcher in a silent entreaty. Nobody had noticed it but me.

"You know what it's like being somebody's last resort."

Deirdre looked away, unable to argue. "I don't want to lose you. Sometimes it feels like you're barely with me. That your only true companion is the guilt you've harbored for thirty years." She put her head in her hands and when they came away, her voice was trembling. "The only person who can forgive you is yourself, Tim. It will come from here," she said, tapping her chest, "but only when you let it all go. Don't you see that?"

I looked into the darkened hallway behind Deirdre, clawing at shadows. Deirdre stood up to leave, then turned back to me. "Aren't I enough? Haven't I filled up the dead spaces inside?"

CHAPTER FIVE

Later I found myself in the workshop, which I'd converted from the two-car garage after I bought the place. It was quiet as a church, the extra sound-damping insulation I'd installed when Deirdre moved in working all too well tonight. None of the outside noises of traffic or wind were able to intrude, and the silence became oppressive and intimidating. Usually I could come out here and not have to think about anything—occupy my attention by working on some small, intricate item. Or use the noise of the power tools to drown out everything else.

Now I wandered aimlessly between the benches and machinery, idly inspecting various pieces of unfinished work, turning them over in my hands without really seeing them. The polished metal equipment gleamed under the soft fluorescent light, and I could smell the sawdust I'd neglected to sweep up. One of the fixtures began to buzz and flicker randomly; the ballast would probably have to be replaced.

I drifted toward the blinking bulb, thinking about everything Deirdre had said a few minutes earlier. She was in the shower now, washing off the day's dirt while I brooded out here, sticky with sweat. In the solitude of the shop, the right thing to do became less clear-cut. Who was I really serving by not staying out of it? If I answered honestly, I knew it was only myself, not Deirdre and certainly not the victim, whom I didn't even know.

The bulb was still flickering over my head. I reached up and gently twisted it, felt one of the contacts engage in the socket. The fixture lit up brightly, no longer blinking.

Deirdre was right. The boy was dead. I wouldn't indulge my tendencies toward guilt or self-pity any longer. I was out of it.

My head clear for the first time since yesterday morning, I walked over to the bench where I'd left several of the smaller pieces for a French provincial dresser I was building. The design had come from an old friend I hadn't seen in a while.

In prison, an old trustee named Walter had befriended me. Over the course of a few years, he taught me everything he knew about woodworking, his trade before being convicted of murder. He'd killed his granddaughter's preschool teacher, who'd been caught by a custodian molesting her after hours. Filled with rage, Walt took matters into his own hands, then turned himself in. They gave him ten years, a long time for a man his age. Federal time because the molester was a teacher for the Head Start government program. But Walt was treated like royalty in prison after word spread that he'd gotten rid of a child molester. Many privileges were his for the asking: cigarettes, snacks, a TV in his cell. Another perk was the job of running the prison woodshop, where he built and repaired tables and chairs from the mess hall and library, and furniture from the administrators' offices, among other things. With over thirty years in woodworking, he had a lot of knowledge and expertise to impart. Just watching the touch he had in his strong, nimble, well-worn hands gave me a great respect for the craft. It seemed ironic, though, that a prison term could have provided me with such a fulfilling and gratifying trade, one that also paid so well.

After moving out here, I'd built a steady business slowly, one customer at a time. Most of my tools came from garage sales and business liquidations. I rented a space at Village Fest, the weekly craft fair and farmer's market held in downtown Palm Springs. There, I sold the furniture I built and refurbished, and developed a discriminating clientele who appreciated the craftsmanship of my work. The piece I was working on now was for a customer in Las Palmas, the wealthy, old money section of Palm Springs.

The bottom rails for the dresser were the first things I looked at. They'd been kerfed, soaked in water, then bent by using clamps tightened on the wood until the proper curve was attained. By now, they were sufficiently dry, so I removed the clamps and inspected the rails. They perfectly matched the contours of the cabriole legs sitting next to them.

I brought the legs to another bench, where I'd left the molded drawer fronts I recently assembled and shaped. Those needed some light sanding to smooth out the seams, but I decided to finish off the legs I'd just put down instead. I found the headset radio and turned on KCLB-FM. John O started a set about drug abuse with a Guns N' Roses song called "The Garden." I wondered if Deirdre was listening inside.

I began the final shaping of one of the dresser legs by tightening a vise around the lag screw bored into it. Picked up a wood rasp to round the foot, turned up the music a little and set to work. I'd just gotten into a rhythm of short, even strokes in time with the music when I thought of something that had been bothering me since yesterday, niggling at the back of my brain.

I put the file down and removed my headphones, not bothering to switch the radio off. I went into the house. Deirdre was in the bedroom with the TV on and no sound, and I got no response from her when I turned it off. She was asleep on top of the covers, the house still warm at this hour. I watched her for a moment. Her breathing was deep and peaceful. A faint smile on her face. What was she dreaming about?

The clock on her side of the bed glowed a liquid green. Almost ten. It sat on one of the night tables I'd built when Deirdre moved in, and I remembered the time a few months later when she spilled nail polish remover on the tabletop. It damaged the finish and left an ugly mark. Deirdre had been upset for hours, crying that she'd ruined the only bedroom set we would ever have. Before then, I'd been unsure of her thoughts on marriage. The following day I proposed.

I went out the front door into the electric desert night. My car was sitting at the curb. I opened the trunk and peered inside, searching for the heavy duty flashlight we kept there for emergencies.

The flashlight hadn't been used in years and I hoped the batteries weren't dead. But the light barreled out brightly, stabbing the darkness. I hurried across the street to where Branson and I had talked yesterday morning. I pointed the flashlight into the gutter, sliding the beam back and forth. Nothing. I wondered if I had the right spot, looked up at the house and knew I did. Remembered the wind blowing Branson's cigarette ash and widened my search. A moment later, found what I was looking for.

It was in the street now, flattened by a few tires. An empty matchbook. I turned it over and saw

BLUE BIRD MOTEL

INDIO, CA

in blue letters across the front. A small bird between the name and the location. The cardboard had been dimpled from the gravel in the street. One of those narrow ones, looked like eight matches, all gone now.

The cops had missed it. They probably hadn't come anywhere near it, other than when Branson had parked here, since it was across the street and two houses away. I looked up and down the block. Nothing moved. The wind had died down, and an expectant pause seemed to hang over the area. The hair on my arms was standing up, as if there were a static charge trembling in the atmosphere.

I sat down at the curb, thinking. The matchbook didn't appear to be very old despite having been run over. I tried to remember what Branson used to light up yesterday. Saw him flick a lighter and put it back in his pocket. So I knew the matchbook wasn't his.

Pure luck that I'd found it. My eyes had seen it yesterday, but my brain hadn't. Rattled around upstairs for two days, until my hands were busy and my mind was relaxed. But where did it come from? Did it even matter?

I decided to do my thinking inside. Locking the front door behind me, I went into the kitchen and put the flashlight and the matchbook on the counter. The phone was sitting there, now without its mating handset. That was still lying in pieces on the floor, under the dent in the wall on the other side of the kitchen. In the shadowed room, the hole looked deeper than I knew it was. I went over and inspected the drywall, running my fingers over the damage. A little of it flaked away and fell to the floor in tiny chunks next to the broken phone, tapping the polished hardwood as they landed. The sound was amplified by the silence of the rest of the house. The harm I'd done to the wall looked repairable, but I couldn't say the same for the phone. I picked it up and laid it on the kitchen table where it sat in silent rebuke.

There was a bottle of bourbon on one of the top shelves. I poured three fingers in a glass, and sat down at the table with the drink and the matchbook. Absently turned it over in my hand, as though I was doing a card trick. I gulped half the bourbon and it burned on the way down.

The Blue Bird Motel. I'd never heard of it. Probably a low-rent, pay-by-the-week or -month place off the beaten track, light-years away from the glitzy resorts that populated the Palm Springs area. The fact that it was in Indio, and not part of a chain, suggested that.

Again I wondered if the matchbook had anything to do with anything. Probably just a random piece of trash. But the cardboard was still shiny and stiff, the only mark of wear being the pavement dimples. So it hadn't been there too long.

If the matchbook belonged to the murder victim, then he was staying at the Blue Bird. That much was obvious. A drug addict would fit, paying weekly rent in a run-down motel. Comes out here for Deirdre's help, maybe had some inside information on the area's drug trade. Which would explain someone trying to stop him.

I saw the guy standing outside, getting his nerve up. Smoking. Empty matchbook discarded. Or being dropped in a struggle and blowing down the street. Any number of things. The matchbook may have been the culprit's. If the death wasn't drug-related, that left Turret in the scenario I'd related to Deirdre this morning. Maybe the boy was simply in the wrong place at the wrong time. Saw Turret lurking and was killed because of it.

The police hadn't found a vehicle belonging to the victim, though. If he'd driven here, he probably wasn't alone. Someone had taken the car after what happened. The killer himself? A companion who escaped?

One thing was certain. I wouldn't find out just sitting here. I should call the cops and tell them about finding the matchbook.

Which now had my fingerprints all over it. I hadn't thought of that, and silently cursed myself. At the very least, Branson would be furious with me for contaminating a piece of potential evidence. He wouldn't hesitate to make things tough for me, judging from his outburst this morning. And I should have kept my mouth shut as I was leaving the interrogation room.

I wondered where in Indio the Blue Bird was. Got the phone book and opened it to the Yellow Pages. The place was nowhere to be found, which didn't surprise me given my earlier guess about it. I flipped to the white pages, the fine print straining my eyes in the dimly lit kitchen.

There. Halfway down the page. Indio was a thirty-minute drive south on I-10 or one hour if you followed Palm Canyon Drive as it curved against the base of the mountains through most of the other valley cities.

An obvious choice presented itself. Call the cops or check it out myself first. Maybe if I pursued it on my own, I'd find that the Blue Bird had nothing to do with the murder and I wouldn't have to risk Branson's ire for no reason.

Then the possibility of Turret being involved hit me again. Maybe he was the smoker. Maybe he was staying at the motel right now. I could make a quick call and find out if he was registered there, but I didn't want to chance alerting him in any way. If Turret was behind this, and I could surprise him, take him down myself... the idea had a certain *mano a mano* appeal to it. And boy, did he have it coming from me—an old score I'd never imagined being able to settle.

In the end, my earlier decision to stay out of the case wasn't a factor. Here was a gift from the karmic gods. I couldn't say no.

CHAPTER SIX

I tried not to think about what I was doing, afraid that if I debated the pros and cons any further, good sense would prevail or I would chicken out entirely. Still, I took more time than I needed to moving around the house, making sure the windows were shut and locked, closing and locking the sliding glass door in the kitchen. I wrote Deirdre a note saying I went out for a drink and would be back around two. Left it on her night table in the small pool of light from the bedside lamp. I lied because I knew she wouldn't approve of what I was doing, convincing myself if the trip proved fruitless there was no reason to upset her. Like most married men with their wives, I was afraid of Deirdre.

I made a last circuit of the house, then checked the inside door lock in the shop. Just before I shut the light off, something occurred to me. In one of the bench drawers were some gloves I used for staining furniture and I grabbed a pair to take with me. Probably wouldn't need them, but if it came to it, I wanted to be more careful than I'd been with the matchbook. In the living room, I set the burglar alarm to allow movement inside for Deirdre but no outside entry, then double locked the front door behind me.

Outside in the car, I clicked on the dome light and found a map in the glove compartment. I checked the address I'd written down on a scrap of paper. The Blue Bird was on Highway 86 in Indio, just off the Dillon Road exit from the interstate. I started the car, telling myself I was doing the right thing. The engine came to life immediately. I felt bad about not talking it over with Deirdre, but I knew that one word from her would keep me home tonight.

Rolling silently over the empty streets, the nighttime breeze whispered through the open windows and dried the sweat on my skin. For all my attempts to avoid thinking about it, I was still apprehensive about what to do once I got to the motel. Check things out first, try to determine if Turret was staying there. I resigned myself to telling the cops what I'd found no matter what happened, despite my earlier inclination to avoid that if I could. I'd just have to deal with Branson and his attitude. So that was settled.

I turned on the radio, finding KCLB again. The overnight guy, known as the "Night Manager," introduced a band called Mazzy Star. He described them as a cross between the Velvet Underground and the Doors. Their chiming guitars and echoing voices blended together into a woozy, hypnotic sound that soothed my jangling nerves as the freeway on-ramp came up. The traveler's stop was still open, but only a few gas station and restaurant customers were visible, wraithlike figures in the sodium glow shuffling to and from their vehicles.

I got on the freeway going east. The engine heaved briskly up to speed as the wind and the music on the radio filled the car. Mazzy Star was still on, and the song featured a spooky organ sound that was like the Doors at their most psychedelic. It brought back a smoky, hallucinatory night I'd experienced some thirty years ago, a party where the drugs and alcohol were freely offered and nonstop. Loud music had pounded my eardrums all evening, until a bizarre conversation with Glenn Turret later on in a quiet corner of the house.

On a fishing trip with his parents, he'd watched the lifeguards administer CPR to someone who'd almost drowned. The victim survived, and Turret remembered wondering what it felt like to have that much power in a life or death situation. He went on and on about the godlike qualities of those lifeguards. If I hadn't been so stoned at the time, maybe the story would have scared me.

Twenty minutes later, I was at the Highway 111 turnoff. The bright lights of the Indian casinos glared in my windshield as I made a right off the highway and entered the city of Indio.

Indio is a dusty old place with a grungy southwestern flavor that I normally found appealing. On more carefree evenings, Deirdre and I would drive past the quaint old buildings here, through relaxed, siesta-like streets, catching the aromas of Mexican cooking on the musty, crop-scented air. Sometimes we'd hear *ranchera* music drifting in the wind, and watch the falling sunlight burnish the town a twilight gold.

Now the area was enshrouded in darkness that felt stifling in my unease, and I had to force myself to go on. I turned off the radio and slid through the dim city light toward the motel. The Union Pacific tracks at Indio Boulevard jarred me to attention; I made a right just after them, following the boulevard as it turned into Highway 86. The Blue Bird would be just a few blocks down, I remembered from the map. I slowed down a bit, squinted at the address numbers on my left. To the right, the railroad tracks paralleled the road. The silent hulks of two boxcars, massive and dark, sat on some siding next to the tracks, sentries standing guard.

In the light from a streetlamp, I verified the address number I'd written down. 82-420. I was still in the 83s. A little farther on, across more tracks, was a U.S. Border Patrol office, and the police station I knew, was just a few blocks east. That made me nervous. If I'd given myself half a chance, I would have turned around and abandoned the whole venture. Instead, I concentrated on the street numbers.

I entered the 82-000 block, then passed under Golf Center Parkway. The Amtrak station loomed on my right, followed by another bridge overhead, this time for Jackson Street, and I thought maybe I'd missed it. If I hit Monroe, I'd definitely gone too far.

Suddenly, it appeared. Its name was lit up in pale blue letters under the jaundiced light from the streetlamps. "*By the week or month.*" I read further, and saw that no credit card logos were present. I tried to swallow the lump in my throat as I went by, taking in the scene as it rolled across my field of view like a painted canvas backdrop on a movie set.

The Blue Bird was a small place set back from the street by a shallow parking area. Weeds shot up through cracks in the concrete. A dusty old Plymouth that looked as if it hadn't been moved in months sat in front of the office, inert under a thick coat of dirt. A tumbleweed had blown up against its side. The only other vehicle was parked in front of one of the rooms. A small pickup truck with an old camper shell on its back.

The building itself was a one-story strip of about fifteen rooms badly in need of a facelift. Disheveled and run-down, paint faded and peeling. A dozen or so roof tiles missing, probably blown off in the gusty winds that sometimes hit this area. The office at the far left end was well-lit, with a neon vacancy sign hanging in the window. About half the rooms' porchlights were burned out though, including number 2 with the pickup truck in front. Its front door was in shadow, the curtains in the unlighted window closed. The porchlight for number 12 was illuminated, the room faintly lit behind closed curtains.

I slowly accelerated past the Blue Bird and made a U-turn up the block, hugging the curb as I inched closer to the motel. I stopped two doors away and turned off the engine, my heartbeat going up a few notches. It was now or never, I thought, and got out of the car.

I started toward the motel as nonchalantly as I could. Passed an auto body shop, then the pest control business next door. When I reached the motel parking lot, I realized I'd left the gloves on the front seat of my car. Cursing under my breath, I wheeled around, feeling naked and exposed, and saw my headlights going full-blast, shining like beacons by the side of the road. Hurrying back to the car, I realized I wasn't made for this. I'd brought gloves for the remote possibility of a surreptitious search, but no weapon if I had to deal with Turret. Not smart. But the frustration I felt pumped me up and gave me a reckless courage. I switched off the headlights and grabbed the gloves, stuffing them in my pocket as I approached the motel again. I noticed that all the rooms except 2 and 12 had their curtains open wide to the night. The place was practically empty.

I wasn't expecting that. I decided not to talk to anyone in the office just yet. Instead, I'd knock at the doors of the two rooms that looked occupied. If Turret answered one of them, I'd take him down immediately—I'd been in enough fights in prison to be confident in that area. Plus I'd have the element of surprise. If someone else answered, I'd apologize and say I had the wrong room. Either way, I'd bring in the cops afterward. I'd try number 12 first, since it was the one with a light on.

When I reached the door, I paused to give the parking lot and street one last look.

Nobody.

I knocked, more tentatively then I'd planned. "Manager," I called out, improvising. I turned away from the window in case Turret peeked out.

No response.

Another three knocks, this time louder. "Manager."

Still nothing.

Looking around again, I saw that number 2 remained dark and undisturbed. No swaying curtains from curious neighbors. The empty street and quiet parking lot seemed to urge me on.

Five firm knocks got nothing but silence from room 12. Surprising, given the light behind the curtains. Thought I'd see about number 2 with the truck in front. I turned to go that way, then, on a whim, tried the door in front of me instead.

Unlocked. An even bigger surprise. I hesitated. Looked around once more and found myself alone, still. I almost wanted someone to notice me and demand what the hell I was doing.

Okay, think. Light's on inside but the door's unlocked. No car out front and no response to my knock. Seemed a little off. The room was either empty, or the occupant was asleep or taking a shower or something and hadn't heard the door. But why was the door unlocked if the person had left? Who sleeps with the lights on? And a knock should have wakened him if he was sleeping. Unless . . . unless there was something wrong.

I wasn't thinking of Turret now, I was thinking of the kid on my front lawn. Decided I should just go in, make sure no one needed help. If I heard the shower, I'd be out of there.

I pushed the door open. Nobody greeted me with an angry question. I didn't hear running water.

"Hello? Anybody here?" If someone was, they weren't answering. Or couldn't.

My shadow extended into the dimly lit room from the bright porchlight, and I was inside before I knew it. I shut the door behind me. Snapped the deadbolt home and paused a moment to let my eyes adjust to the light. The bedroom was empty. I crossed to the bathroom quickly to check there, with the same result.

No one here. A musty smell of old carpet and unlaundered linen, as if the window hadn't been opened in a long time. And smoke. Place like this probably let you smoke all you want. I went back to the door, thinking I should leave. Turned around instead, gave the room a closer look. It was larger than it seemed from outside, about fifteen by twenty feet. A double bed on the left, against the wall and parallel to the front window. Two small night tables with lamps flanked the headboard. Across the room on the right, a small closet with a flimsy, louvered wooden door that folded shut in two sections, next to an ancient TV on a stand. Against the back wall and directly facing me, a table and mirror that reflected where

I stood unmoving at the door. The mirror was too short to catch the uneasiness on my face. A chair stood on one side of the table.

A wall extended along the far side of the bed, separating the bathroom alcove from the rest of the room. The light came from a ceiling fixture with one of its bulbs burned out. It was covered by a translucent glass shade which held the corpses of various flying insects, dark spots against the frosted glass.

The place had the air of someone having left in a hurry, and I got the impression they weren't coming back. No clothes, suitcases or toilet articles were visible anywhere in the room, which was untidy and disordered. Something didn't sit right.

I took the matchbook out of my shirt pocket. Considered it. Looked over at the two night tables, each with an ashtray next to the lamp. Only one of them held a book of Blue Bird matches.

Those were pretty long odds. The one in my hand came from this room, I was sure of it. A quick look around wouldn't hurt anybody. I put on my gloves and started on the night tables first. Both were cheap wood veneer, with one drawer at the top and an open space beneath it for linens. I went to the one closest to me first and opened the drawer.

A phone book inside and nothing else.

About to close the drawer, I thought better of it and pulled out the directory. Flipped through it to see if there was anything, a note or a marker, tucked between its pages. I didn't find anything and tossed it on the bed. Then I recalled something I'd said to that reporter on the phone earlier tonight. I picked the book up again, going to the R's in the residential section. It was hard to turn the pages with the gloves on.

"Come on," I whispered impatiently. Finally I got to the page I wanted.

And couldn't believe my eyes.

CHAPTER SEVEN

The "x" was marked in black pen-ink, and it was right next to our name. Which should have been unlisted, but that was the least of my problems. Now I knew that whoever had stayed in this room was looking for me or Deirdre. Maybe both of us.

Was it the boy who'd died on my lawn? Or Glenn Turret? Whoever it was, hopefully his name would be listed in the motel register, although in a place like this, which probably preferred cash, that wasn't a sure thing. I'd have to find a way to ask as soon as I finished in here.

I put the phone book down and went to the opposite side of the bed. The other night table accommodated the phone, and I briefly wondered why the phone book was in the other drawer, then decided it didn't matter. Without thinking, I almost picked up the receiver to check for a dial tone, not sure why that would help me, but I thought better of it, worried that it would somehow alert the office to my presence. Instead, I pulled open the drawer and found a small Bible in a plastic cover sitting inside. Hoping for lightning to strike twice, I went through it in search of any telltale scraps of paper, but found nothing.

I crossed the room to the closet and slid the door open. Nothing inside but an empty shelf and a few bare hangers on the rack, and a luggage holder folded in the corner.

I turned and took a few steps past the mirrored table and the chair. The bathroom was small, with the sink, toilet and bathtub all crammed in together. First I checked behind the door for anything hanging there. Nothing, just an empty hook. The shower curtain was old and brittle, open and bunched at the end of the tub. A smudge of dirt near the drain, but the tub looked completely dry. I took off a glove and checked the shower curtain, lightly sliding my fingertips over the plastic. I felt a few drops of water in the deeper creases near the bottom.

Someone had showered here a while ago, but not too long. Two days at the most, I guessed.

It was time to bring in the police. They'd print the room, get a name or description from the desk clerk and quickly identify the person who'd stayed here. If it was the victim, whose prints they obviously already possessed, this would be a huge break. Knowing the victim's identity would bring them that much closer to the killer.

Unless I had the wrong room entirely. It didn't seem that way, especially with our name marked off in the directory, and I didn't feel like knocking on any more doors anyway. Just make the phone call and let the cops do their jobs.

In the back of my mind, I knew I wouldn't admit I'd come out here. I'd simply tell them what I'd found in the street and they would take it from there. Glad I'd been careful wearing the gloves, I put back on the one I just removed, feeling confident I hadn't left a print on the damp shower curtain. Even if I had, it was probably in an obscure enough place to remain undetected.

I started toward the door, intending to call the police from home. On the way out, I noticed one of the pillows from the unmade bed sitting on the chair. I grabbed it as I walked past, expecting to find nothing underneath.

A small, leather-bound notebook sat in the middle of the seat cushion.

It looked like a diary. Whomever it belonged to had vacated the

room in a hurry, had probably flung the pillow into the chair hap-
hazardly without noticing what was there, perhaps in the act of
gathering up clothing to pack. Now the small book stared up at me
as I tried to decide whether it was worth it to crack the binding and
step further into whatever was going on.

I dropped the pillow, picked up the notebook and brought it
over to the bed. Turned it over slowly in my gloved hands as I took
a seat on the mattress. I knew I was pressing my luck by taking the
time to do this. Knew it wasn't smart to linger in a room I'd basically broken into while there was still the possibility that its occupant would return. The sensible thing to do was get out as quickly
as possible, leaving the book behind, and let the cops handle things
from here. But I couldn't resist looking through what was sitting in
my hands right now. I just wanted a few more minutes. Five at the
most, I promised myself.

The covers had nothing printed on them. Just smooth black
cowhide worn shiny in a few places. I went to the front page, hoping to find a name there or inside the cover. Nothing. Same for the
back. The handwriting inside looked masculine, for some reason,
and the day and date headings told me that it was in fact a diary.
I skimmed the material and got snatches of what he'd written, but
nothing concerning the events of the last few days. Stuff about
school ... he was in some kind of communications degree program. What he did with his friends ... the band he saw last night at
a club. None of it so far told me anything concrete about who he
was or where he lived, and my patience was wearing thin. I skipped
to the last few entries and found one for Saturday, April 14th. Just
two days ago, right before the murder.

*... it's so dry out here, and hot! Not like the humidity I'm used to ... it
irritates my skin so it itches constantly ...*

My eyes flew over the page, desperate to find something useful.

*... when you get out of the car to take a piss or get something to eat, it
feels like stepping into a blast furnace ...*

I forced myself to read faster.

... It's been such a long drive, I sure hope this is all worth it ...

I was beginning to wonder whether reading this cold would tell me anything at all. However, it was apparent that the author wasn't from around here, which was at least a start. And if he was coming from the east or south, Indio would have been on the way in to Palm Springs.

A little further down, same day: *Got off the freeway for some food and found this dump after dinner. What kind of a name is the Blue Bird for a motel?*

I skipped ahead, turning the page to the last paragraph that had been written.

Just got out of the shower and I'm already sweating. This is miserable. The air conditioner is blowing warm air around the room. Nine o'clock at night and it must be close to ninety. There's no way I'm going to sleep tonight. Too hot, and too much on my mind. Might–.

I looked up, thinking I'd heard a car creep past on the road outside. It was probably nothing but I checked anyway, moving the curtain aside a fraction of an inch for a narrow view of the parking lot and street.

Which were empty.

I craned my neck to see the far end of the lot. The same two vehicles were parked there; nothing had changed since I'd come in. If anything, it looked more peaceful than before.

Deciding it was random traffic or just my frayed nerves, I returned to my seat at the edge of the bed and picked up the diary. I thumbed through it to find the last entry. The gloves slowed me down again, but I eventually found the right page. I tried to relax, but the scare with the passing car had given me a greater sense of urgency. I knew I was pushing the edges of my self-imposed time limit. It just wasn't smart to sit here like this. But I couldn't help myself.

–Might as well drive over there right now, get it over with. I'd have to–

I heard footsteps from outside, saw a shadow flick across the window. I flew to the still-open closet, got inside and crouched in a position that faced the room. Slid the door shut as a key was inserted into the lock.

The room was visible in fractured strips through the louvered closet door. The door opened and I saw his shadow knife into the room before I saw him. After coming inside, he quickly surveyed the room. His gaze stopped on the diary I'd left on the bed, then he closed the door behind him.

A light leather jacket and blue jeans were all I saw before I shrank back into the closet, hoping to remain invisible as long as possible by avoiding the strips of light finding their way through the slats.

The man moved further into the room and stopped directly in front of the closet, in my line of sight again. I held my breath.

Thankfully, his immediate goal was the edge of the bed and the diary I'd dropped there. His back was to me so I couldn't see his face. But he was tall and had short, reddish brown hair. Not Turret, unless he'd gotten a dye job and grown a couple of inches taller. Whoever it was picked up the book and opened it. Leafed through it a few moments before stopping to read something. He nodded to himself, and I got the feeling he'd found what he was looking for.

Then the man stiffened, as if sensing another presence in the room.

CHAPTER EIGHT

Without turning, he slowly stuck the little book inside his jacket. When his hand came out again, it was holding a gun.

Shards and splinters of wood exploded outward as I burst through the closet door, ripping it from its hinges. The slide at the top tore out of its track with a loud shriek and I caught a surprised look on his face, eyes wide as he turned toward me. Part of the closet door was still between us. Then my forward momentum toppled him backward onto the bed, knocking the gun from his hand when I crashed into him. I heard it thump on the floor somewhere behind me amid the crazed bellow I'd let out in the attack.

He was pinned under me and what remained of the closet door, struggling violently to get free. I had a piece of wood pressed into his Adam's apple, and heard the breath wheezing in his throat. His eyes were bugged out inches from mine, fixed on me with frantic pleading. He clutched both sides of the slat, trying to force it upward to catch a breath.

I let up on the pressure slightly and asked him, "You with Turret?" my voice tight with exertion.

His eyes flickered back and forth, struggling to come up with an answer. Then he settled on one. "Yeah ... he sends ... his ... regards."

That surprised me, which gave the man an opening. He slammed his open palm under my chin and threw me off the bed, backward onto the floor. I landed hard amongst the splintered fragments of the door. The gun was right there. I grabbed it as he took a step toward me, and I'm sure the weapon in my hand was the only reason he didn't stick around to beat the hell out of me.

Instead, he stumbled to the door, throwing it open as I spun to my left, still on the floor, and pointed the gun at him through my upraised legs. He was briefly framed in the lighted doorway as he fled, distinct as a paper target on a shooting range. The gun shook in my hands. I probably could have hit him with my eyes closed, but I couldn't bring myself to pull the trigger. He sprinted through the small parking lot to the street, then headed toward where I'd parked my car. And he still had the diary in his jacket pocket.

I dashed out the door after him, not seeing anyone else around. As I reached the street a car blew past me, headed in the direction I'd come from. It was him. Again, I chose not to shoot, cursing myself afterward, certain I could have blown out one of his tires.

Too late now, the car speeding away too quickly for me to even get a plate number. My car was down the street the opposite way. I rushed over, praying the man hadn't punched a knife into a tire or something. No time, I was sure.

Precious seconds were wasted removing a glove so my hand would fit in my pocket for the keys.

Finally, I got them out, unlocked the door, threw the gun on the seat with both gloves and jammed myself in behind the wheel. The car started immediately, coming to life with a guttural roar. I gunned the engine and accelerated down the block, hoping to pick up the man's tail, which I'd already lost sight of. Traffic lights, red or green, meant nothing to me; I raced through the deserted streets, desperate to overtake the fleeing vehicle and the man I knew was somehow involved in the murder. Streetlamps and store signs and traffic lights blurred together in an unbroken stream of color, like those time-lapse photos of nighttime traffic.

I thought I saw brake lights flash in the distance several blocks ahead, then slide around a corner and disappear. I accelerated further, the engine humming, and almost clipped a pickup truck advancing into an intersection I'd barreled through against the light. The driver was so startled, I didn't even get a horn.

The close call made me a little more cautious going through the next couple of lights, removing my foot from the gas pedal momentarily as I neared the intersections, then mashing it to the floor once I determined they were clear. In my excitement, I wasn't sure I could identify the exact street the taillights had turned into. But I took my best shot and made a screeching left back toward the highway, retracing the way I'd come into the city.

Banging over the railroad tracks again, my car bottomed out, its underside scraping against the humped concrete and iron rails. Sparks flew out behind me in the rearview mirror. Up ahead to my right, I caught a lone pair of taillights streaking down the southbound lanes of Highway 111, leaving me no choice but to assume they belonged to the car I was chasing. After crossing over the Coachella Wash, I wrenched the wheel to the right and shot up the onramp in pursuit.

The taillights I'd just seen, no more than red pinpricks of light, were now nowhere in sight, and I was afraid I'd lost him. He could have made a U-turn over the dirt median and onto the northbound lanes, but if he had I'd missed it. Maybe he'd continued south, I thought, rocketing past the exit on my left for Avenue 50, its presence a mere twitch in my peripheral vision that registered a split second later. Instinctively, I slammed on the brakes, fishtailing down the road, leaving the smell of burned rubber in the air and thick black treadmarks on the pavement. I could see them trailing behind me in the red glow of the brake lights, which changed to pale white as I jerked the car into reverse, craned my neck around and sped backward toward the exit I'd missed, the transmission whining loudly in protest. Luckily, I was the only one on the road at that hour.

At the exit, I stopped and got out of reverse in one motion, then followed the exit lane to the left, through the median and over the northbound lanes, disregarding the stop sign there. Then I was in relative darkness beyond the highway, the streetlamps few and far between in this agricultural section of Coachella. My headlights stabbed the darkness when I came off the highway, momentarily illuminating a cloud of dust hanging in the air beside the road to my right, a few hundred yards away. It was either the remnants of a solitary dust-devil on this relatively windless night at the far end of the valley, or evidence of a man-made disturbance, like a car veering into the roadside dirt.

Without hesitation, I swung to the right, cutting the corner and throwing up dust clouds of my own, then followed the curve way too fast, straddling the orange center line as I tried to keep the car under control. In the field to my left, three radio towers stood skeletal and erect, reaching up into the nighttime sky, their red aircraft warning lights blinking solemnly.

The road had just straightened out on its long trek east toward the Mecca Hills when I made out a lone car parked in the dirt on the other side of the road, faced the wrong way. Its lights were out and I couldn't tell yet if it was the car I was chasing. I squinted through the dusty windshield from several hundred yards away, and quickly closing the distance, thought I saw movement behind the vehicle, like someone crouched near the trunk. I slowed down, realizing too late that this detour was probably a trap, and a moment later he poked his head above the car's back end and leveled a rifle my way.

I ducked to the right, taking the wheel with me, and skidded off the road into the dirt as my side window blew inward with a deafening pop, showering the interior with a hail of glass, the sharp, crystallized particles cutting into my skin and covering every surface in the cabin. The other side window was gone too, taken out by the bullet's continued trajectory over my head. Razor-like shards and splinters extended from the window opening, trembling and breaking apart as the car plowed through the furrows and irrigation ditches of the field I'd driven into.

Bouncing around like a pinball, I struggled to keep my foot on the pedal, with my head just above the dashboard to see where I was going, but low enough to avoid getting shot. The suspension was taking a hell of a beating, the car jolting violently over the cultivated rows of produce and the channels between them. The headlight beams seesawed crazily in front of me, then winked out abruptly when the car slammed nose first into a large irrigation ditch. The front end burrowed into the soft, wet soil. If I hadn't been trying to evade the rifle shots, I might have gone through the windshield. Instead, my upper body was thrown against the instrument panel, the gear-shift lever punching into my chest, the side of my head bouncing off the radio console. I went blurry for a few seconds and tried to shake it off, but couldn't stop the ringing in my ears. Then I realized I'd held on to the steering wheel for dear life during the crash, so that my left arm was pressed down on the horn. It was blaring continuously, piercing the night with a shrill cacophony. When I let go it stopped, and I could hear the engine idle roughly, then splutter and die.

CHAPTER NINE

Forcing myself to move quickly, I untwisted my legs and waist from beneath the steering wheel, sore all over. Blindly, I felt around for the gun I'd flung onto the seat beside me, and found it on the floor wedged up near the heater vent. I pulled it out, then pushed open the passenger door, desperate to get out of the car in case the shooter decided to finish me off. The door swung open easily, bouncing on its hinges before settling. I tumbled out into the dirt, crawled to the back of the car, and peeked over the trunk toward the road.

The man's car was gone, nowhere in sight. All I saw was the empty road and the unplanned exit lane I'd carved into the dirt. The pungent scent of farmland hung in the air, along with the steady buzz of insects. A placid calmness resettled over the evening. A few miles away, the interstate traffic cut through the hills, moving in slow motion silence as it entered and exited the valley. To the right: the road I'd skidded off stretching toward an ancient beach, powdered silver by grains of sifted moonlight. To the left: Highway 111 disappearing southward, not a speck of traffic on it. It seemed I was alone.

Then I became aware of the faint sound of music somewhere behind me. Turning, I saw a small house about two hundred yards away, illuminated by glaring security lamps. In my panicked flight through the field I'd missed it. Now I could see shadows moving against the brightly lit background of the house, several silhouetted figures making their way toward me. As they approached, I put the gun in the car, not wanting to seem a threatening presence on this darkened property. I wondered if the shooter would have been scared off so easily if not for those lights.

There were three of them. One was holding a flashlight, a full-moon circle of light bobbing up and down in the darkness. Tall, wearing a red baseball cap stained dark with grease, a tanktop and dungarees. The other two both wore T-shirts and one had a tattoo on his forearm.

They stopped on the other side of the ditch in front of my crippled vehicle. The leader pointed the flashlight at me, running the light up and down before settling on my face. The glare obscured my view of them.

"What are you doing here?" he asked warily.

I thought quickly, came up with something about a drunk driver running me off the road. "Didn't you see him?" I asked. No response. "Could you get that light out of my eyes?"

The light dropped to my feet. They were probably migrant workers, leery of dealing with the police. That was fine with me. "He was driving the opposite way and he came right toward me," I continued, pointing back along the road.

"What about your windows?" one of the others asked, as the flashlight played over the car.

Shit. I hadn't thought of that. Kept my mouth shut, hoping they'd just want me off the property. I could see them thinking, obviously suspicious of my story. One of them circled around to the opposite side of the car, looking at the damage. The gun was right on the front seat, another question I couldn't answer. So far, they hadn't seen it.

"You need help with your car?" the first one finally asked.

Twenty minutes later, after a lot of grunting and heaving, we managed to get the car out, first by digging the driveshaft out of the dirt, then starting it up and pushing.

Back on level ground again, I shook their hands and said I owed them a cold one, but we all knew that would never happen. I backed out the way I'd come, so as not to further damage their crop by turning around. Slow going, the car sluggishly negotiating the dips and ruts and raising clouds of dust. Eventually, I reached the edge of the field and stopped on the shoulder of the road. The head-lights, undamaged when they hit the soft dirt bank of the canal, threw twin rivers of light that shifted and swelled in the swirling dust.

The men watched me leave. Just before I turned into the road, I gave them the high-beams as a farewell, but they had already turned back toward the house.

CHAPTER TEN

My car seemed to guide itself back toward Indio and the Blue Bird Motel as I tried to make sense of everything that had happened. It wasn't easy with the headache pounding in my skull. I drove slowly to give myself time to think.

If not for my bruises and the sprinkles of glass all around me, I would hardly have believed that the last few hours weren't some half-remembered episode of a TV cop show. In fact, the whole night seemed like one of those hallucinations you get just before falling asleep, your imagination running wild while the rest of the world goes on normally.

Tonight had been as far from routine as you could get without ending up dead, and I thought about what I should do next. I was lucky those men had helped me with the car. And glad that my car was old enough to not have airbags. Without a tow-truck driver to report the accident, I didn't have to tell the police about anything other than discovering that matchbook. Leaving out the rest of it, though, meant they wouldn't get my description of the motel room intruder, and more important, the gun that was now sitting in my back seat.

The gun. My prints were on that gun.

I could wipe it clean, but that would remove the shooter's as well. Out of the question. I wanted to give the police every chance of solving the crime. I'd take my chances and play it straight.

Pulling into the motel parking lot a few minutes later, the second thoughts began to take over. There was no chance I wouldn't spend the night in jail. My prints on the weapon could get me convicted of murder. I didn't think it would come to that, but it was possible.

I had to bite the bullet though. Finding that boy's killer was too important to me.

I parked in front of the office beside the dust-covered Plymouth and turned off the ignition. The office windows were still lit from within. The neon vacancy sign buzzed and flickered, then seemed to synchronize with the ticking of my engine as it cooled. Looking to my right, I noticed the other vehicle parked in front of number 2. That room's lights were still off, and I could see number 12's door hanging ajar, the way it had been left in my sudden departure.

Eager to get this over with, I got out of the car and swung the door shut. Broken glass fragments rattled around inside. The office door, like the rest of the place, was covered with old peeling paint, and a dingy blind was closed in the window. It had a "Manager" sign at eye level and a doorbell to the left, identified as the night bell and feebly illuminated under a layer of grime. I pressed it and heard a strident buzzing inside, followed by the faint sounds of someone grunting and moaning as if he'd been injured.

The door wasn't locked when I tried it, swinging open slowly on squeaky hinges. Stepping inside the well-lit office, I noticed a blank-screened TV in the upper right corner and a counter running across the room in front of me. The sounds of muffled struggle turned more frantic, coming from the floor behind the front desk.

He was tied up down there, hands and feet, squirming in the tight space behind the counter. Eyes bugged out in fear. His mouth was duct-taped and his breath came out in a rapid, shallow whistle.

An open door on my right said "Private." Beyond that, a dark alcove that I went through to get to the area behind the front desk. A short corridor on the right presumably led to the proprietor's living quarters.

Someone had done a thorough job incapacitating him. His legs were bound together at the knees and his feet were crossed one over the other and secured, preventing him from getting up to a standing position. The man's throat was working, his Adam's apple bobbing up and down as he struggled to get enough air around the duct tape. I ripped it off in one quick motion. He gasped several times, filling his lungs. There was a small patch of blood on the back of his head, a shiny, dark red spot congealing in his thick hair. Sweat beaded his face, which was as red as a bad sunburn. It was obvious he'd been getting pretty worked up over his predicament.

"You okay?"

"Who are you?" he asked, still breathing hard.

"My name's Tim Ryder," I answered, undoing his hands from behind his back.

"That guy isn't still around, is he?"

"You mean the one who did this to you?"

" 'Course. Who else would I be talking about?"

"What did he look like?"

I got the last of the tape off, and he rubbed his hands together, getting the circulation back.

"Tall, maybe six foot. Leather jacket and jeans. Red hair. White dude," he added, reaching for a pair of scissors under the counter. Next to them, a roll of duct tape with its ripped end hanging off. The manager was lucky it had been there, I thought. Those scissors could have been buried in his neck right now instead.

"Why? You know him?" the man asked, cutting the tape from his knees and feet.

"Not really," I answered.

A nervous look. "Not really? What does that mean?"

"Relax. He's no friend of mine."

"So who is he, then?"

"I'm not sure," I said, helping him up. "I'll tell you what I know after we call the police."

"You don't look so good yourself," he said, eyeing the bruise on the side of my face.

I brought my hand up to it and felt a bump. "I'll be all right."

Nodding, he brushed past me, and I followed him into a sitting area in the back that was part of the living quarters. He veered toward an easy chair next to the couch and sat down heavily.

"Dizzy," he said, touching the back of his head.

"You should get that looked at." I went into the kitchen to get him a glass of water, which he drained in several long gulps.

"'Preciate it, bud. I was beginning to think I'd be there all night." He got up and took the empty glass to the kitchen sink. "I gotta take a leak somethin' terrible. Be right back." Just before he left the room, he turned back to me and asked, "You ain't gonna rip me off, are you?"

"I would have left you tied up," I answered, shaking my head. "We should call the police, though."

"Soon as I'm done," he agreed, then disappeared down the hall past the kitchen.

I went to the phone sitting on the kitchen countertop and picked it up. Dialing my number, I recalled the way it had been marked in the phone book inside room 12. It rang three times before Deirdre answered. She sounded groggy, her voice thick with sleep.

"Deirdre, it's me. Are you awake?" I glanced at my watch. After one.

"Tim? Where are you? When did you leave?" she asked, perking up.

"I'll explain everything when you get down here." Or the cops will, I thought.

"Down where? What are you talking about? You're scaring me."

"Everything's fine," I assured her, trying to sound less worried than I felt. "I'm just going to need your help." I paused, looking for a way to put it. "I'll probably be in police custody within the hour." That sounded bad.

"Under arrest? For what? Damnit, Tim!"

"Nothing serious," I lied. "It won't stick. But I'd like you to be here."

"Fine. Just tell me where you are. I'll get there as soon as I can." Her voice hardened, all business now, no stranger to late night phone callers needing her help. Deirdre was always at her best under pressure and I relaxed with that thought.

"The Blue Bird Motel down in Indio. On Indio Boulevard as it turns into Highway 86."

"Dillon exit?" she verified, on the ball as usual. God, I loved her.

"You got it. Make a right at the tracks and follow Indio Boulevard north. The Blue Bird is on your left, three miles or so. Can't miss it." *Especially with the cops that will be crawling all over the place.*

"Gimme thirty," she said.

"Deirdre?"

"Yes?"

"Don't get a ticket." I felt her smile at the other end.

"You either," she countered. "See you soon. And stay out of Branson's face if he shows up. I don't want to get there and find you in a choke hold."

"I'll try to be nice. I love you."

"Oh, Tim," she said. "I'm sorry about earlier."

"I know. I'm sorry too." A forgiving silence. "You better get going."

When I hung up the manager was standing in the hallway. "Your wife?"

"Yeah," I said, pushing the phone toward him.

He came over and picked it up, punching in the numbers. I heard him give his name–Ken Sutter–to the dispatcher as I walked back to the front office for a quick peek outside. It seemed as normal as it could be under the circumstances. I double-locked the door just in case. Went behind the front counter and took a look at the key rack on the wall. Sixteen rooms, two keys for each. Attached to big plastic tags with the room number on it but not the name of the motel. Probably for security. The credit card-type ones at the hotel chains didn't even have the room number.

I saw that room 2 had one key out. Both keys gone from the space for number 12. The guy I'd fought with had one of them, probably not legitimately. I looked around for the motel register, but didn't see it. No computer either. I went back into the living room.

Sutter was still on the phone. I took a seat on the couch, under a faded painting of Palm Valley, as it was called in the early days. There was a glass-topped coffee table in front of me, chipped, and the recliner next to it didn't match the couch. Between them, a small end table and lamp. A rickety entertainment center sat against the opposite wall, and the kitchen was separated by the countertop and bar. Faint light filtered in through threadbare curtains covering the room's one window.

"That's right, the Blue Bird," Sutter said into the phone. "No, no, I'm all right . . . Yeah, I'm sure . . . Okay . . . We'll be waiting for 'em. Thanks."

Sutter hung up, came over and sat down. "They'll be here in a few minutes."

He was a big man with a paunch that hung over his belt and pallid, doughy skin. He told me that he'd been running the place for about ten years now, and lived here too, as I could see.

"Indio's stayed pretty quiet all this time," he said, " 'cept for the drug flare-ups every now and then." There it was again, I thought.

"Hasn't grown around here like it has in Palm Desert and some of the other cities," Sutter continued. "Shopping centers, golf courses." He shook his head. "Just brings in a lot of traffic. 'Course, we see a little more with the casinos down here."

"What about tonight?" I prompted.

"Well, everything seemed pretty normal up until about eleven or so," he began. "That's when I stepped outside for a cigarette. I don't like to smoke inside," he explained. "Smells bad enough in here as it is."

"What time did you say?" I asked, trying to tie it in with what I'd been doing.

"After eleven, ten minutes after maybe." I was in number 12 then, nosing around. "I usually step out around that time. Anyway, I'm just about to light up when I see this guy walking in like he owns the place."

"Where, in the parking lot?"

"Yeah."

"Toward room twelve, down at the other end?"

"I guess so. Could have been in that direction. How did you know?"

"I'll tell you later," I answered. "Go on."

"So he stops when he sees me, like he was surprised or something, and I could tell he was up to no good." He shook his head. "I shoulda turned around right then and come back inside and locked the door. But I'd only gotten one puff, didn't want to waste it." A chuckle. "Funny the little things that can screw you up. Tied up and gagged in my own place 'cause I wanted to finish my cigarette."

"Ever seen him before?"

"Nope, didn't know him. But then again, it's not unusual to see strangers walking in and out."

I wanted to ask what type of residents he normally got, short-term, long-term, out-of-towners, but knew we were pressed for time. The police would be here any second.

"What happened next?"

"He walks up to me and asks if I'm the manager, then wants a room. I tell him it's cash only, which is fine with him, so he follows me into the office. Never did get to finish my cigarette. Anyway, once we're inside, he pulls a gun, and I'm thinking 'Oh shit, is he gonna rob me?' But instead he asked me about the guest register. Told him it was in a drawer below the counter. Next thing I know I'm on the floor with a knot on my head, tied up with that tape."

"Can I take a look at the register?" I asked, hoping the guy hadn't taken it.

"Why?"

"Like to see who was in twelve."

I could see he was about to ask why again, but instead he shook his head and got up. "Follow me."

Sutter opened a drawer behind the lobby desk and put the book on the counter. It was big, too big to fit in a pocket or stick in the waistband of your pants. I opened it and found something that didn't really surprise me. The pages for the last few days had been ripped out.

"Jerk," Sutter muttered, seeing what had been done.

"You wouldn't have this information somewhere else would you?" I asked.

Sutter shook his head no.

"Damn." I thought a moment. Someone was going to some trouble to make sure the victim on my lawn wasn't identified, assuming the victim was the one who'd rented the room. Because after he'd died on my property, they'd spent a few seconds taking his wallet and ID. And the motel room key, most likely. Now this.

"I assume you're going to tell me what's going on eventually," Sutter said, interrupting my thoughts.

CHAPTER ELEVEN

The police arrived on the scene then. We heard their big engines in the parking lot outside as they pulled up, followed by the squeal of brakes and thumping doors. Red and blue shadows snuck through the gaps in the blinds, and seconds later they were pounding on the office door.

Sutter opened it.

"You the one that called in the assault?" one of the two officers asked. They were from the Indio Police Department.

"Yeah, that was me."

"Who are you?" the officer asked, turning to me.

"I'm the one that found him. After it happened."

"Hadn't been for him, I'd still be tied up down there," Sutter offered, looking between both of them. "It was damn uncomfortable, lemme tell you."

"You hurt?"

"No, I'm fine. Just a bump on the head."

"How 'bout you?" he asked me.

"I'm okay."

They both came in and gave the place a quick once-over, their gunbelts squeaking as they moved. The one doing the talking was in his late thirties, about my height and bulky, with a sun-worn complexion and light brown hair. His nameplate said "Regan." His partner was younger and shorter. Slim, with gelled, jet-black hair and an Asian cast to his skin. I saw his last name was Roy.

"Where'd it happen?" Regan asked.

"In here."

"The assailant took off right after, I assume."

"I guess. He knocked me out. Asked me for the guest register first." Sutter paused and continued. "Demanded, more like. With a gun."

"He had a gun?"

"Yeah. That's what he used to knock me out. Cracked me on the back of the head with it. Gave me a hell of a headache," Sutter explained, touching the tender spot.

"Actually," I interrupted, "it's in my car right now."

Everyone swung toward me with looks of surprise.

"The gun? You have it?" Regan asked.

I nodded.

"Show me," he said, moving to the door.

We all followed him outside to my car. Both officers noticed the broken windows and Roy asked what happened.

"It's a long story," I said, approaching the passenger side and reaching for the door.

Regan put a hand on my shoulder, pulling me back. "Don't touch it. It's in there?"

"Right on the seat."

He found the gun using the flashlight he pulled from his belt.

"Come over here a second," he told Sutter, shining the light on it. "That the same gun?"

Sutter leaned over and looked inside the car. "Looks like it. Yeah, I'd say that's it. Probably an impression of it on my head where he hit me," he joked, but didn't get a smile from either cop.

They both straightened and Regan said, "Okay, we better start at the beginning. What exactly happened?"

"You may want to call the Palm Springs Police Department," I advised.

Regan raised an eyebrow. "Why would we want to do that?"

I told them about the murder on my front lawn and why I thought it might be connected. "There's two detectives on the case. Branson and Tidwell. They'll probably want to hear about this."

Regan turned to his partner. "Have dispatch contact the sergeant. See if he wants to bring in Palm Springs. And get some backup too."

Roy nodded, then stepped away to make the call. Regan turned back to Sutter and me, taking out a notepad and pen.

Just then, I saw the light in room 2 come on over Regan's shoulder. Two people came outside, curious about all the commotion. Regan followed my gaze and saw them too. He didn't notice number 12 at the far end.

"How many guests you have tonight?"

"Just two rooms booked," Sutter answered, lifting his chin at number 2. "Room two over there, and twelve farther down–" That's when he caught sight of the splintered door hanging open, dim lamplight visible from inside. "Hey . . ."

Regan turned around again and saw the damage. "You had a break-in too?"

"Same guy that assaulted him," I explained, nodding at Sutter.

"This gets better every time you open your mouth," Regan said, as Roy finished calling it in and rejoined us. Sutter was eyeing me questioningly, wondering what exactly had gone down over there.

"Sergeant's coming out," Roy said. "He's getting Palm Springs over here too."

"Okay. See about those people over there," Regan directed, gesturing toward number 2. "Find out if they saw or heard anything. Then check out twelve."

"You got it," Roy said, wheeling around.

Another patrol car arrived then, adding to the kaleidoscope of red and blue light splashing over the old motel. Regan told us to wait while he conferred with the other officers.

Sutter leaned toward me when Regan was gone and lowered his voice. "What the fuck happened over there?"

"You'll find out in a second," I said, with an urgent hand on his shoulder. "But I need to ask you something first. It's very important. Was it a young man who rented that room?"

"Yeah."

"Early twenties?"

"I guess so."

"Yes or no?"

Sutter stopped to think. "Yeah. That seems about right."

"When did he check in?"

"Saturday night. Eight or nine probably."

It had to be him, the same guy on our front lawn.

Sutter interrupted my thoughts. "What's this all about? You know the guy who rented that room?"

Before I could answer, Regan came back. The two newcomers were rummaging around in the patrol car's trunk. One of them handed his partner a roll of yellow tape and took his own toward number 12. The other one headed to the front office.

"All right, somebody tell me what happened," Regan prompted, then turned to Sutter. "We'll start with you. You called in the assault."

"Right."

"Go ahead. From the beginning."

Sutter recounted the story he'd told me, from the time he saw the man in the parking lot to when I discovered him tied up on the office floor. Regan got a description of the assailant and verified a few things about exactly what the man had said and the time it all happened. At that point, Roy rejoined us after talking to the other tenants. They were standing in the doorway of room 2 in bathrobes, an older couple disturbed from their sleep by the unexpected activity.

"They didn't see or hear anything. Said they were real tired and slept from earlier tonight until now. I got their names if we need them later."

"Good enough," Regan responded, then turned to me. "Now how did you come to be in possession of that gun?"

I told him why I'd come out here, and about going into the room. Roy listened to the story while Regan wrote everything down.

"You shoulda just called the police," Regan said.

"I wasn't sure this place was even related to the murder. It was just a matchbook."

Regan shook his head. "You knew it could be important, or you wouldn't have come out here," he said. "You still have it?"

I pulled it out of my pocket, and Regan took it by the edges and put it in my car.

"There was something I wanted to tell you," I said to him when he came back.

"I'm all ears."

"My name was marked in the phone book in room twelve. Someone was looking for me or my wife. I think it was the kid who ended up dead on my lawn."

"How would you know that?" Regan asked.

I looked at Sutter, who was absorbing all this silently.

He shrugged. "Maybe the same guy. Young. Rented the room Saturday night." Then Sutter turned to me. "But what time did you find his body?"

"Right after six, Sunday morning. Why?"

He shook his head emphatically. "Couldn't have been him then."

"Why not?" Regan and I asked simultaneously.

" 'Cause he rang my doorbell Sunday morning asking for the duplicate key. Said he lost the first one. It was definitely after six o'clock."

There went my whole theory.

"You get his name on the register?" Regan asked.

"Yeah. But it doesn't help us now. Guy who hit me ripped the pages out of the book. No record of the last few days."

"Did your tenant say what happened to the first key?" I asked Sutter, still stunned at his revelation.

"No, and I didn't ask. I did tell him I'd have to charge him for a replacement though. He threw a five on the counter, which more than covered it. Then he took the second key and I haven't seen him since. Kinda seemed in a hurry."

"He checked out?" Regan asked.

"Well, not formally. Didn't say he was, anyway."

"You been in the room since he left?"

Sutter shook his head. "No. The deposit covers three nights. He didn't ask for it back, so I assumed he was still here."

"Who cleans the rooms?" Regan asked.

"I do." Sutter shrugged. "Probably not as often as I should."

Regan thought for a moment. "The key that guy used tonight was probably the one your tenant lost. It all fits."

"Except he wasn't the victim on my lawn," I said. An earlier thought resurfaced. The victim could not have come to my house alone, since his car wasn't found. Unless the killer, maybe with the help of an accomplice, took it.

"We'll get to that later. Hopefully, there's something in the room that'll help. Let's get back to tonight. You were in there yourself."

"Right." I told him about the diary I'd found. Then how I'd lost it during the break-in and gone after the man.

"And you're positive it was the same person that assaulted Mr. Sutter?" Regan asked.

"Absolutely. Tall white guy with short reddish hair. Leather jacket and jeans."

Regan looked to Sutter for confirmation.

"That's him," Sutter agreed.

"Where did your windows get shot out?" Regan asked me.

"Out in Coachella, off Avenue 50. I could show you."

"Let's go." He turned to Roy. "Bring Palm Springs up to speed when they get here." Then to the other two officers, who'd finished with the crime scene tape: "You guys follow us. We may have some evidence out there."

I followed Regan to his patrol car, a little worried. Deirdre should have arrived by now; it had been a good forty minutes since I'd spoken to her on the phone. But I decided not to say anything–she'd probably be here when Regan and I returned to the motel. Maybe she had to stop for gas or something; she wasn't the type to get lost.

"Buckle up," Regan told me when I got in the car.

CHAPTER TWELVE

The drive over was anticlimactic after the high-adrenaline car chase a few hours ago. The empty streets seemed static and one-dimensional, like partially developed photos. As we moved through the becalmed city toward the highway, I tried not to think about Deirdre's no-show, or the possible identities of the young motel guest and the intruder.

But Regan wouldn't let me relax.

"You know, what you did tonight can be a pretty serious crime. Involving yourself like that, there's no telling what could happen."

"And Sutter could still be tied up in that office with tape over his mouth," I replied in my own defense. "He wasn't doing so well when I found him."

Regan nodded. "I'm not inclined to take you into custody, although I do have grounds to arrest you for interfering. Or tres-passing for that matter. But I don't think Sutter would press charges."

"Thanks," I said, meaning it. He seemed to be a stand-up guy, a good cop and a fair man. "I appreciate it."

"Of course, I can't guarantee what Palm Springs will do if this turns into their case. They could see it a different way."

You don't know the half of it.

"There's something I didn't get a chance to tell you back there,"

I said, and waited while Regan sped up the highway on-ramp. "Somebody else may be involved in all this."

Regan gave me a quizzical look. "Who?"

"His name is Glenn Turret. He just got out of prison last week. I used to know him."

Regan had no idea of the background on this, it hadn't appeared in the papers yet. That would change tomorrow, I thought, remembering that reporter on our doorstep tonight.

"Used to?"

"It was a long time ago. Over thirty years."

"What makes you think he has anything to do with it?"

"The guy I fought with tonight told me."

Regan looked at me with disbelief. "You had a conversation with him? In the middle of a fight?"

"He fell backwards when came I out of the closet and I ended up on top of him. I had him pinned under me on the bed." Regan raised his eyebrows further, and we both chuckled. "And I hadn't even bought him dinner."

When we were done laughing, I continued. "Anyway, part of the closet door had come with me, and I used one of the broken slats on his neck. I was scared. I let him up for a little air and took a shot in the dark–asked him if he knew Turret. He admitted it." I thought about it. "I don't know. Maybe he was lying."

"Who is this Turret? And what made you ask that guy about him?"

I hesitated, reluctant to get into my criminal past. "You'll probably read about it in tomorrow's paper."

"Tell me about it."

Halfway through the short version, the turnoff for Avenue 50 came up. "Here it is."

Regan slowed down. "Which way?"

"Left."

We went over the median, stopped at the stop sign, then proceeded over the northbound lanes to Tyler.

"Take a right," I told him. "Just beyond the bend up here."

The other patrol car was still behind us as we followed the sharp curve in the road, which I'd shot through practically on two wheels a few hours earlier. A few miles away, the Mecca Hills looked destitute and ghostly in the pale moonlight that fell on this rural part of the valley. The radio towers on our left continued their solitary rhythm, red warning lights pulsing a perpetual heartbeat. The field I'd been forced into was now quiet and dark, and I could barely make out where my tires had dug into the dirt shoulder. Sprinkles of window glass sparkled like diamonds on the ground there.

"That's where my windows got shot out."

Regan slowed down and looked. "Where was he?"

"Farther down," I said, pointing ahead.

He crept up a few hundred feet.

"There," I said, making out some tire marks in the dirt by the side of the road.

Regan stopped and left the engine idling. "So how did it go down?"

"I was a few hundred yards away when I first saw him here," I began, before being interrupted by one of the officers from the vehicle behind us, who'd walked up to the car.

"What's going on?" he asked when Regan rolled his window down.

"See the disturbance there?"

The officer turned around and looked. "Yeah."

"Drive up fifty feet or so and block off that shoulder. I don't want anyone driving through there. If we're lucky the shooter left shell casings or something."

"Right," he replied, and went back to his car.

"You came speeding down this road after him and he took out your windows when you got close?"

"Yeah, you saw where he got me. I wasn't sure it was him until I was practically on top of him. I swerved off the road and into the field." The patrol car behind us rolled past, lights flashing. We watched it nose diagonally onto the far shoulder, its back end partly in the roadway ahead.

"And then what?"

"He took off."

"Just like that? He didn't come after you?"

"I know, I was surprised too. I would have been easy pickings– my car stalled just off the road. Although I did have his gun."

"Probably what saved you."

That and those farmworkers. But I'd keep them out of this if I could. "Could be," I agreed. "Or he'd accomplished what he wanted to by getting me off his tail."

"Let's take a walk back there," Regan suggested. He put the car in park but left the lights on and the engine running. He got out, pulling his flashlight from his belt, and I followed him. We stopped at the edge of the pavement. Regan squatted on his heels, pointed his flashlight. The light played over the skid marks I'd left behind and the scattered particles of glass in the dirt, turning the ground at our feet into a shimmering carpet.

The beam followed the tire tracks into the field. Then Regan stood up, looking into the distance and surveying the area. He stopped when he saw the house, now quiet but still illuminated by security lamps, then moved on. Apparently, he thought it was too far away for any useful witnesses. That was fine with me.

"How did you get out of there?"

I shrugged like it was no big deal. "Put it in reverse and backed out the same way I came in." A complete lie, but the simple ones work best.

He seemed satisfied with that, and we walked back to his car. Regan got on the radio and told the dispatcher exactly where we were. Then he backed up to a spot near where I'd gone off the road, marking and securing the area until the detectives arrived. I could hardly wait. Branson was sure to be among them.

As if in response to that thought, two vehicles, one of them a black and white, the other a nondescript four-door sedan, exited the highway and sped toward us. Headlights on high-beam but no sirens or emergency flashers. They pulled up on the shoulder behind Regan's car in a cloud of dust. He approached the lead vehicle, the sedan, and stooped to confer with the driver. I couldn't hear what he said, but saw him point to the other patrol car parked on the opposite shoulder, say a few words, then look up at me, nodding in response to something the driver said.

One of the two officers who'd followed us out here came up and stood beside me. A few yards away, Regan straightened, allowing the driver of the sedan to get out. As I'd expected, it was Branson. The two uniforms in the black and white followed suit: Palm Springs PD, not Indio.

"Been a long night, hasn't it?" the officer standing next to me said as Regan approached us. Branson and the other two hung back, watching.

"The detective from Palm Springs is here and he's not real happy," Regan informed me. "He wants to talk."

"I'll bet."

I started toward the sedan. Branson leaned against the hood, arms folded on his chest. He was chewing gum, his jaw working up and down vigorously as he watched me approach.

"What the hell did you think you were doing?" was the first thing out of Branson's mouth when I stopped in front of him. The two officers he'd brought with him stood off to the side.

"I don't know what came over me," I said, as Branson got off the car.

"Don't give me any bullshit on this, Ryder," he shot back, throwing spit. "Jesus Christ, I get rousted out of bed at one in the morning 'cause some idiot wants to play cowboy! This is a police investigation, for Chrissake! You think you can just waltz in any time you feel like it?"

I kept quiet.

"What's the matter? No smart-mouth comments tonight?"

"Look. I shouldn't have said what I said the other day. I apologize."

"Too late for that, Ryder," Branson said. He spat his gum on the ground, ticked off.

"You're going in. See how much of a wise-ass you are in jail." He turned to the two officers. "Read him his rights guys. Interfering in a police investigation." Then he turned back to me. "I'll deal with you in the morning, after you've spent a few hours in the can. And you better hope I don't find your prints on that gun." He strode off in an angry huff, finished with me for now.

"I need to talk to my wife," I called out after him as the cuffs were being snapped on my wrists.

CHAPTER THIRTEEN

"Did you guys happen to notice if there was a woman at the motel?" I asked from the back seat of the police car. "My wife was supposed to be there and I'm kind of worried about her."

No response. Both officers just stared straight ahead after a quick glance to each other at my question. My hands were twisted awkwardly behind me in the cuffs. The seatbelt shoulder strap cut tightly across my chest. I couldn't get physically comfortable in that position; leaning back was impossible because of the cuffs, and the seat had no cushions—it was merely hard molded plastic, unyielding as a park bench. No accommodation was made for the comfort of anyone unlucky or foolish enough to be riding back here, and I considered myself a little of both.

We were taking the direct route to the Palm Springs police station, the radio occasionally squawking a too-loud dispatch framed by scratches of static. Off the highway, the Spotlight 29 and Fantasy Springs casinos were still garish novas of light, even at this late hour.

My unexpected arrest in Coachella meant I couldn't reconnect with Deirdre at the motel. At the exit for Palm Springs I tried again. "Look, I know there was a lot going on at the Blue Bird, but I need to know if my wife showed up."

The officer in the passenger seat turned around and answered through the metal screen that separated us. "The only woman I saw was about sixty years old, and she was with another man. I'm assuming that wasn't your wife."

"There wasn't a younger woman hanging around by herself?" He shook his head. "Maybe she'd just driven up?"

"Look, I just told you, there was only the one older woman. Not that we need to be answering your questions. Now keep quiet and enjoy the ride."

But I couldn't let it go. It wasn't like Deirdre to be that late; all told, she'd had over an hour to get there before these two would have arrived. Something must have happened, I was sure of it. "Can't you swing by my place and check it out, just to make sure she's all right?" I pleaded, knowing how ridiculous the request sounded. "Or send somebody else?"

"I'm not going to make a welfare check in the middle of the night just because you miss your wife," the driver told me. "You can call her in the morning from jail."

"You don't understand. She could be in danger." I felt the sweat on my forehead, but couldn't wipe it away because of the cuffs. Some of it dropped into my eye, and I shook my head to clear it.

"So why did you leave her alone?"

I didn't have an answer for that.

"You heard what the detective said. We get a call from your wife, I'll take it myself. But right now, you're going to jail."

I gave up, knowing there was nothing I could say or do. My only hope was that she'd arrived at the motel after my departure and, seeing that I wasn't there, assumed from our phone conversation that I'd already been taken into custody. Maybe she was waiting for me right now at the Palm Springs police station. Please God, I thought, let her car be in the parking lot when we drive up.

A few minutes later we were there, the street quiet under the hard yellow light from the streetlamps. There wasn't a solitary vehicle parked at the curb in front, and the only ones sitting in the small parking lot were patrol cars and a few civilian vehicles that weren't Deirdre's. My heart sank as I glued my face to the window, checking again in the feeble hope that I'd somehow missed it the first time. But Deirdre wasn't here. I cursed myself under my breath for not saying something to Regan earlier, certain I could have convinced him to check on her.

Now I was about to be jailed, over two hours since Deirdre told me she'd see me in thirty minutes. Worried sick, and not a damn thing I could do.

In back, they pulled me out of the car and escorted me through a heavily secured metal door. It slammed shut behind us, a re-sounding bang echoing through the holding area, which was brightly illuminated. The walls were painted an institutional gray-green and the floor was unadorned concrete, pockmarked and dented in numerous places.

One officer went over to a counter to confer with the officer on duty. The other one led me further inside to one of three holding cells, where he patted me down in front of the metal bars. A prisoner slouched against the far wall and watched us without interest, obviously out of it. After taking my watch and everything in my pockets, the officer uncuffed me and told me to remove my shoes, which he deposited in a plastic bag. Then he put me in the cell.

"What about my phone call?" I asked, turning around.

"Later," was the curt reply. "After you're processed."

The officer walked off with my stuff without another word. I nodded to my cellmate, who was occupying the sole bench. A big white guy with greasy brown hair and stubble on his face. Dressed in a threadbare T-shirt and blue sweatpants. He didn't say anything, just watched me a few moments, then sighed loudly and stretched out on the bench with his arm over his eyes.

I was about to sit on the floor against the wall, then I changed my mind and jabbed him hard on the shoulder. "Move, buddy. I'm taking the bench."

Startled, he lifted his arm from his face and studied mine. Seeing something he didn't want to mess with, he quietly complied, shuffling to the spot on the cold concrete floor where I'd been about to sit.

It felt good to let off steam at someone else's expense, small-minded and petty as it was. I thought about my situation, got more and more pissed as I waited. I cursed myself for every wrong move I'd made. Starting with not calling the cops as soon as I'd found that matchbook.

There was still the possibility that Deirdre had eventually made it out to the motel and then returned home, knowing there wasn't much she could do until morning–a tiny flame of hope that I tried to keep alive. It wasn't easy. I wanted to scream at the top of my lungs, punch a hole in the wall. But that would do no good. There was no choice but to stick it out.

The booking officer came to get my cellmate about half an hour later. My request for a phone call got only a noncommittal "*Later*," a response that didn't surprise me. The holding area became as quiet as a tomb after they left, my own ruminations the only sound in my head. Eventually, those thoughts turned into an incoherent haze and I actually dozed off.

I awoke what seemed a short time later. Dazed and mushy-headed, like I'd been sleeping off a bender. The booking officer was unlocking the cell door.

"Come with me, Mr. Ryder," she said, swinging the door open. Her nameplate said "Brock." I followed her in my stockinged feet, while her patent leather shoes clicked smartly on the concrete floor. We turned down a short corridor and entered a small room where she took my picture and my fingerprints.

When we were done I asked about my phone call again.

"First thing in the morning," Brock told me, looking at her watch. "That's only a few hours away."

Easy for her to say. "What time is it?" Time had a weird way of distorting itself in here, and the absence of any windows magnified that feeling. It was like being stuck in the hold of a ship lost at sea, the queasiness of incarceration replacing seasickness.

"Four thirty."

"So how long do I have to wait?" I asked as evenly as I could.

Brock gave me a stern look that said *don't push it.* "After seven," she answered, then nudged me out of the room. "Follow me, Mr. Ryder. We'll get you a blanket."

I went with her to an unmarked door, which she unlocked and opened. A small room filled with shelves of bleached white towels and musty blankets. "Take one," she said, indicating the blankets. "You'll get a shower in the morning."

"Has anybody called here tonight asking about me?"

She'd closed the door to the linen closet, and now I was following her deeper into the jail complex, toward another heavy metal door with reinforced glass in it. I was hoping Deirdre had phoned to verify my whereabouts and situation.

But Brock shook her head. "No one's called for you tonight. At least not while I've been on duty."

"What time did you come in?" I asked a little too quickly.

"What's with all the questions?"

"I apologize," I told her. She stopped when we reached the end of the corridor. Regarded me coolly. "Really. It's just that I was supposed to meet my wife earlier tonight and she never showed up. That's not like her. I think something's wrong."

"Like what?" She'd heard it all before.

"There might be someone after her."

That got a raised eyebrow. She folded her arms on her chest, but didn't say anything.

"You know about the murder in North Palm Springs yesterday, right? They found him on somebody's front lawn?"

"I know who you are."

"Then you know how important this could be. I need that phone call. Now."

But Brock only shook her head, as if to clear it of any compassion she might be feeling. "None of that makes any difference," she told me, picking a large key from the assortment in her hand. She stuck it into the slot and pulled the heavy door open, her voice hardening. "You'll get your phone call in the morning." She held the door open for me, gesturing with her head. "Go on."

The jail area was dimly lit at this early hour, a maze of squared-off hallways and dead ends. The cells weren't enclosed by metal bars. Instead, they were sealed with thick sheets of a transparent Plexiglas or Lucite material that looked bulletproof, like the clear windows that sometimes protect bank tellers. Unlike the ones in banks, however, which were probably cleaned nightly, these were scratched and smudged with dirt and grease and saliva. Most of the cells we walked by were unoccupied. A few housed indistinct human forms laid out in the shadows of the bunk beds, some of them wide awake and watchful, others loudly snoring. In one of them a man stood urinating into an aluminum toilet, his stream a thick arc that bubbled noisily in the bowl; I could smell its strong, acidic odor. He stared at us frankly as we passed, but Brock ignored him, kept her eyes straight in front of her. The next corridor came right after an empty shower area, also enclosed but completely visible behind the clear walls. Four shower heads protruded starkly from plain tiles. A few cells past that, Brock stopped and selected yet another key from the crowded ring and unlocked the door. The constant rattle of those keys was a grim reminder of the freedom I'd lost.

I stepped inside with my blanket, and she closed the door behind me. The lock engaged firmly, with a metallic click that echoed sharply in the small space. When I turned around, Brock was gone, the sound of her footsteps quickly diminishing down the narrow passageways.

There was a man lying on the bottom bunk. His breath whispered rhythmically, betraying sleep. He stirred when I threw my blanket on the top bunk and hoisted myself up. A thin, plastic-covered mattress. No pillow. I bunched the blanket up at one end and laid my head on it. Stared up at the ceiling at least seven feet above me. Not surprisingly, the height did nothing to make the room seem less confining.

A few minutes later, the guy below me stirred again. Sniffled and cleared his throat noisily. He got up and went over to the toilet and spat in it, took a long piss, returned to his bunk and lay down.

"Hey man," he said, kicking the underside of my bed. "You awake up there?" I didn't respond, hoping he'd get the message and leave me alone. But he didn't.

"What are you in for, bro?" my cellmate asked, undaunted.

"Do you mind? I'm trying to get some sleep."

He continued obliviously, as if I hadn't said anything. "They got me for indecent exposure," he explained proudly. "A weenie-wagger." Pause. "Did you see that shower area over there? All open like that? When I get my shower in the morning, I'll show that bitch what a real man looks like."

That was it. I leaned over the bunk. "I don't want to hear any more about your perverted pastime, all right? So why don't you shut the hell up?"

He didn't respond, just gave me a shit-eating grin, and I could barely restrain myself from jumping down there and slapping it off. Instead I promised, "and if I ever see you on the street doing that shit, I'll kick your ass."

His smile only got wider. "Maybe you'd enjoy it."

"Yeah. Just like all the women that laugh at what you got."

"Oooh. Good one."

He wasn't worth it, I decided, and lay back down, muttering one final insult. "Freak."

He was quiet after that. A few minutes later I heard his breathing slow and become more regular. Dozing again, apparently at peace with his unnatural compulsion and the trouble it brought him. There was no way I'd be able to sleep. Not with the hours until morning lined up like miles of desert sand dunes between me and what I hoped wouldn't be a mirage. That phone call I waited for had to give me Deirdre's voice on the other end, awake and alive and wondering what all the fuss was about.

CHAPTER FOURTEEN

My first few months in prison weren't as bad as I'd feared. Of course I was petrified from day one, not knowing what to expect, and the reality was as brutal and demeaning as anything I'd imagined. You could never afford to let your guard down. Violence exploded instantly and seemingly without provocation at any time of day or night; constant vigilance was required to stay out of it and avoid becoming a victim.

I got into several serious scrapes those first few months, as the bullies and intimidators tested the new guy. Was I going to stand up or punk out? I'd answered that question to myself before even getting there and was determined to make it stick, no matter what the cost. Hitting rock bottom was almost liberating. My staunch refusal to succumb to the threats and intimidation that were second nature to so many of the inmates became a form of therapy that helped rebuild my dignity and self-respect. The old military adage *if it doesn't kill you it makes you stronger* may once have seemed macho and trite, but in prison it became a new outlook on life. I scratched the phrase on the wall beside my bed over the course of a few days. Some nights, when I wasn't sure I would make it into the next day, I'd run my fingers over the letters I'd carved in the concrete. Trace the words out one by one while the lights were out until I fell asleep.

Gradually my life inside became less frightening and dangerous. I've heard that if you make it through the first few months behind bars you'll probably be okay, as long as you keep your nose clean. For me, that was true. I learned how to act and what to say to defuse a situation without giving in. When to crank it up a notch and get in someone's face even if it meant getting the shit kicked out of me. Who to stay away from and who to get close to. How to deal with the gangs that virtually ran the cell block. Day-to-day existence became less random and more predictable. As time went on, I acquired the right kind of associates to watch my back.

But even before then, when my physical survival was most in jeopardy, I drew a strange comfort from the realization that I'd brought it all on myself. The fact that I deserved what I was going through and was able to accept it gave me a certain serenity which enabled me to go on.

That peace eluded me utterly now. I lay there on a plastic pad staring up at the smooth concrete ceiling, while an unrepentant flasher snored peacefully below me. If I could get away with it I'd smother him with my blanket just to have something to do.

With no real sense of time, my hearing strained for any sound of activity that would point to the coming of morning and an answer to Deirdre's whereabouts. Every now and then I heard the faint rattle of keys, or the sound of patent leather shoes pacing on the concrete floor. The unintelligible murmurings of the guards as they went about their nightly duties. Sometimes, the percussive sound of a cell door being opened or closed, bouncing a sharp echo through the building like the report of a small caliber pistol. Each time I heard one of those sounds, I prayed that the footsteps were coming for me, that the key would be inserted in this lock, that my door would be the next to open. My heartbeat skipped in Pavlovian response countless times throughout the early morning hours, only to be disappointed when the noises faded into silence.

I fell into a fitful dream eventually. I was in a small boat on a sparkling blue lake under a sky that matched the color of the water. The lake was surrounded by stark, crumbling mounds of red-tinged soil, the edges of the water lapping gently at the shoreline. It was unbearably hot and still. The surface of the lake shone brightly in my eyes, mirroring the relentless rays of the sun. I shaded my eyes, becoming aware of someone in the boat with me. He had a cap on his head, the brim pulled low on his forehead. A fishing pole in his hands extended out over the water, the line disappearing tautly into the depths. The man pulled his rod up and withdrew a shimmering silver fish that danced in the sunlight, throwing glittery drops of water into the air as it struggled on the line. After reeling it in, he tossed the fish in the bottom of the boat. It flopped and twisted frantically, drowning on oxygen. I reached down, tried to grab it to throw it back in, but it squirmed and slipped out of my fingers. The man watched the fish slowly dying, its tiny pebble eye pointing upward unblinkingly while its scales dried and dulled in the blazing heat. When it finally stopped moving, he grabbed the fish by the tail and held it over the water. It hung lifelessly for a moment before he dropped it into the lake. A tiny splash, then it disappeared. I looked over at the man, trying to see his face. The boat started rocking and I awoke to the shaking of the bed.

The guy below me was kicking it, trying to rouse me. "Dude. She's here for you, man."

Thinking he meant Deirdre, I shot up immediately, instantly awake. But it was only the guard, motioning me to follow her. She held the door open and I jumped down to the floor, anxious to get in touch with Deirdre.

"Come with me," Brock said as I approached the door. I followed her past the other locked cells, more of them occupied now than earlier.

"Can I call my wife?"

"We'll see. You may not need to."

"Why, is she here?" I asked anxiously, the *may* part of her answer failing to register at first.

We continued toward the main jail door, passing the shower area where a man stood unmoving under the water, eyes closed as the spray misted around him.

Brock didn't seem to notice him. "No, she's not. But they want to talk to you."

"Who?"

"Just follow me sir," she responded tiredly, pulling her keys out again. We went back into the holding area. Brock stepped behind the front desk, unlocked a cabinet and took out the bag containing my shoes. She watched as I put them on. At the far end of the room, a carpeted corridor led to the front of the building. It ended with the door I'd noticed from the other side yesterday morning on the way into the interview with Branson. That seemed so long ago.

I tried one last time. "I'd still rather make my phone call first."

Brock unlocked the last door without a word. We entered the squad room. It was empty and quiet this early, except for the coffee machine hissing and bubbling in the corner. The aroma hung in the air, adding an out-of-place domesticity to the official environment. The clock on the wall said just after 6:30.

She let me into one of the interrogation rooms, where I was greeted by the brooding presence of Detective Branson pacing agitatedly in the corner. Detective Tidwell sat at the table, more relaxed with a steaming cup of coffee in front of him.

He looked up as we entered. "Thanks, Ronda."

Brock nodded once, closed the door and left us alone. Tidwell told me to sit down, indicating a chair already pulled away from the table. I took it, and regarded Branson standing still a few feet away, eyeing me heatedly. He looked disheveled and bleary-eyed from the long night.

I started before they had a chance to. "I have to get in touch with Deirdre. I think something's happened to her."

Branson leaned over the table toward me, his fists gripping the opposite chair-back. "You're not in any position to be making demands, Ryder."

"You can have a lawyer before we start, but that'll just delay things," Tidwell said. "You don't want that, do you?"

"Whatever. Let's just get it over with. But if anything's happened to Deirdre—"

"What?" Branson interrupted. "What're you gonna do? Sue us? Hunt one of us down? You're the one that screwed everything up. This is all on you."

I didn't reply. He drew back, taking the chair opposite me. I really rubbed him the wrong way, I thought. From the start, without even trying.

Tidwell took a sip of coffee. "Tell us about last night. Start with that matchbook you found. And don't leave anything out."

"I already told them everything last night. Nothing's changed."

"And now you're going to tell us," Tidwell replied evenly. Branson gazed at me balefully, hands folded together in front of him.

I outlined everything that had happened, eyeing the large mirror on the wall behind Tidwell, aware of a presence behind the glass watching and listening. I sensed I was being appraised along with the story I was telling, and tried to make it as accurate as possible, while downplaying the things I'd done to bring it to this point. Tidwell interjected periodically with questions and clarifications. Branson remained silent and fuming. When I finished, Tidwell got up and left the room. Left me alone with Branson, who didn't wait two seconds to start in on me.

He leaned back in his chair, one arm still on the table. "I had an interesting conversation with some farmhands out in Coachella last night."

I kept quiet.

"What did you think, I wouldn't find out about that?"

"So what. They helped me with my car. Big deal."

His voice hardened. "Why didn't you tell us about those men?"

"I guess I forgot."

Branson's eyes lasered into me.

"I didn't think they'd want to be involved. What difference does it make?"

"What else are you leaving out?"

"Nothing."

"Was that motel room really empty when you broke into it?"

"Why would I lie about that?"

"Maybe you're protecting somebody. Just like those farm workers."

"There was nobody there."

"I'll find out if there was. Then I'll arrest you for obstructing."

"I'm telling the truth."

"You still got that mystery diary?"

"You know I don't. You probably searched my car already."

Branson leaned forward, completely calm. "You hold out on us again and we'll take you down, Ryder. You clear on that?"

"I heard you."

He started gathering up his notes from the table, shaking his head. "Not helping anybody here," he muttered.

"I disagree."

He stopped with the papers. "Really."

"If I hadn't done what I did, all you'd have is an empty motel room, with a manager that might not have made it through the night tied up like that. Nothing about the diary. And no gun."

"You haven't changed a bit have you?"

"What do you mean?"

"You can do whatever you want because you're smarter than everybody, right?"

"I never said that. I think you have the wrong impression of me."

"How's that?"

"I got no problem with authority. But you made this personal the other day, remember?"

"Yeah, okay. My fault."

"Look, I screwed up, all right? You think I don't know that? You think I wouldn't undo it if I could? But I can't. It's done. And I gotta live with it."

"You stay outta my case, Mr. Ryder."

"Out of your–goddamnit, I'm not talking about last night!"

Branson seemed as surprised as I was. He watched me for a moment, then picked up his notes and stood.

Tidwell returned then. "You're free to go, Mr. Ryder."

"Just like that?"

"Just like that."

"What about Deirdre?"

"What about her?"

"She never showed up at the motel last night after I called her." I looked at Branson, who remained stone-faced. Turned back to Tidwell. "Can't you send someone out to my place to check it out?"

"Why? You'll be home soon enough. I'm sure she's fine."

"You should feel lucky we're not throwing the book at you," Branson told me. "So count your blessings and get out of here."

Tidwell didn't say anything, just folded his arms and nodded. I decided to stop beating my head against the wall and got up. Muttered a few things under my breath.

"You got something to say?" Branson asked.

I faced him calmly. "Where's my stuff? And what about my car?"

"Oh, that'll be here for a while," Branson replied. "Four or five days, maybe."

"You'll get it back when we're done going through it," Tidwell said. "You can get your other stuff though. Follow me."

Back in the holding area they gave me my wallet, keys, watch and change in a large manila envelope. As I emptied it on the counter, Tidwell put his hand out.

"We'll need the car keys."

I took them off the ring and handed them over. After signing for the rest of it, I checked my wallet for the cash and credit cards I'd had in there.

"Don't trust us?" Tidwell asked.

I put the wallet in my back pocket without answering.

Tidwell opened the rear door on bright sunshine. "Stay out of trouble," he said, holding the door. "I mean it. Branson was right. We could've charged you with any number of things. Especially with your prints on the gun."

"So it was the murder weapon?"

"Goodbye, Mr. Ryder."

"How do I get home without my car?"

"Call a cab. Or take a bus."

The door slammed shut and I turned around, wondering what the quickest way home would be.

CHAPTER FIFTEEN

The morning was painted with a brilliant, clear light that was all the more blinding after my long night inside. Everything possessed a diamond-hard sharpness. The crisp contrast between sunlight and shadow projected a sense of hyper-reality, as if the world had been amplified and clarified overnight. Long early morning shadows extended from the objects and buildings around me, making them seem larger and more threatening. The shiny police vehicles in the back lot glinted menacingly, like poised mechanical beasts, as I walked around to the front of the building.

The bank clock across the street said 7:27. Three minutes ahead of my own watch. I felt like I'd already missed something important, that I'd be forever chasing something just out of reach. I hoped I wasn't too late for Deirdre if she needed help. Her car was nowhere to be seen, so I hurried to the pay phone in front of the bank, jingling in my pocket for change, wondering what I would do if Deirdre didn't answer. My hand shook while I deposited the coins. A steady dial tone, the image of a flatlined heart monitor flashing through my mind.

With enough change for only one call, I punched in the numbers carefully. Listened to the relays click into place. Then the calm, measured pulsing of the line as it rang on the other end, a rhythm that did nothing to slow my erratic heartbeat.

Four rings, each more excruciating than the last. I squeezed my eyes closed, imploring Deirdre to answer. The machine did instead. Her voice warm and resonant but stored in memory. A digital ghost. Then the strident beep in my ear, and I heard my voice shaking on the edge of hysteria, full of fear and desperate hope and the realization that something had gone terribly wrong.

"Deirdre, pick up, please pick up." Sobbing now, hand on my forehead, then through my hair. I thought I would vomit if she didn't answer. "Oh God, Deirdre, where are you, please be there." Nothing but silence and my own hitched breath in the earpiece.

I looked up and saw a bus pass by belching blue smoke into the clear morning, the words NORTH PALM SPRINGS VIA INDIAN AVE scrolling on the ticker. Dropping the phone, I ran for it. I made the bus stop thirty yards away just behind the lumbering vehicle. It slowed down for a man sitting on the bench, who waved it on with his newspaper. I got there just as it was pulling away, reached up and pounded loudly on a back window. The bus jerked to a stop and I got on, out of breath and once again going through my pockets for cash. I folded up a one and put it in the box as we lurched into motion.

The bus was completely empty, and I took the first seat up front. I caught sight of the phone booth I'd just abandoned, with the receiver still dangling on its cord. Transfixed, I watched it recede into the distance as we moved away.

We made a left on Tahquitz Canyon. Passed the courthouse and city hall, their walls scrubbed white and brilliant in the morning light. I silently willed us to make every light, hoping for a clear ride through downtown. But most of the stops seemed to have people waiting, some of them wearing uniforms for the various hotels and restaurants. I cursed under my breath at each stop and each missed signal.

At Indian we made a right, nearing Deirdre's clinic, and it brought back the uneasy tension between us yesterday. Now all I wanted to do was feel her heart beating against mine, breathe in the clean scent of her hair. Listen to her soft voice in my ear telling me everything would be all right. I clung to a last vestige of hope, that maybe Deirdre had been out on one of her morning jogs when I called. She'd do that sometimes, get real quiet, struggling with her demons, and I'd know to leave her alone. She'd buzz around the house, try to keep herself busy with the mundanities of housework. Eventually she'd give up and take an exhausting run into the surrounding desert on one of the many old dirt tracks that crisscross the landscape. Return with her eyes afire, as if they'd stored the light reflected from the burning sands. Her skin would glow with sweat and exertion, temporarily cleansed of the toxins inside.

We passed over the interstate into North Palm Springs a few minutes later. The freeway was no longer the colorful river of moving light it had been yesterday evening. I looked down and saw broken, gray concrete and painted lane markers worn away by endless traffic. The travel stop bustled with commuters going about their business.

I got up to stand anxiously on the steps in front of the door, watching as the Thomas Avenue stop got closer. The brakes squealed and the door folded open in front of me with a metallic screech. Bounding onto the pavement, I was stunned by the blast of heat and light after the air-conditioned coolness of the bus. It pulled away with a groan as I stepped away and ran toward home, picking up speed as I got closer, needing to be there *now*, yet dreading what I'd find.

By the time I reached our street my lungs were burning and my vision was spotting. Rounding the corner at full speed, I almost got run down by a kid driving an old foreign car, his hair waving behind him in the open window. I stumbled and went down, ripping my pant leg and scraping my palms. Leaving skin on the pavement, I kept going, my heart doing triple-time. As I approached the house, I saw Deirdre's car sitting in the driveway, gleaming under the blazing sun. Racing past it to the front door, I noticed that everything seemed normal–no signs of struggle anywhere on our property–until I tried the door and found it shut firmly but un-locked.

I pushed it open and entered the static dimness of our living room. The house was quiet except for the heaving of my chest, and when I called out Deirdre's name, I could barely hear my voice.

I walked down the hallway to our bedroom, still panting.

I stepped into the open doorway.

And felt a piece inside of me break off and fall away.

For a moment I wanted to let it pull me down with it. But then I swallowed the lump in my throat and knelt beside the bed, feeling her neck for a pulse I knew wouldn't be there. The room suddenly got smaller, and I saw my reflection in the clouded glass of the sy-ringe buried in Deirdre's arm.

I collapsed on the bed beside her, burying my face in her hair, the pain rippling through me. I stayed there until the trembling stopped and the grief became a dull ache in the pit of my stomach. I reached for the phone and picked it up. Gave the information to the police, and after hanging up, tried to banish the thought that I'd driven her to it.

I laid back down beside her, treasuring those last few moments alone with her in our hot bedroom. I heard Deirdre's voice in my memory, hushed and reverent, as if recalling the receiving of a sacrament or sacred gift. It was in Idyllwild, where we'd gone ski-ing for the weekend, inside our cabin toward midnight. We were in front of a roaring fire, listening to the crackle and hiss of the logs.

"I remember when I used to fix," Deirdre had begun, her face glowing in the firelight, framed by the window behind her and the moonlit snow outside. "I always used those wooden matches, the thick, long ones that came in a box. Strike it and get that life-giving flame. At least it felt that way then. A bright orange flower, dancing in front of my eyes. And then that sizzle as I cooked it. Sometimes I'll hear something in the kitchen, you know, the spatter of grease or something, and still get a chill up my spine. It brings it all back to me. Drawing it into the glass. The prick of the needle, and then that warm liquid rush. God, it felt good." She stopped, and her eyes came back to mine. "But it doesn't last. It's a lie. The doorway to damnation. It takes so much more than it gives. And you never really know that until it's too late."

A warm glow spread across my back. I opened my eyes, found us bathed in a golden shaft of sunlight from the window. Deirdre's face flushed and lifelike in the healing rays of light. A robin was hopping on the fence just outside the window, deep red as a desert sunset. When it saw me it froze, regarded me calmly, then fluttered off lightly when the doorbell rang.

CHAPTER SIXTEEN

I stumbled to the front door, tears blinding my eyes. I let the two uniforms in without a word, pointing back to the bedroom. If they said anything to me, I didn't hear it.

When I saw Branson and Tidwell approaching through the dried grass, the dam finally broke. The blood rushed in my ears. My voice was an incoherent torrent of accusation and blame. I struggled past Tidwell, who tried to hold me back, into Branson, who went down in the grass at my feet with blood running from his nose. Then I was on top of him, my fists pummeling his face and chest, with Tidwell shouting in my ear. He pulled me off in a tangle of flailing arms and flying fists. I landed on my back with his knee on my chest and his gun in my face.

"Right there, buddy!" he warned. I heard the hammer click back, the black hole of the gun barrel offering infinity if I chose it.

"Do what you have to," I whispered. Tidwell uncocked the gun and holstered it, roughly pulled me off the ground.

He whirled me around and slammed on the cuffs. "You better get it together, man, and fast."

The two patrol officers had come outside, and they were re-holstering their weapons. Tidwell marched me past Branson, who was muttering under his breath and brushing dead grass from his rumpled suit, to the dark sedan sitting by the curb behind the black and white. He shoved me into the back seat. Rolled the window down before slamming the door shut.

"Stay there, Ryder. Don't even think about moving."

Tidwell joined Branson in the middle of the yard and said something to him. Branson silently shook his head in response, dabbed at his nose with a handkerchief. Blood spotted his white dress shirt. They both turned to look at me in the car watching them, Branson with a frown on his face but no apparent rancor toward me. Tidwell just shook his head disgustedly and went into the house; Branson nodded solemnly in my direction before turning to follow him inside.

An ambulance and a second patrol car pulled up. Lights flashing, sirens blaring. One of the officers on the scene met the two who'd just arrived, conferred with them briefly, then directed the medics into the house.

Another officer approached and leaned toward me through the open window. "I don't have to worry about you out here, do I?"

I ignored him. He shrugged and leaned against the back of the car, watched the crime scene tape being strung up around the front of the house. Evidently, he'd been assigned to guard me.

Closing my eyes, I let my head fall back to the seat. I tried to block out everything that was happening. No luck. I heard more vehicles pulling up, brakes squealing and doors thumping shut. Hurried footsteps going back and forth. Orders being given and acknowledged. Shocked whispers and conjecture from the neighbors gathered once again in the street. The news people finally arrived, drawn by their ever-vigilant police scanners.

One reporter made it to the car. "Is that your wife in there, Mr. Ryder?"

The question startled me. I opened my eyes to see a microphone jammed through the window, before the cop rushed back over and grabbed him. "How does it feel to be going through this again?" he yelled over the officer's shoulder as he was being escorted away.

I watched all the activity swirling around me, trapped. Tidwell came out of the house and got into the car. He twisted around in the front seat and pushed the hair back from his sweating forehead. "You okay?"

I looked away, not answering.

"I'm sorry this happened," he said.

"A lot of good your sorrys do for Deirdre. If somebody had listened to me last night, or even this morning, she may have had a chance. So take your apology and shove it."

Tidwell's eyes flashed angrily. "Watch it." He was about to say something else, but then stopped himself and sighed.

"I guess I'll be going to jail again for hitting Branson."

"No. We're not going to arrest you for that. Branson feels as bad as I do about this." He paused for emphasis. "But you really gotta cool it."

I practically spat the next words at him. "Cool it? My wife is dead." I shook my head, tired of being angry. "You guys should have been here. As soon as I told you something was wrong. You fucked up and Deirdre paid for it."

"Look. I told you there was nothing we could do. We can't go running all over town every time someone thinks something *may* be wrong. We'd never get anything done. And you gave us a lot to do last night."

"I'm not interested in excuses," I told him. "Just find the guy who did this to her."

A steady look from Tidwell, like something was on his mind. He blew air out of his mouth and his eyes slid away.

"What?" I asked apprehensively.

"I hate to tell you this, but right now we're not even sure it's a homicide."

"You gotta be kidding!" I shouted, barely able to restrain myself. My voice lowered a notch. "What are you talking about?" Out of the corner of my eye, I saw Branson watching the exchange from the lawn.

Tidwell glanced his way for a second, as if for support, then told me, "We've only taken a quick look so far, but there's no sign of violence or struggle anywhere in the house, including the bedroom." He stopped, reluctant to go on, but I already knew what he was going to say. "And with her history of drug–"

"Fuck you. She's been clean since I've known her. Not one relapse."

No response.

"You think this is all a big fucking coincidence? Some guy ends up dead on our front lawn, and two days later my wife OD's?"

An earlier thought resurfaced, but I pushed it away.

"There is no way she did that to herself, no fucking chance. That's the most ridiculous thing I ever heard. I told you what happened last night. She was all set to come out to Indio for me. What do you think, she decided a quick nod would be the thing to do before getting behind the wheel?"

Branson was suddenly there, standing outside the car. "Maybe she was already high when you called her."

That took me aback. Deirdre had sounded out of it when she first answered the phone, and I'd assumed that was from sleep. But she'd recovered quickly, and seemed clearheaded and razor-sharp when I told her what was up. Branson had to be wrong. I'd have known if she was using. Wouldn't I?

"No," I said, putting it out of my mind with an emphatic shake of my head. "Didn't happen that way. She had help with that syringe."

"I don't know what to tell you," Tidwell said. "If there's evidence of that, we'll find it." He looked up as the coroner's wagon arrived and backed partway into the driveway. Branson went over to meet it and led them into the house.

"I just can't believe I let her down," I said to myself. Grief was waiting to pull me under, a dark undertow.

"I promise, if your wife was murdered we'll get the guy. Just let us do our jobs." A pause. "We're going to need a complete statement from you about how you found her. At the station. You up to that?"

"I guess so." I was suddenly very tired. Shock was beginning to set in. "Whatever."

"Let me go tell Branson." He left me alone and I stared straight ahead. Unmoving, barely breathing. Retreating into myself. The flashing red and blue lights blurred together, the sounds of emergency activity fading away. Why hadn't she fought? The question came out of nowhere, and with it, a stinging shame for thinking that way. Maybe Deirdre thought she could handle the dose. Or that I'd make it back, or send the cops her way in time to revive her. Either way, it was better than accepting the finality of a bullet in the head.

Tidwell reappeared beside me. Opened my door and turned me around to take off the cuffs. He returned them to the case on his belt and shut the door, then circled around to the driver's side and got in. I sat back, hands still clasped behind me, unable to look back as we drove away.

CHAPTER SEVENTEEN

Back at the police station for the third time in two days. Tidwell sat me down in the conference room and left to get some coffee. He brought in two styrofoam cups, but I didn't touch mine, leaving it sitting in front of me. The glass-topped table reflected the lighted fluorescent squares above as the steam from the coffee curled upwards.

"Wait here," Tidwell told me and walked across the squad room to a large office, where he spoke with someone sitting behind a desk. Presently, Tidwell turned to look at me. The other man nodded, saying one last thing before Tidwell stepped out and closed the office door. On the way back, he stopped and talked to one of the other detectives for a moment, then went to his own desk. Rummaged around in there until he found a cassette tape, which he removed from its wrapper and slid into a small tape recorder. He brought it in with him, along with a dog-eared legal pad and pen. I heard phones ringing and the chatter of a typewriter before he closed the conference room door and sat down.

"Branson should be here any minute. We'll start without him." After clicking on the tape recorder, Tidwell recited our names and the date and time.

"You got out of here about eight this morning. Did you call her first thing?"

The coffee was hot under my fingertips, and I dug my nails into the styrofoam. "I used the phone booth at the bank."

Tidwell nodded at me to go on.

"The machine picked up." The cup buckled inward, snapping. Hot coffee spread over the table, burning my hand. We both got up to avoid the spill, but it soaked Tidwell's legal pad. He got the tape recorder just in time.

"Sorry."

"You said you were up to this."

I didn't know what to say.

Tidwell shook his head. Picked up the tablet and turned it sideways so the coffee dripped off. Then he ripped off the wet pages and threw them into a trashcan in the corner. He was fuming, his voice low and calm. "That's all you get, Ryder. Next time I punch your ticket."

"Understood."

"Sit down."

I did. Tidwell went out to the coffee machine and brought back some paper towels. He tossed them over the spill and I watched the coffee soak into the paper.

"Let's try this again," he said.

The next few minutes were a painful recollection of the events this morning after my release, everything described in meticulous detail.

"How did you find her?"

I looked at him stupidly. "I walked into the bedroom."

"No, I mean ... I'm gonna have to ask you about the condition of the ... how she looked."

"You saw her."

"You didn't—did you try to revive her?"

"She was cold."

"Move her in any way?"

"No."

"Hold her in your arms? Anything like that?"

"I lay on the bed with her until you guys showed up."

"So we saw her exactly as you found her."

"Yes."

"And you didn't disturb anything in the room."

"I used the phone. That was it."

"How about the needle?"

"Didn't touch it."

"Okay." Tidwell wrote something down. "Did you see anything, *anything,* that made you think she was forced?"

The question hung in the air a moment. "She had to have been."

"Is that a yes or a no?"

"I didn't do a whole lot of looking around."

"But you didn't see anything?"

I knew the direction this thing was taking. "No. But I told you, the front door wasn't locked and the alarm wasn't set."

"You sure you locked the door last night before you left?"

"Yes."

"And set the alarm?"

"Absolutely."

Tidwell studied me a few seconds. "But you were pretty wound up weren't you? You could have forgotten."

"What are you saying?"

"It's possible you left without thinking."

"No way. Not a chance. I can picture myself doing it right now." More scribbling.

"Look, I'm positive that door was locked and the alarm was on. Somebody was in that house."

"Who?"

"I don't know. The guy I fought with last night."

"What makes you think that?"

"He had enough time to do it. Probably went there right after I got stuck in that field. He'd be free and clear."

"Uh-huh. Let's go back to last night. You called her from the motel."

"Yeah. Right before the police got there."

"How did she seem?"

"Tired. I woke her up."

No response.

"It was after one in the morning."

"And you woke her up."

I realized what he was getting at—if it had gone the way I thought, the man should have been there already. "I got my car back on the road pretty quick."

He nodded. "So she sounded groggy."

"Only at first."

Tidwell waited.

"She wasn't high."

"And then what?"

"I told her where I was. Gave her directions."

"She leave right away?"

"She said she would."

"You get the feeling she wasn't alone?"

"What?"

"That someone was with her? Telling her what to say?"

I couldn't say I had. "No."

He wrote that down. "Was she mad at you? For going off like that?"

"No. In fact, she apologized for something that happened earlier." I wished I hadn't brought that up.

"What?"

"It was nothing. Just a personal thing."

"Nothing to do with the murder?"

I didn't want to answer. "Look, I know what you're gonna say, but it wasn't like that."

"What did you two argue about?"

"It wasn't an argument. She thinks–thought–I was getting too wrapped up in it. Because of Turret."

"She was upset."

"I'm telling you she had no reason to start using again."

"You told me that in the car. But you've got to prepare yourself if she was. The fact remains that you were both dealing with a lot, even without Turret. And I don't have to tell you how addicts–or ex-addicts–sometimes handle stress."

"I resent you telling me what my wife was about."

Branson walked in. He looked at the coffee I'd spilled, then at me before sitting down. He'd washed the blood off his face and changed his shirt.

"We were just about done," Tidwell told him.

Branson nodded and addressed me. "There's a hole in the wall in the kitchen, like someone punched it. You know how it got there?"

"I lost my temper last night when every reporter in the city was calling us. You'll find the phone in pieces."

"That was my next question," he said, and turned to Tidwell. "You wanna go on?"

"I think I got all we'll need for now," he answered, switching off the tape recorder.

"We should be done at the house by tonight," Branson told me.

"Doesn't matter. I don't think I'd make it through the night alone in there."

Branson frowned. "Where did you plan on sleeping?"

"I haven't really thought about it."

"We need to know where to reach you."

"I'll let you know." I felt like driving, and never stopping. "I'll need my car."

"We're not done with it yet."

I looked at Tidwell. "What about Deirdre's?"

"It has to be printed."

That made sense. If the guy accosted Deirdre as she was leaving to meet me, he might have touched a door handle or something. But it left me in a lurch.

"I can't have my car. And I can't have her car either?"

They looked at each other, and Tidwell leaned over and punched a number into the speaker phone sitting on the table.

"Mitchell," someone answered on what sounded like a cell phone.

"Steve. This is Tidwell. Print the car first, okay?"

"You got it. Anything else?"

"No. See you in a bit. And thanks." Tidwell ended the call and turned to me. "You hungry?"

"I guess so."

"I'll pick up some burgers," Branson said, turning to go. Tidwell followed him into the squad room. I heard him ask if there was anything new at the scene before their voices faded. Then he came back in.

"You mind waiting in here?"

"I need a restroom."

"Down the hall to your right. Come on back when you're done."

He followed me out of the conference room and sat down at his desk. I took a short corridor to the restroom, which smelled of disinfectant. A bulletin board above the urinal had the sports page tacked to it, but I didn't read it. At the sink, I found the soap dispenser empty. I turned on the water anyway, splashed my face with cold water. Cursed under my breath when I saw they had one of those drying machines, forcing me to use toilet paper. In the mirror, I wiped the remaining water off my face and ran my fingers through my hair. None of it did any good. I closed my eyes. Gripped the sides of the basin and squeezed, putting my head down. The door opened behind me, and I realized I'd been knocking my head softly against the mirror. I looked up, embarrassed, as one of the detectives came in.

"How's it going?" he said without interest, eyeing my reflection before going into the stall. I caught the door and left.

Back in the conference room, I watched Tidwell doing some paperwork at his desk. The phones in there rang every few minutes, but otherwise it was pretty quiet. Then Branson came in, the smell of grilled meat and fries following him.

After eating, we went out to their car again. Neither of them spoke. Tidwell glanced back at me every now and then in the rearview mirror. It was late afternoon but the air conditioner was on full blast, whistling through the vents.

"Where's Turret?" I asked.

"He's not a suspect," Branson answered.

"Why not?"

Branson turned around. "I'm sorry for your loss, Mr. Ryder. But we work better without interference."

Tidwell's eyes kept coming back to me in the mirror. "Turret was still in jail at the time of the first murder," he said.

I couldn't believe my ears. "What?"

"Paperwork screwup. It happens."

I wanted to rip the car apart. I wanted to grab both their necks and throttle them until my strength gave out or they crashed the car. I'd been chasing smoke, and now Deirdre was dead.

"My wife had a miscarriage three months into our first pregnancy," I heard Branson say over the roaring in my head. "Took me a long time to convince her it wasn't her fault."

I saw myself last night, working in the shop. Finishing up and going into the house. Stopping at the bedroom door as I'd done and seeing Deirdre asleep on top of the covers. But in my mind, I got into bed beside her, and watched the rise and fall of her chest until I fell asleep, no thoughts of Turret to invade my dreams.

CHAPTER EIGHTEEN

"You coming?" Branson said, leaning into the car with his door open behind him. We'd stopped in front of the house.

I got out into the heat. Two of my neighbors were standing in the front yard next door, talking quietly. Most of the official vehicles were gone. The crime scene tape marking off the property was still there, and a white police van was parked in front. A man in shirtsleeves and slacks took a large toolbox from the back of the van into the house ahead of us. We ducked under the yellow tape and followed him.

"Anything I can do to help, Tim," Ralph from across the street called out. I lifted my hand to him without turning around.

Inside had already acquired the sterile, clinical environment of a laboratory. Two technicians worked in the bedroom, gathering prints under a bright floodlight they'd put in the corner on a stand. The hot bulb must have added a good five degrees to the already warm room. It left nothing to the imagination, showering everything with a radiance so strong I half expected to see my bones through my hands. Deirdre's body had already been removed, and the bed seemed huge and empty without her. I looked away quickly.

Branson got the okay from one of the investigators for me to take a bag from the open closet and stuff it with some clothes. Next

I went to the dresser, which was covered in fingerprint powder. I looked to Branson for approval. He nodded after the tech told him he'd finished with it. I took some underwear and socks out of the top drawer, then glanced around the room.

"You guys have her purse?"

"We haven't gone through it yet," the second technician said.

"I need the car keys."

"You don't have your own?" Branson asked.

"Not to hers."

"You got spares somewhere?"

I nodded at the nighttable on her side of the bed.

"How about it?" Branson asked the guy.

"Let me see," he answered, walking over to it. He opened the drawer with a gloved hand and looked inside. Pulled out the small key ring, holding it up for me to see. "These them?"

I nodded, and he looked to Branson. "Okay with me," Branson said.

Tidwell, who'd been standing in the doorway, agreed. "I can't imagine finding prints on them and nothing else."

I caught the keys as they were tossed to me. Told them I was ready to go, wanting to get out of there as fast as possible. Outside, I got in the car. Deirdre's scent lingered inside, a lavender soap she used. I put my head on the steering wheel, eyes squeezed shut to cut off the tears that threatened once again.

A knock on the driver's window. I looked up and rolled it down. "You okay to drive?" Tidwell asked. I nodded, started the car. "Hey," he said, getting my attention. "Don't leave town, all right? We may need you."

"Where would I go?"

"You're going somewhere now."

"I just have to get outta here."

"If I call in tonight, they'll know where to reach you, right?"

"Soon as I know," I said, putting it into gear and backing down the driveway.

I drove without thinking. No destination in mind, a hot wind blowing through the car. Turning corners yet escaping nothing, the choices I'd made following me wherever I went. Last night at the kitchen table, Deirdre had sensed what was coming, that I wouldn't let go until it was too late. She'd known it wasn't Turret who tormented me, and I realized that even if we'd been told right away he couldn't have done it, things wouldn't have turned out any different.

I kept driving, the pain and loss I felt hardening into a tight knot in my stomach. Eventually I found myself on Highway 111 going back toward the city. The valley around it was bronzed with the fading evening light. Every day, from early morning to mid-afternoon, the sun was all-powerful and merciless. A glowering, un-quenchable ball of fire. But as it neared its nightly resting place beyond the western peaks, it lost much of its ferocity, becoming more muted and buttery. The sky, bleached bone-white with the sun at its zenith, was now regaining its azure splendor, and the soil, pale and wrinkled in the noontime hours, reawakened like a ripen-ing orange.

Just before Windy Point at the edge of the desert, I turned off into the packed hard sand by the side of the road, and the small, cleared circle of land a hundred yards into the scrubland was flat and empty and still. Tire tracks and the remains of campfires were the only signs that anyone ever came here. This was where I'd pro-posed to Deirdre three years ago, the Desert Angel looking down on us while the wind buffeted the car like something alive.

Now the area was windless and silent. I parked and got out of the car, searching for that familiar imprint upon the mountain. The mountain stared back down at me, offering nothing. It grew in solemn ranks, each more imposing than the last. My eyes swept its surface, back and forth and up and down. But I saw only hard, faceless dirt. I felt my heart drop into the dust at my feet, then the sun crashed into the mountain and ripped open on its jagged peaks, and I screamed until my throat was as raw and parched as the desert around me.

CITY

CHAPTER NINETEEN

Dusk now, the city in shadow, recovering from another long hot day. I was parked across the street from Deirdre's clinic. Streetlamps flickered to life. Traffic lights had that weird, watery luminance when the last minutes of daylight float in the atmosphere before evaporating into the night sky.

An hour earlier, I'd ended up at Nate's on Palm Canyon Drive. I almost ordered a whiskey, but didn't want to start down that road. Settled for a ginger ale instead. The place had been pretty quiet. I watched the bartender polish glasses so I wouldn't have to face myself in the mirror above the bar. Tidwell's words kept coming back to me, though I tried to force them away. Maybe he was right. Maybe Deirdre couldn't deal with the possibility that my past was about to pounce on us. Or that she would lose me in the process, not just physically but emotionally. Either way, I wouldn't be there. All the things she'd overcome by herself, maybe she just didn't think she could do it again.

Deirdre had grown up in New York, where she was sexually abused by an uncle while still in grammar school. It had continued for a few years, until she reached junior high, and the repressed shame and guilt eventually caught up with her. Her sister died in Deirdre's senior year of high school. She stopped caring about herself after that. Heroin dulled the edges of her ravaged self-esteem, and her early and mid-twenties were consumed by the addiction before she'd finally cleaned up and moved across country to this desert. I'd come out here about the same time, both of us fleeing demons we'd so far been unable to shake. We used to laugh that maybe they couldn't stand the heat. But we both knew what it really was, and now, in my stubbornness, all of it had been lost.

The ginger ale in front of me had turned to water, the ice melting and sending condensation down the sides of the glass. It was slippery and cold in my hand as I turned it back and forth. The news about Turret took everything out of me. With no focus for my anger I was impotent. I went over the interview at the police station, then thought of how quickly they'd finished with Deirdre's car. Her keys were sitting next to my glass on the bar, and I knew then what I had to do. I left without touching my drink.

The palm trees along the sidewalk rustled in the breeze that came down off the mountain. An empty paper cup skidded on the pavement past the car. It had little company, with vehicle and pedestrian traffic beginning to thin out as evening descended. I'd give it a few more minutes. I felt raw and scraped out, as if my insides had been scoured with steel brushes. There was no getting around the fact that if I hadn't left last night, Deirdre would still be alive. Probably getting off work right about now, her long hair blowing in the breeze as she glided down the sidewalk.

She gets in the car and sits beside me, shutting the door to seal in the silence. Her warm hand rests on my arm, and I hear her whisper, "Stay with me, Tim. Here. Now."

I took Deirdre's spare keys from my pocket as I approached the clinic. Once inside, I locked the door behind me. The alarm whistled faintly, waiting for someone to key in the proper code. I had less than a minute before it would go off in a keening blare that would alert the police. On several previous visits here with Deirdre, I'd observed her punching in the code on the alarm's keypad. I couldn't remember the actual numbers she'd used, but I was fairly confident of being able to recall the pattern once I saw the keyboard.

Hurrying to a small closet a few feet in, I opened the door and found the green alarm control panel. Hoping the code hadn't been changed since the last time I was here, I tried it out. The whistling stopped and the LCD screen told me I'd been successful.

Relieved, I went to Deirdre's office without turning on any lights. I closed the door before switching one on. There was a wedding photo of us in a gold frame on her desk. A casual picture taken by one of the guests, showing us dancing arm in arm. Deirdre had a loopy grin on her face, her hands on my back clutching both of her shoes. Her bare feet were on top of mine as I struggled with the dance steps, all five-foot-ten of her leaning into me. I picked up the picture and smiled, remembering that perfect day. My thumb caressed the smooth glass in front of her image. Putting it back, I went straight for the file cabinet in the corner, used another of Deirdre's keys to unlock it. The current client files were in the top drawer, about ten of them she dealt with personally. I removed the top page from each, which listed personal information like addresses and telephone numbers, stacked them in the automatic document feeder and turned on the machine. While it warmed up, I opened the second file drawer and saw that it held previous patient files, going back about six months, and I prepared to copy those too.

Everything I thought could be useful, about forty files in all, I copied. It went quicker than I expected with the automated machine, and I was done in about twenty minutes. After recollating the files, I found an empty folder for the copies. Before I left, I grabbed our wedding picture and included it with the documents in the folder, switched off the lights and reset the alarm.

Outside, I turned around to lock the door behind me. As I did so, the picture of me and Deirdre slid out of the folder and clattered on the pavement. I was afraid it had broken, but found that it was okay when I picked it up. I locked the door, knowing I'd probably never return. Back in the car, I put the sheaf of papers on the seat beside me with the photograph on top. As I drove away, the streetlights slid over the picture frame's glass and reflected into my eyes.

There was a Denny's next door to the motel off the freeway. I ordered the first thing I saw on the menu, not caring what it was. It was strictly for nourishment, fuel for the following day, and I didn't really taste any of it. I sat at the counter and watched the waitresses scurry back and forth. The cooks behind the order window worked methodically over hissing clouds of steam and sizzling grease. It brought back the time I'd spent working in the prison kitchen, first doing post-meal cleanings, then the cooking itself. I'd been out a long time, but it didn't feel that way.

As I ate, I went over my plans for tomorrow. I'd taken Deirdre's case files in order to begin tracking down her clients, hoping to speak to as many of them as I could about the possible identity of the young man shot down in our front yard. It was the only thing I could think to do. If both deaths were related to the area's burgeoning drug trade, I'd do my damndest to prove it. I was absolutely convinced, unlike the cops, that Deirdre's death wasn't self-inflicted or accidental.

I finished the meal and left a ten on the counter, then checked into the motel next door. The room was plain and impersonal, exactly what I needed. I sat down on the bed, looked at the phone. Didn't want to deal with it, but I decided to get it over with. Someone picked up after three rings.

"Can I speak to Allie?"

"Is that you, Tim?"

"Allie?"

"Oh, Tim, I'm so sorry. We're all just in shock. How are you doing?"

"I don't think it's hit me yet. I mean, I've had some moments, but . . ." I started over. "I'm going to need your help."

"Anything."

"Can you call anybody that may not have heard yet? I'm just not up to it."

"Everybody at the clinic knows. I don't have Terry's number though." Terry. Deirdre's friend from Triumph Outreach.

"I'm sure it'll be in the Rolodex on her desk in the office. I'd give it to you but I'm not at home."

"Are you going to be okay?"

"I think so."

"The news said . . . what happened, Tim?"

"I don't know."

"She seemed fine."

"She was. Allie, she didn't do that to herself."

"I knew it. I knew she didn't." A shaky breath. "But the police think . . ."

"They don't know her the way we do."

"What about you, Tim?"

"I don't know. I'm still trying to sort it all out. First the other murder. Now Deirdre. I don't know."

"She called me last night."

"What?"

"I talked to her last night."

"When?"

"You were in the shop."

I couldn't seem to absorb the news. "What did she say?"

"She was worried about you."

It just couldn't get any worse. Everything I'd done was wrong. "She tried to talk me out of getting involved. And I didn't listen."

"It's not your fault, Tim."

"I wasn't there for her."

"It's not." I knew she wanted to ask why I'd gone down to Indio, but she didn't. "When's the funeral?"

"I'm not sure yet." I had to end this, now. "Allie, I may not be in touch for a couple days."

"I understand."

"But I'll call when I have the arrangements."

"Okay." A pause. "God, I'll miss her. I miss her now."

"I know. Goodbye, Allie."

I hung up. The phone at home was probably ringing off the hook from other friends, but they'd just have to fill the machine. I got up and turned on the TV. Went to the window and pulled the curtains. The room reflected back at me, obscuring the night outside. I switched off the lamp and stood in the darkness with the TV flickering in the background. Watched the traffic zoom by on the freeway, my reflection coming and going with the light from the television screen.

CHAPTER TWENTY

The next morning was bright and hot, and I woke up sweating to the sound of a morning news show. I switched it off, took a long hot shower until steam filled the bathroom and my skin prickled with heat. Still wet, I went into the bedroom and turned on the window air conditioner. Let the cold blast of air dry my skin and shock me into wakefulness. Then I dressed, combed my wet hair back and went down to the restaurant. I ordered a large breakfast and drank cup after cup of strong black coffee, steeling myself for the coming day.

Back in the room, I spread the copies I'd made last night on the bed, and started with Deirdre's most recent clients. The first number didn't answer. The second one was answered by a man who sounded in a rush.

"I'm looking for Michael D'Angelo."

"You found him," he said before speaking to someone else. "Not now, Trish." Then he was back. "Who's this?"

"I'm sorry. This is Tim Ryder. I think you knew my wife, Deirdre."

"Yeah," he said, drawing it out warily. "I know a Deirdre."

"I don't know if you heard–"

"Look, I'm on my way to work. What's this all about?"

"I guess maybe you didn't see the news."

"What news?"

"She's dead."

I heard a woman in the background, and his voice got muffled before he came back. "Did I hear you right?"

"You did."

"My God! That's . . . that's terrible. I don't know what to say."

"Can we talk sometime today?"

"You said you're her husband?"

"Yeah."

"I'm really sorry. I can't . . . what did you want to talk to me about?"

"Maybe we could meet somewhere."

"I guess. But I don't see how–"

"Where do you work?"

"I don't know if I feel comfortable–"

"It would really help me out. Deirdre too."

"How did she die?"

"Can we talk about it later?"

"Well . . . if you can make it out to the San Gorgonio Inn. What's today?"

"Wednesday."

"I get a break around ten."

"I could be there then. Where at?"

"The parking lot. Don't ask for me, I'll find you. My boss is just looking for a reason."

"No problem. I'll see you at ten."

The next one had an answering machine, which I didn't bother with, and the one after that rang and rang. Number five picked up just before I was going to move on.

A woman, speaking very quietly. "Hello?"

"Is this Monica?" The TV was on behind her.

"Yeah." Tired, without inflection.

"My name is Tim Ryder. I–"

She started crying. "I just saw you on TV."

"I'm sorry."

"How could she do this?"

"It wasn't what you think."

She didn't seem to hear me, and her next words were loud and distorted in the earpiece. "Where were you?"

I waited until she got herself under control. "I have to talk to you."

"Deirdre was going to help me find Cameron. I had an appointment with her and everything."

"Who?"

"My son. I haven't seen him in five years."

"I have to talk to you."

"I don't want to talk to you," she said. The next thing I heard was the dial tone. I called her back, but she didn't answer, and I realized then what I was up against. I put the phone back in the cradle, her question echoing in my mind. Found the next name and dialed.

"What," I heard over loud music in the background. He sounded young.

"Bobby Callejo?"

"Just a sec." He dropped the phone, and the music didn't get any quieter before Bobby answered.

"Bullet the blue sky," he sang off-key with the music, obviously drunk, then shouted into the phone, "U2 *rocks*, man."

This wouldn't be easy. "Hey. You got a counselor named Deirdre?"

"Oh. Yeah. Cool lady. I don't think she's too happy with me though."

"Why not?"

"Well, you know how it is. I blew her off the last couple weeks. Nothing personal, man." He started singing again.

This was a waste of time. Maybe when he was sober. "Yeah, okay. Thanks for your time."

I hung up without waiting for a response, completely discouraged. One out of six, but I was luckier with the last few, getting three other people to meet me later in the day. The final call I made was a disappointment, though, to Patrick Reed, the kid from the fountain. His phone was disconnected. With the rapport Deirdre had obviously shared with him, it seemed more likely that he would give her name to a friend in need. I jotted down his address so I could try his place in the evening.

After filling the car with gas, I set out for Banning, about fifteen miles west on the interstate. Most of the city pushed up against the San Bernardino Mountains north of the freeway, except for the sprawling Sun Lakes retirement community on the other side. The San Gorgonio Inn was an older place visible from the freeway, and I made a few rights into the parking lot. It was hot and still, and the mountains rose up in different shades of brown against the blue sky. Eventually, the smog from L.A. would get pushed out here. I sat against the hood of the car, sweating, keeping an eye out for someone who might be looking for me. It was a few minutes to ten. On the second floor walkway I saw a man in a white shirt and pants pushing a cleaning cart. He stopped it in front of one of the rooms and glanced my way. Looked at his watch and came down the stairs, pulling a pack of cigarettes from his shirt pocket as he approached.

"You the guy I just talked to?"

"That's right."

"I forgot your name." He was in his thirties, Caucasian, with a short beard, and very thin.

"Tim."

He nodded, took a cigarette out of the box. "It really sucks. I been thinking about it all morning. She was a good person." He sounded matter-of-fact, maybe a defense mechanism against the hardships in his life.

"Thanks for seeing me."

"No problem," he said, patting his pockets. "You got a light?"

"Sorry."

"You mind coming to my car?"

"Sure." I followed him to the edge of the lot, toward an old Pontiac with weathered paint and peeling vinyl on the roof. He stopped when he saw the flat tire in the back.

"Ahh, hell. Musta been that metal I ran over on 18th."

I looked at my watch. "You need help with the spare?"

"It'll have to wait till later. But thanks." The windows were all rolled down, and he leaned over and reached in for the cigarette lighter. When it popped out, he lit his cigarette and tossed the lighter onto the seat. I saw duct tape and burn marks on the vinyl.

"You were going to tell me how she died," he said, blowing smoke out of his nose.

"The police think it was an accidental overdose."

The cigarette stopped halfway to his mouth.

"I don't," I said.

He nodded, taking a puff.

"It looks like you agree with me."

"I'd be surprised. What was in her system?"

"Heroin."

He pondered that, tapping ash onto the pavement. "So someone else put it there?"

"That's the only other explanation."

"Why?"

"I'm trying to find that out."

"What do you want from me?"

"You heard about the body they found the other day, right?"

"Yeah. In North Palm Springs."

"It was on our property."

"Whoa. I didn't know that."

"Deirdre didn't know him. But we'd been talking about the possibility that maybe he knew her. Through one of her clients." He studied me, not saying anything. "You know, like a recommendation."

"Not from me. Maybe to the clinic."

"No. They'd have to have her name."

"I wish I could help." He dropped his cigarette on the pavement and ground it out. "But I don't see what one would have to do with the other."

I didn't feel like getting into it. "I don't know. I had to start somewhere."

"I gotta get back."

I walked with him over the hot concrete, toward the motel and my car.

"How did you find me?"

I hesitated. "Your file."

"I figured. My life's an open book anyway." He turned to look at me. "I reported someone last week. Smelled ammonia in one of the rooms. I don't know if that helps."

"Drug lab?"

"That was my assumption."

"What happened?"

"They carted him off in the back of a police car."

"You didn't know the person, did you?"

"No."

I tried to make it fit, but couldn't. "Thanks anyway." We stopped at the bottom of the stairs. "I appreciate your time."

He stuck out his hand, and I shook it. "When's the funeral?"

"The police still have her. I could call you."

"Do that. I should be there."

The rest of the day I spent circling the fringes of the valley. I stopped at the nature preserve midday to kill some time. It was dusty and still, completely deserted in the heat of the afternoon. I sat on a bench surrounded by palm trees, listening to the silence. At a mobile home park in Desert Hot Springs I'd learned nothing. The lady had fanned herself with a newspaper and spoken of how much she looked forward to her meetings with Deirdre. She didn't know what she would do now. I'd left more dejected than ever. Took Dillon through the Indio Hills, past Sky Valley to the preserve. Before I knew it, an hour was gone, and I headed down to La Quinta, where I met another recovering addict who had nothing more than sympathy to give me. Palm Desert was the next stop, with the same result. Afterward, in no hurry to get home, I found Palm Canyon Drive. It wound through Rancho Mirage and Cat City on its way to Palm Springs. Landscaped retirement communities glistened on my right. On the left, rocky foothills rose up in stunted heaps.

Patrick Reed's place was on Palm Canyon Drive, near the outer edge of the city. An ancient looking little apartment complex, nine units arranged in a shallow U formation around a flower and weed infested courtyard. It was done in the traditional southwestern style, with adobe colored walls and faded pink roof tiles. A Subway sandwich shop was right next door.

I parked in the street out front and went into the courtyard, headed for number 6. A large horsefly darted in front of my face. I batted it away. There were cactus and wildflowers crowding the walkway, baking under the late afternoon sun. Overgrown weeds threatened to choke off the area. A dry fountain stood in the middle of the courtyard, its discolored surface crumbling and flaking away. The place was empty and silent except for the buzzing flies, and seemed straight out of an old western.

Going up to the door at number 6, I noticed an old cat, gray and dusty, sprawled in the meager shade beneath a wilted rosebush in front of the apartment next door. It panted tiredly, one milky eye following me warily.

I knocked on the door in front of me and waited. No answer. The unit didn't seem abandoned; there was a partially closed curtain in the window and I peered through the crack in the center. Too dark inside to see anything, so I tried next door, whose window was also closed and curtained against the heat of the day. The residents would probably venture out later, like the nocturnal wildlife that lived in the area.

This time the door was answered by a short, thick Mexican

woman. She stared out at me from her dim living room. The cat at my feet darted into the house, but she didn't seem to mind. I heard faint music inside and smelled grilling meat, which made me realize how hungry I was.

"Sí?" she asked.

I inquired in Spanish whether she knew the man next door and told her his name. She nodded and said yes, he lived there, but couldn't tell me when he'd be back. When I thanked her, she closed the door quickly, eager to shut out the intense heat.

At the Subway I bought a sandwich and sat down facing the window. Kept my eyes on the street outside. The only customer in the place, I ate slowly and began to relax from the long day. But I'd be ready if I caught sight of anyone who might be Reed.

When I'd finished the sandwich, I got up to refill my drink. I turned away from the window momentarily, and almost missed a young man walking by outside. Rushing out of the store, I just caught him going into the courtyard: thin and medium height, short, unkempt hair. He wore a T-shirt over dusty blue jeans and battered old sneakers.

"Excuse me, are you Patrick Reed?" I asked from right behind him.

Startled, he turned around, looked me up and down. "Yeah, that's me. But I don't want anything, man. I'm off that shit."

"I'm not here to sell you anything," I said, then hesitated. "I'm Deirdre's husband. I need to talk to you."

"Deirdre?" he asked uncertainly.

"You haven't heard?"

"Heard what?"

"She . . . she's dead."

"Dead?" He put his hand on his forehead and rocked back on his heels, clearly surprised. "How? I just saw her the other day."

"Can we sit down or something? I need to ask you a few things."

"I can't believe it."

"You live here?" I asked, nodding at the apartments.

"Yeah." Reed looked back at them, shaking his head slowly, then told me to follow him. When we got to his door, he pulled out his key and unlocked it. "Wait here, it'll be roasting inside," he said, then offered me a soda. I held up my Subway cup, and he nodded dazedly and disappeared inside, telling me he'd be right back. He came out a few moments later with a clean shirt on and a sweating can of Coke.

We sat on the porch step, Jimi Hendrix gazing at me from Reed's T-shirt. We talked while the courtyard succumbed to the encroaching shadow of the mountain. I told him how Deirdre died, and also what had happened Sunday morning.

Reed studied the drink in his hand, which was still unopened. "Yeah. I heard some of the guys talking about that."

"The guys?"

"I work for a gardening service. Deirdre found it for me." He popped the top on the Coke and took a sip.

"Patrick, I'm wondering if you gave anyone Deirdre's name without telling her."

"What do you mean?"

"Someone that may have needed her. Like a referral."

"No."

I looked away, disappointed. A man across the courtyard came outside, put a small hibachi grill on his doorstep and lit it up.

"So the guy who got killed may have known one of her clients?" Reed asked.

"Could have."

"I can't believe she's gone. I guess I thought she'd always be there to help. You know?" he said, and it went like that for a while. As we spoke, the dwellings around us seemed to awaken from a long slumber. Windows were opened and lights came on; Reed went inside and opened his own place to the night air. Came back with a pack of Marlboros and matches. He left the door open and sat down next to me, his back against the doorframe, and pulled a cigarette out of the pack with his teeth.

"Smoke?" he said, extending the pack toward me.

I shook my head no. He lit his cigarette and took a long drag. Tilting his head back, he looked up at the sky, blowing the smoke out in a forceful rush. "I loved that lady," he murmured. "You were lucky to have been with her."

I gazed toward the street, where an occasional car sped past, oblivious to this quiet little world. "I know."

Reed's eyes were shiny in the darkness, and he couldn't seem to look at me. "She really helped me out. Got me back on my feet." He sniffled and wiped his nose. "I'm really going to miss her."

I could barely speak. "Me too."

"I was the guy in the fountain a few weeks ago."

"Yeah? I think I read about that."

"Got a bit of notoriety for it," he chuckled. "My fifteen minutes."

"I know the feeling," I said, and he gave me a quizzical look. "All this shit that's happened."

"Oh. Yeah." Drag on his cigarette. He lit another from the first one and dropped the butt between his feet, grinding it into the dirt with his shoe. Then he looked up at me. "I know this'll sound corny, but . . ." I waited. ". . . she was my savior."

I knew what he meant.

Reed sighed deeply, then went on. "My girlfriend's pregnant."

I wasn't sure what to say. "Congratulations. Did Deirdre know?"

"No." He looked down. "Didn't get the chance to tell her."

"Well, wherever she is . . . ," I started, then couldn't go on. It was time to go. "Thanks for your time," I said, standing. "And your sympathy. It means a lot." I stuck out my hand.

Reed took it. "Can I come to the funeral?"

"I'd appreciate that," I replied, shaking his hand. "In a few days. After the autopsy." Saying that, I thought I'd be sick and lose the entire meal I'd just eaten on Reed's doorstep. "I'll let you know. You have a phone?"

"I'll give you my girlfriend's cell number," he said. I handed him a pen and my Subway receipt and he wrote it down. I told him I'd be in touch, and we said goodbye.

Halfway back to my car something occurred to me. "Patrick?"

He was still seated on the step, the glowing red ember of his cigarette suspended in front of his face. "Yeah?"

"Ever hear of a band called Gravity Throttle?"

"Gravity Throttle?" He thought for a moment, then shook his head. "Can't say that I have. Sorry." Another drag from his cigarette. "Why?"

"That kid the other day. On my lawn. He was wearing one of their T-shirts."

"You think he knew them?"

"Maybe."

"Have you tried the Web?"

I hadn't thought about that. "Good idea. I'll do that. And I'll call you about the funeral."

"I'm really sorry about Deirdre. I hope you find who did it."

"Thanks again," I said, turning back to the street. The place had begun to recover from the scorching heat of the day, welcoming the darkness with the faint sounds of music, the warm glow of incandescent light and the sweet aromas of dinnertime cooking. Across the way, Reed's neighbor had what smelled like marinated chicken grilling on his little hibachi. Bright orange flames licked hungrily at the meat, while the dripping fat sizzled and popped, stoking the fire. I thought of the contrast between this community, open and receptive to the night, with the different aromas and sounds all mixed together, then of my own neighborhood as I'd experienced it late the other night: insular and detached, closed off and protected from the night by locked doors, drawn curtains and the incessant hum of the air conditioners that stole the warm nighttime air and converted it to something artificial and cold.

Approaching the street, I saw the broad face of the San Jacintos, their lower reaches glazed pale gray by the city lights, the topmost elevations disappearing into a sky of polished obsidian. I wondered if, in the end, what I was doing would make a difference to anyone but myself and my own guilt-ridden conscience.

CHAPTER TWENTY-ONE

The city library had closed hours before, so I had to use the computer at home, reluctant as I was to go back there. I needed to learn more about the band on that T-shirt as soon as possible, before the night was over.

Parking in the driveway, I noticed the yellow tape had been taken down. I wondered if the police even considered it a crime scene anymore. Inside, the house was mostly as I'd left it the day before, though the master bedroom still betrayed signs of the investigation. Drawers were half open, traces of fingerprint powder dusting their surfaces. The sheets had been removed from the bed. Unless my eyes were playing tricks on me, I thought I could make out an impression of Deirdre's body on the bare mattress. My mind painted a picture of her lying there, peaceful and content and alive, her chest rising and falling softly to the rhythm of my own heartbeat. I shut the door quickly.

The smaller bedroom across the hall, which we'd used as an office, was less disturbed. I went to the computer and turned it on, drumming my fingers impatiently while it booted. On the wall next to the computer was the wildlife calendar Deirdre used, the days crossed off in red as they went by. Saturday was the last day she'd marked.

The modem's dial tone took me back to the phone booth I'd

used yesterday morning, making that desperate call home. Then the white noise static of the Internet connection, and I found myself wishing for a peaceful incoherence like it to keep my grief at bay. Now I could feel why so many people surrendered to drug abuse. I wondered where the heroin that killed Deirdre had come from, who'd brought it into this house. Then my eyes refocused on the screen in front of me. I typed in "Gravity Throttle," hit "search" and waited for a hit. The top ten matches for my request came up onscreen. One of them was for Pynchon's *Gravity's Rainbow,* a few others for scientific articles and Web sites. The one I wanted was somewhere in the middle: an item for an independent, unsigned rock band that had recently released a self-produced CD. I clicked on the listing. Seconds later, I was in.

Their site was done in a gothic style, with psychedelic green lettering on a black velvet background. The first page was a group portrait, with the band members' names listed beneath. They wore black clothing and silver jewelry, high collars and fringed leather jackets. They all looked to be in their early twenties, close in age to the murder victim, whom I'd been hoping to recognize as one of the musicians. But it was obvious, even behind the makeup and unusual hairstyles, that that wasn't the case. Unfortunately, only first names accompanied the instruments they played, which meant it wasn't going to be easy tracking them down. Plus, if the murder victim was merely one of their fans, there'd be little hope of finding out who he was. But I held on to the small chance that he was somehow connected to the band on a higher level. Maybe a roadie or something, anybody they would know personally.

I scrolled down the page, where it showed the links to other pages. A band bio, live photos, tour dates, and a list of MP3 downloadable songs. After clicking on the bio, the screen filled with more of the same distinctive typeface, the first letter of each paragraph enlarged and intertwined with vines, flowers and serpents.

They were a Brooklyn, New York, band who'd been together for three years. One CD on their own label, available through the Web site. That gave me a place to start, even if it was on the other side of the country. I wondered if it was just coincidence that it was the same city as Deirdre was from. I clicked on the concert calendar, hoping for a date and location where I could hook up with them. But the schedule was out of date. The last concert listed was over a month ago, and I saw that the page hadn't been updated since longer than that. Not sure of what to do next, I tried to think of a way to track them down. I typed in "The Village Voice," crossed my fingers while its homepage assembled. When it came up I went straight to the show listings and scrolled through the week's events. There were dozens of bands at numerous small clubs and venues, but I couldn't find Gravity Throttle anywhere. My eyes were tired and burning from looking at the monitor, but I forced myself to go on. The listings covered Friday to Thursday, which was only up through tomorrow. Exactly when a new edition would show up on the Web I couldn't say, but I didn't want to wait until then anyway. Unless I found something tonight, there was no way I'd get any sleep.

I tried the advertisers' pages, hoping they'd publicize future events farther in advance. There were pages and pages of ads. Concerts, poetry readings, album release parties and gallery showings. Some ads were large and elaborate, others smaller and more plain. I went through every single one of them, my eyes blurring with fatigue. My wrist ached with each movement of the mouse, clicking, scrolling and sliding.

Didn't get a hit. Gravity Throttle was nowhere to be found in New York, at least as an advertised attraction. My head was pounding, and I was just about to call it a night. Then something caught my eye. A small notice for a band called Spine, who were playing their debut show at a club called The Coven tomorrow night. What intrigued me about it was the lettering in the ad; it was similar to the style Gravity Throttle used in their bio, with the "S" in Spine enlarged and intricately decorated.

After saving the page, I hit the "back" button a few times until I got to Gravity Throttle's Web site. I perused the material looking for another "S" like the one in Spine, and found one starting the third paragraph of the bio: *Sparked by the addition of a new singer . . .* For comparison, I minimized the screens and put the two of them side by side.

An exact match. Hoping the script style wasn't particularly common, I kept the advertisement displayed, snatched up the phone on the desk, and punched in the number of The Coven. I glanced at my watch. 9:32. Which would make it 12:32 in the morning on the east coast, still early for most club-goers.

After four rings the line engaged. I heard what sounded like a big crowd over a heavy background of music. Someone answered "Al's Bar," above the din.

Momentarily taken aback, I raised my own voice and stuttered, "Oh, I'm sorry. I thought I was calling The Coven."

"Not till tomorrow night."

"Excuse me?"

"Only on Thursday nights. It's Al's Bar the rest of the week. What can I do for you?"

"Your band tomorrow night—"

"Spine? We been getting a lot of calls about that." Then, like an answered prayer: "Former members of Gravity Throttle. They forgot to put that in their ad." The music in the background ended and I heard applause.

"How many former members?" The more, the better.

"Three out of four, guy. Another new singer." Pause amid clinking glasses and laughter. "Look, we're pretty busy. Come by tomorrow night. You won't be disappointed." He hung up then, abruptly cutting off the crowd noise.

"Thanks," I said to a dead line.

I knew without thinking about it that I'd be on the first plane to New York City. Screw the mandate from Tidwell not to leave town.

It would be a short trip; either the band knew the victim or they didn't. If they didn't, I'd be wasting my time. But if they did know him, finding his identity might lead to Deirdre's killer, and I'd hand the information over. A long shot, but I had to take it. And nobody needed to know about the unauthorized trip if nothing useful came up.

As I threw some stuff into a small overnight bag, it struck me how similar my thought processes were to those of the other night, when I'd convinced myself to go out to the Blue Bird Motel, and promised that anything I stumbled across would go directly to the police. A series of decisions that had ultimately allowed Deirdre's death.

I tried not to think about all that as I finished packing and turned off the bedroom light. After checking my wallet for cash and credit cards, I left the house without bothering to set the alarm. There seemed nothing worth protecting now. Back at the motel, I retrieved the other overnight bag, Deirdre's client paperwork and, finally, our wedding photo which I'd propped on the night table. It seemed horribly out of place there. Then I checked out.

I got to Palm Springs International Airport just before eleven and hurried past the putting green outside, unused at this hour. At the terminal, all the ticket counters were closed until the next morning. The last scheduled flight had landed, and the boarding areas beyond the security checkpoints were now inaccessible behind rigid fencing. Only a few travelers remained in the terminal. Two security guards prowled the hall in tandem.

I spent the night right there in the parking lot. In the cramped back seat of Deirdre's car, I could feel sleep coming on quickly. The last thing I saw before closing my eyes was a blue-white point of light glowing above Mount San Jacinto. I thought it was a star at first, but then recognized it as the light for the tramway's summit station, anchored to the mountain high above the valley.

The next morning I awoke at sunrise, stiff-necked and groggy.

I bought a round-trip ticket to New York with an open-end return date. After breakfast in the cafeteria, I found a pair of phone booths and picked one. Closed the door to shut out any telltale airport noises, and took out Branson's card.

Tidwell answered instead. "Tidwell, homicide."

"It's Tim Ryder. I was calling about the autopsy."

He hesitated, and I knew that wasn't a good sign. "I hate to tell you this, but it's just like we thought. The coroner can't rule it a homicide. Not with what we got."

"Which is nothing," I finished for him. I'd expected this, and it strengthened my resolve to pursue things on my own.

"Basically. No foreign prints we could find, not even on the syringe. Same with the spoon and the lighter and the other stuff. No evidence of a struggle in the house or on her person . . . sorry, I know that sounded kind of cold."

Next to me, a man took the other booth. "What about the cause of death?"

"Heart stoppage due to heroin overdose."

"So that's it?" I could hear the airport public address system faintly through the glass, and hoped it wouldn't be audible over the phone.

"I don't like it any more than you do, but our hands are kind of tied. Branson and I don't set the priorities around here." I didn't respond. "We can still talk to a few people, but beyond that, I can't promise anything. We'll do our best."

"You find anything new on the first murder?" I wanted something, anything, to point me in the right direction for Deirdre.

"I can't really talk about that. It's ongoing."

"What about funeral arrangements? When can I have her body?"

"The coroner still has to wrap up a few things, but tomorrow should be okay. Call me."

"All right." I couldn't think of anything else to say, so I quietly hung up. I knew what he meant by *wrap up a few things*, an unfortunate way to put it, and the thought sickened me. They had to put Deirdre back together.

I was startled by the door rattling loudly right next to me. Someone wanted to use the phone. A young guy with a questioning, irritated look on his face. Fuck him, I thought.

"Fuck off. I'm not done yet."

His face reddened. Then he noticed the other phone booth free up and took it, shaking his head. I closed my eyes, rested my forehead on the phone in front of me, alone inside the glass case again. I was dying in here. The finality of Tidwell's news was a bigger blow than I'd thought it would be. All around me, travelers went on about their business. The muffled sounds of commerce barely reached me as I stood there, visible to the outside world yet sealed off from it. I felt as if it had always been this way before Deirdre, and always would be in her absence. Then I opened the door and walked toward the departure area.

CHAPTER TWENTY-TWO

I ordered a beer with lunch, then had another. We hit a long patch of turbulence and the plane's swaying and dipping, coupled with the alcohol, soon gave me a pounding headache. I put on the headphones and dropped into a restless nap. I kept seeing myself standing in our bedroom doorway the other night, wanting to get into bed with Deirdre. But I couldn't get past the threshold no matter how hard I tried. A voice was echoing in my head, and when I woke up it was the captain announcing our landing.

It was close to five in the evening New York time. Looking out the window, I saw clouds below us, the sun in the west lighting them from above. Through the cloud cover, Manhattan suddenly appeared, a great, gray, spiny beast. Skyscrapers packed together like bristles. I remembered the golden sunlight this morning and how it burnished the inert rock face of the San Jacintos, then took in the stainless steel monotone of the city below us. Up ahead, the Atlantic Ocean was a dull sheet of crinkled tinfoil. Ships belching blue smoke were visible on the horizon, where it met the fading gun-metal sky. The Statue of Liberty was lost at sea, her upthrust torch extinguished by the gathering clouds.

I looked away and spoke to the passenger next to me, a woman in a gray pinstriped business suit. "Excuse me. Uhh . . . do you live in New York?"

The plane took a sudden dip, and we both tensed.

"It's just that I've never been here before," I continued after we smoothed out.

"You need help with something?" she asked, closing her laptop.

"You know how much cab fare into the city will cost me?"

"Manhattan?"

"Yeah."

"Thirty bucks, flat fee. But why would you want to do that? The subway's cheaper. Faster too." And when I didn't reply: "What part of Manhattan?"

"Greenwich Village."

"A train'll get you there."

"A train."

"Yeah." She had a pretty face that needed little makeup, and her skin, one shade lighter than her dark brown hair, was smooth and unblemished. "Air Train first, then the subway. You can ride with me if you want."

"That's very nice of you. Thank you."

"Just don't let anybody sell you the Brooklyn Bridge," she said, and laughed.

"I won't," I replied sheepishly.

"You here on business?"

I didn't know quite how to answer that. "Yeah."

The seatbelt sign came on with a soft ding. I strapped in as the landing gears rumbled into position below us.

After landing, I picked up a map of Manhattan. We boarded the Air Train, then transferred to the subway at Howard Beach. Miraculously, we each found seats across the aisle from one another. Finally we introduced ourselves, and she told me her name was Lynn. She flashed me a quick smile as the subway moved out, but it was too noisy to really talk. A guy standing near the door holding on to a handrail was checking her out, until he noticed me looking at him.

"Pizza-man can't throw anybody out," I caught from a few seats away. A young man with sunglasses over his head.

"He's still going to the Hall," his companion said. "I mean, come on. . . . "

The train ran more smoothly than I expected, with a rhythmic sway as it traveled through Queens and Brooklyn, each stop identified by large black signs with white letters. The stations were colored with splashy murals and graffiti, and the music of street performers could be heard from the platforms. Next to me, a lady with a baby in her arms cooed softly to him. Lynn had pulled an appointment book out of her jacket pocket and was paging through it.

When we stopped again, I leaned forward into the aisle. "I . . . ahhh . . . I'm not sure where to get off." The smell of food wafted into the train car along with the pungent odor of oil and hot metal and electricity.

"Oh, I'm sorry," Lynn said, putting the book back in her pocket. "You're just two stops after mine."

"Thanks. I really appreciate your help."

"No problem," she said around someone that had just stepped in front of her. "I know it can be kind of intimidating."

"You lived here long?"

"Few years," Lynn said as we jerked into motion, and that was it for a while. A bridge took us over the river to Manhattan, then back in the tunnels again, which were punctuated by recurring strips of yellow tracklighting. Halfway there, I was startled by another train whipping by in the opposite direction.

The seat to my right was vacated eventually, and Lynn came across the aisle to sit next to me. "What about you? Where are you from?"

"California. Palm Springs area."

She nodded, smiling. "Desert playground for the rich and famous. Which one are you?"

"Neither one, I'm afraid." Was she old enough to remember the war that had brought my notoriety way back when? Probably just barely; she looked to be in her late thirties. I glanced down at her bare ring finger, surprised that she seemed interested in me. But she wasn't Deirdre, and no woman ever would be.

Feeling a sudden pang, I looked away quickly, and Lynn, picking up on the expression that must have clouded my features, quieted. Suddenly we were two strangers on a crowded train.

In the darkness of another tunnel, I saw my face reflected in the opposite window, and the noise all around me began fading away. Deirdre had told me once about how, when she was in high school, she used to come down here and randomly pick a train, then stay on it until the end of the line. Just to try and get away from what was eating her up inside.

"Never worked," she said, sitting on the hood of our car out near Garnet Hill, while the Southern Pacific freight lumbered past. Deirdre had always liked traveling songs, and a taped collection was playing on the stereo. "Sometimes I'd end up near the airport, watching the planes take off, wondering how far I could get. Maybe I'd find one that would never land, just fly off and never come back." She shook her head and smiled faintly. "Then I'd get back on the subway, thinking I'd be stuck in New York forever."

Lynn spoke from miles away. "My stop's coming up. You're going to be looking for the West Fourth Street station."

I nodded, still with Deirdre in that hot desert. "West Fourth. Okay."

She didn't respond, just held my gaze for a moment. Took a breath like she was about to speak, then swallowed it. We came to a halt and she stood with the other debarking riders, laptop under her arm and overnight bag in hand. Somebody bumped her on his way out, but she didn't seem to notice. She pointed to a plastic subway map inside the door with colored lines all over it.

"This is us," she told me, putting her finger on the blue line. Just above her head, I saw strips of advertisements in English and Spanish. *Got a drug problem? Get help!* "West Fourth is two stops from now. Here." She indicated a white dot further up the line, then gestured outside. "See the signs?" Hers was Chambers Street.

"I got it. Thanks again."

Lynn turned back to me just before she left. "Take care, Tim," she said, and I couldn't think of a damn thing to say before she was gone, high heels clicking on the platform outside as the door slid shut.

Needing some fresh air to clear my head, I got off at the next stop, one before the Village. I jostled my way off the subway carrying the bag I'd packed at home. I stopped to watch the train pull away, its taillight blinking slowly as it receded into the tunnel. Then I went up the steps into the graying evening light.

CHAPTER TWENTY-THREE

A blast of warm, supercharged air hit me when I reached street level, and the city moved all around me. Pedestrians rushed by on the sidewalks. Traffic ebbed and flowed in slow-moving packs, yellow cabs lined up like marching ants. Fleeting clouds of steam escaped from curbside subway vents. Across the way, neon signs advertised tattoos and piercings in a shop window. The din of the streets vibrated in my bones. It was the sound inside a seashell amplified a thousand times.

Pulling out the map, I tried to fix my bearings. On one side, Canal Street extended west to the crowded Holland Tunnel exit. Toward Chinatown, it was lined with a vast array of shops and businesses: electronics and hardware stores, furniture dealers proclaiming the best prices on futons, and a varied assortment of bargain retail outlets. Across Canal and down: Tribeca, the "triangle below Canal," I remembered from somewhere. Soho was in the opposite direction, just before the Village.

I went that way, north on Sixth, moving away from the steel and concrete thickets of the downtown high-rises. At Grand, I waited for the light to change. An imposing presence loomed over my shoulder, and I turned to see a fifty-foot model staring down at me from a huge Gap billboard plastered to the side of a building. As I stepped into the crosswalk, I felt the man shadow me, keeping track of my progress. I actually seemed to be making better time than the gridlocked traffic inching forward a few feet away. I passed sidewalk vendors hawking magazines, flowers and food. The smell of singed pretzels made my mouth water.

A few minutes later I was wishing I'd stayed on the subway. The humidity in the air seemed to suspend all the dirt and grit and exhaust rising from the pavement. I was more used to the dry desert heat. A young woman wearing snakeskin pants handed me a coupon for free admission to some nightclub, which I put in my pocket without really looking at.

"Doors open at ten," she said after me. "I'll be looking for you."

I pushed on, through milling throngs of shoppers, tourists and businesspeople. Streetlamps and headlights were coming on in the dusk. Together with the lights from shop windows and signs, they bled into the atmosphere like viscous smears of colored oil on glass.

In Soho, I looked up at the cast-iron facades with their identically painted fire escapes. The metal staircases zig-zagged up and down the buildings, bisecting large windows that reflected back the twilit city. Back in the early seventies, when Deirdre was living in New York, this area was just another fading commercial district, inhabited mostly by artists. Then, she'd told me, the developers began moving in and, from what I could see, they'd been entirely successful in transforming the place into a dining and shopping mecca for the trendy elite. I passed open-air cafés and coffee houses, hair salons and art galleries, jazz clubs and hip bars, all vying for attention and dollars.

Houston Street divided Soho from the Village, and I found a small hotel a few blocks in. The bored-looking desk clerk gave me a room on the second floor, accessible only by stairs. It was hard not to collapse next to my bag on the bed. But if I slept now I might not wake up for hours, and I had too much to do. Al's Bar wasn't far away.

Outside again, I found MacDougal, and walked up toward
Washington Square. The Village, with its coffee houses, jazz clubs
and cafés, had an aura that reminded me of its long-standing reputation for radicalism. It felt like I was walking through my own
counter-cultural past. Somewhere nearby was the townhouse
that the Weathermen had accidentally blown up during the height
of the Vietnam War protests in 1970. They'd been making pipe
bombs in the basement.

Still on MacDougal, I passed a used record store blasting fero-
cious speed-metal onto the sidewalk. My attention was drawn to
the front window, where a poster advertising tonight's Spine
concert was taped. Hoping to get some useful information on
the band, I ventured inside. It was dark and incense-filled. Racks
of used vinyl in front. Glass cases holding smoking paraphernalia
lia labeled "for tobacco use only." In the back of the shop,
silkscreened T-shirts, leather and velvet clothing, and candles in
all shapes and scents. The guy behind the counter was reading a
book while the music raged around him. He wore a Misfits T-shirt
and a nose ring. He looked up as I approached, and turned the
music down.

"The band in your window," I said, pointing to the poster.

"Yeah?"

"Know anything about them?"

"Like what?"

"Where they're from. Who their friends are."

He frowned. Flicked off the music, then put the book down,
mystified. "I don't get it."

I decided to get right to the point. "One of their fans showed up
dead on my front lawn a few days ago. In California."

He studied me, trying to tell if I was bullshitting. "You're kidding."

"Wish I was." No reply. "I know it's a shot in the dark, but the
shirt he was wearing is the only lead I have."

"You a cop or something?"

I shook my head. "Nope."

He put his hands on his hips. "But you came all the way from California."

"It's a long story. Anyway, he had a Gravity Throttle T-shirt on. I'm told they mutated into Spine."

"Yeah, that's right."

"Why the change?"

A shrug. "I don't know. The singer ended up in rehab. Heroin or something. Guess they got sick of his bullshit. Kicked him out and changed the name."

Heroin. Another drug thing.

"Do you know them at all?" I asked.

"Yeah, a little. They've done a few in-stores here. But I don't see how that can help you."

"Anything else going on with them that sticks out?"

"They were talking about getting a manager a few weeks ago. But the guy hasn't been around in a while."

"What happened to him?"

Another shrug. "Don't know. I guess he split. You'll have to ask them."

"You didn't know him did you? The manager?"

"No. And there's not much else I can tell you." He picked his book up. "Check 'em out tonight. Maybe they'll talk to you."

"I plan to," I replied, just before he turned the music back on.

Outside, I took another look at the poster in the window, which was vibrating with the force of the music. The club was right around the corner. If I was lucky, maybe I could catch the band now, before the show.

Al's Bar, renamed The Coven one night a week, was between a body piercing parlor and a cheese shop that advertised in its window over one hundred different varieties. Al's Bar had the Spine poster in a glass-enclosed bulletin board by the front door. From inside I could hear music and the crack of billiard balls. A couple of biker types leaned against the wall outside smoking cigarettes. They paid no attention to me as I entered.

It was a large, dimly lit space that looked like it had been converted from another type of business. A bar off to the left once you got through the small foyer. At the edge of the dance floor, in the center of the room, were numerous tables and stools, with some old thrift-store sofas and coffee tables mixed in. Another bar filled the opposite wall to the right, near the pool tables I'd heard from outside. The stage took up the entire rear wall. Drums and amplifiers and guitar stands sat beneath racks of professional lighting equipment. A slowly rotating disco ball, most of its mirrored squares missing, was suspended over the sound console and mixer set up in a cleared space across the room. In the far corner, a strange sculpture stood at least ten feet high. It was filled with Dante-esque figures, all bulging eyes, yawning mouths and grasping claws. Eerily illuminated by a couple of purple spots, it sat in a position of prominence under a stained-glass skylight. Curiously, the whole affair didn't seem out of place.

Nudging my way between two customers, I went up to the near bar and flagged down the bartender. A big guy with an apron and greasy, thinning hair.

"Is the band around?" I inquired.

He glanced toward the stage and shook his head. "You just missed 'em. They just finished soundcheck. Need a drink?"

"Ahh . . . no thanks."

"By the way, you'll need a handstamp if you wanna stick around for the concert. Eight bucks."

"I'll come back," I said over my shoulder on my way out to hunt down some food, but then heard the barkeep say, "Oh, wait a sec, here's one of 'em now."

When I turned around the guy was coming from the area behind the stage. One of the musicians pictured on the Web site. He wore boots over black stretch pants, a fringed black leather jacket and a psychedelic tie-dyed T-shirt. Short hair, gelled over his forehead and dyed a bright yellow. He took a seat at the end of the bar, asked for a mineral water. The bartender put a sweating bottle of Evian in front of him and pulled off the top. I told the bartender I'd pick it up.

"No need," the musician answered. "I'm comped tonight. But thanks anyway." He took a long swallow.

I grabbed a stool next to him as the bartender moved off. "I came out from California to see you guys tonight."

He raised his eyebrows. "No shit?"

"It's not what you think," I explained. "I've actually never heard your music." That admission didn't seem to surprise him, given my age. "But I was really hoping to talk with you. I need some help."

Another swig of the Evian. "Help? How do you even know me?"

"I don't, obviously. But somebody you may have known ended up dead on my front lawn a few days ago."

He'd just taken a drink, and the news provoked a fit of choking. Water sprayed out of his mouth. Staggering off his barstool, he continued coughing, leaning over with the spasms.

"Jesus Christ!" he croaked when he was done choking. Red-faced, he sat back down, breathing deeply as he recovered. "What the fuck are you talking about?"

"Sorry. I shouldn't have just blurted it out like that."

"That'd be a good assumption. Now who are we talking about?"

"I'm not sure. That's what I came here to find out."

"I'd like to help you, but I think you got the wrong person. I don't know anybody who died recently. Especially out in California." He drained the last of the mineral water as the bartender addressed him from near the taps.

"You okay, man?"

"Yeah, I'll live," he replied, raising his voice along with the empty bottle. "But can I get another one of these?"

The bartender came over, whisked the empty container away and placed a new one on the bar. "Everything cool?" he asked, eyeing me.

"Yeah, no problem," the musician answered. "Thanks."

The bartender tossed the empty below the counter, slowly wiped his hands on his apron and gave me a long, deliberate look before leaving.

When he left, I went on. "The victim had a Gravity Throttle T-shirt on. Young white guy, early twenties maybe, with longish brown hair." No response. "Sound like anyone you know?"

"Sure. A few people. But they're all alive and well. Some of them may even show up here tonight."

I looked down to the other end of the bar and saw the bartender on the phone. He turned away when I caught his eye. "I heard you guys were talking with someone about managing the band."

A pregnant pause, his eyes on me, the bottle frozen at his lips. "Who told you that?"

"The clerk at the record store on MacDougal, right around the corner. It wasn't a secret was it?"

"Not really." He gulped the water, then slowly shook his head. "It's just kind of freaky when someone you've never seen before appears out of nowhere and tells you one of your friends may be dead. And knows things about you. See what I mean?"

"I really don't know anything. I'm just trying to find out who that kid was."

"Why's it so important to you?"

"Because the killer didn't stop with him." I hesitated, wondering if I should say it. "My wife was next."

"You're telling me your wife was murdered?"

My eyes must have answered yes.

"Geez, I'm sorry," he continued, and seemed to mean it. He

thought for a moment before admitting, "Yeah, there was some-body that approached us a few weeks ago about taking us on." More thinking. "We'd noticed him a few times at previous shows, back before Rob joined. The new singer. Young guy, like you said. Usually had a friend with him."

"He did?"

"Seemed like it."

"What did the friend look like?"

"Oh, gosh, I don't know. Generic rocker I guess. Not that differ-ent from his buddy. Little rougher around the edges, though."

"What do you mean?"

The musician paused. Scratched his cheek. "I spent a few years in a group home when I was young. This dude came off like he did too. Maybe some time in juvie too."

"How do you know?"

"Well, I don't. Not for sure. But you can kind of recognize the type." He shrugged. "Birds of a feather, I guess."

"Okay," I said. "Go on."

"Anyway. At our last gig—"

"I thought tonight was going to be your first as Spine."

"We opened for another band a few weeks ago. Unannounced. The guy you're asking about was there and he loved Rob's voice, so he came backstage after our set. We got the impression he was try-ing to break into the business. You know, get his feet wet with us. Guess he saw some potential."

"And?"

"And nothing. Just talked with him that one time. Told him we'd think about it." A shrug. "Haven't seen either of them since."

"That was it?"

He nodded, sipping from the bottle.

"What were their names?"

"I don't remember."

"Damn." Another brick wall.

"Look, I'm sorry. We shake a lot of hands, meet a lot of people after a show. I wish I did remember. But it wasn't a very serious discussion at that point because we had other things on our mind. Like breaking in Rob, coming up with some new material."

"Think your bandmates would remember?"

"Beats me."

A tiny glimmer of hope. "Could I talk to them?"

"They left to get something to eat." He glanced at his watch, then at me. "Get ahold of us after the show. Backstage." Then, before I could ask: "*After* the show. I don't want all of us freaked out about this while we're trying to play."

"Sure, no problem." I'd force myself to wait until then even though a voice inside was screaming for information now. I didn't want to risk going away with nothing by being overbearing. Hopefully, the show would go well and they'd all be in a talkative mood. I got up to leave, then realized I was forgetting something. "How's the old singer? Still strung out?"

"Man ... ," he said, shaking his head. "What else do you know about us?"

"Nothing. Other than what's on your old Web site."

"Yeah, we gotta update that. But to answer your question, he made it through rehab and moved back with his parents in Jersey. I just talked to him so he's not the one who was killed."

I asked the next question as delicately as I could. "You think he was mixed up in anything shady? While he was using?"

"Like dealing?"

I shrugged.

"Nothing that would get anybody killed. Far as I know."

"Okay." I hesitated. "So we'll talk later."

"Just come on back." He pointed to the dark corridor beside the main stage.

"Appreciate your help," I said, shaking his hand. "Brad?"

He seemed surprised that I knew his name, then smiled. "The Web site?"

"You got it. See you in a few. I'll be here for the show."

"We go on at ten."

CHAPTER TWENTY-FOUR

On the way out, I handed eight bucks to a girl sitting behind a small desk they'd set up in the foyer. She put the money in a heavy antique cash register and gave me a ticket instead of the hand-stamp. Outside, full darkness had fallen and the area was busy with pedestrians and shoppers. My watch said it was close to eight.

Dinner was pizza and a Coke a few doors down. Afterwards, with over an hour until the concert at ten, I took a walk, hoping to be able to shut down for a while. I passed several small live theaters, an organic food market, and an erotic boutique trumpeting what it called "Weightless Sex!" which, from what I could gather, involved the use of bungee cords. I hurried by. On Sullivan Street, a small, crowded coffee house had patrons spilling out onto the sidewalk. A singer with just a guitar and a microphone was performing inside. I stopped and listened to a few songs. His voice reminded me of Jackson Browne. Next door, in front of a used bookstore, a hand-lettered sign announced a poetry reading later that night.

I'd read in front of a few people once, back in college. Drunk and high, I vomited on the stage halfway through. I thought about the sit-ins and the campus gatherings and the student strikes I'd half-heartedly supported. Scenes of Vietnam War protests, some from vividly remembered TV newscasts and others I'd participated in myself, resurfaced in my mind. If I'd had the strength to put all that behind me . . . but I couldn't outrun what had happened. Then or now.

I headed up toward Washington Square, where cholera victims were once buried centuries ago, back when it was just a swamp. The furtive movements of what could only be dealers shadowed me as I entered the grounds. The park's stone chess tables in the southwest corner were unoccupied. In the distance, at the park's north entrance, the great marble Washington Arch stood richly il-luminated, grand and heraldic as the nighttime trade picked up. I took a seat on one of the benches, knowing it wasn't a smart thing to do with the company I had. But I couldn't bring myself to care, almost hoping someone would give me a problem. There were still a lot of people, mostly young, many of them probably NYU stu-dents from right next door, cutting through the park on their way to the evening's diversions. I thought I saw several transactions take place. A few minutes later, a young guy with tattoos on his arms, wearing a headband to secure his long hair, approached slowly, not speaking but catching my eye as he walked by.

I held his gaze a moment, then shook my head. "Tell your friends I'm not interested too."

He put his hands up in an "Excuse me" gesture and sauntered off.

"Wait a second," I called out after him, unsure of how it worked and even less sure of how to broach the real subject.

All afternoon I'd been going on instinct, taking opportunities as they came with little thought or planning. But this would require the exact right playbook if I expected to get anywhere. In the few seconds it took him to come back, I changed my mind about trying to buy anything other than information. A drug purchase would only have been to loosen him up, not me. I was tightly coiled, ready for action, and wanted to stay that way.

"Make up your mind, bro," he said.

"I don't want any product," I told him, pulling a ten from my pocket, "just information."

"You a cop?" he asked, looking around nervously.

"Relax." I stuffed the ten between two slats on the bench beside me. "This'll be the easiest ten bucks you ever made."

He didn't look convinced but sat down anyway, eyeing the bill. I covered it with my hand. "So whattya want?" he said. "And make it quick." There were slashes all up and down his pant legs, and a large hole left his right knee exposed.

"Heard about anybody turning up missing lately?" I wasn't sure how to phrase it. "Associates? Friends of friends? Enemies?"

"You mean business-related?"

I nodded.

He looked at me like there was a catch. "That's it? That's all you wanna know?"

"A name if the answer's yes."

"What about the dime?"

"Try me." I lifted my hand, leaving the bill exposed.

He looked down at it, then back up at me. "Nope. Haven't heard anything like that."

He reached for the money and I put my hand on top of his, holding it there. "You sure?"

"Yeah. I got no reason to lie." I took my hand away as he stood.

"How about asking a few people?" I inquired. "So I can get my money's worth." A dubious look. "Just your coworkers in the park tonight."

"I got a business to run, man. What's in it for me?"

"Twenty. If you come up with a name."

"I could just make one up. How would you know?"

Fuck it, I thought. This was going nowhere. "Give me a bogus name and I'll come back here tomorrow and kick your ass."

That pissed him off. He planted his right foot and stiffened. Nodded tensely as he surveyed the area. I concentrated on staying relaxed, at least coming off that way. Hands in my lap and one foot crossed over my knee. He reached into his pocket and withdrew a switchblade, which he didn't bother to open. Just tossed it up and down in his left hand. "Even with my friend here?"

"I got friends of my own, bud." Out-machoing him.

He stopped with the knife and pocketed it. "Yeah? Well fuck you and fuck your friends. I don't need this shit." He took off angrily, but turned back after a few paces. "Twenty?"

"That's right."

"Wait there." He circulated a bit. Joined a small group of people near the arch, which looked down impassively at the sordid activity taking place below it. I saw something change hands, then two of them left the park. The other two separated, one of them the person I'd just spoken to. They hung around at opposite ends of the northern perimeter, occasionally approaching people to do business. After twenty minutes he still hadn't returned. I figured I'd been blown off or there was no name to answer my question, neither of which surprised me. The whole encounter had been spur-of-the-moment, unlikely to yield anything useful. I gave it a few more minutes, but nothing happened, so I left.

The brick university buildings glowed a volcanic red in the city light. NYU flags hung lifelessly in the humid warmth like wilted purple flowers. A bowling alley near the school featured late-night bowling until 4a.m. Pounding techno music escaped from its open front doors. Inside was a velvety gloom. Lanes illuminated like airport runways at night, with purple, glow-in-the-dark pins delta'd at their mouths. The pins scattered in eerie, slow-motion silence under the intense volume of the music. I took in the surreal scene for a while, then noticed a lounge further inside. It was no more well-lit than the rest of the place, except for the pool tables squatting under white rectangles of light from the low-hanging "Budweiser" lamps. The bartender was watching two college-age girls playing at one of the tables. Probably trying to think of a way to strike up a conversation. I asked for a beer, and turned to watch the game. The bartender caught my eye and grinned. The girls knew we were looking at them, enjoying the power they had and the ease with which they could so thoroughly occupy our attention. Their hair dropped from behind their ears each time they attempted a shot, and they laughed softly after one of them missed badly, glancing our way without a trace of embarrassment.

I finished the beer, put a tip on the bar, and got out of there, emerging into the relative light of the nighttime city. The heavy threat of rain hung in the air, the clouds overhead bruised an ominous yellow by the city lights.

It was close to ten when I got back to the club on Bleecker. Inside was completely packed. Most of the few dozen tables were taken, and people lounged on the sofas scattered around the room. It was two deep at the bars. Waitresses squeezed between customers with drink trays balanced precariously above their heads. The only space remotely clear was the dance floor in front of the stage. I knew that would change once the show started, so I headed there to claim a spot near the hallway leading to the restrooms and backstage. I wanted to be sure to catch the band right after their set.

Again, as at the bowling alley, it was primarily a college-age crowd. Most of them clustered in groups, having animated conversations over the music on the PA, which fought to be heard over the din. The rumbling bass and thumping backbeat could actually be felt more than heard. I was standing near a speaker cabinet off to the side, and it rattled my bones from those few feet away. I could only imagine what it would be like once the band started playing.

Suddenly the lights dimmed and a cheer went up. The crowd surged forward, filling the dance floor in front of the stage. Fog poured from the smoke machines as the band members slowly drifted onstage.

The guitarist picked up his instrument and plucked a single, distorted note. It washed over the room, then seemed to shatter into brittle pieces. The bass player–the guy I'd spoken to earlier–and the drummer locked into a slow-burning groove, before bursting into a manic, hyperspeed riff. All the lights went on like camera flashcubes, momentarily illuminating the guitarist pounding out chords like his life depended on it. Pandemonium after that, the horde jolted into furious motion.

The aggression and power of the music was cathartic, reverberating in my skull and loosening some of the pent-up anger I'd held inside for the last week. But I kept clear of the moshing that was warming up like a popcorn machine in the middle of the dance floor.

Pretty soon stage-divers were scrambling up and launching themselves, arms spread wide, into the crowd. I couldn't breathe in the relentless press of people against the stage. Before I knew it, I found myself in the maelstrom–sharp elbows, brutish shoulders and stomping boots quickened by the escalating tempo. Everything went black, only to be lit up again in gleaming shards of light, strobes timed to the tribal beat and throwing silver knives throughout the room, now a seizure-inducing display of stop-start motion, a dizzying succession of frozen images flashing across my vision. I didn't know whether to go right or left, but it didn't matter because I was suddenly on the floor, under the writhing hulk of yet another stage-diver who'd picked the wrong guy to catch him because I'd never seen him coming, but who somehow managed to bounce right back up–resilient bastard–leaving nothing but the crowd closing above me like the surface of the ocean after a pebble's dropped into it. Losing air, I felt a boot-tip in my ear and another one in my ribs, then saw a hand reach down, felt two more grab my shoulders and pull me up. A flicker of light showed two men pushing their way toward me. Security, I thought, coming to help, but they were gone in the next lightning flash so I looked the other way, searching for an opening. That's when they grabbed me, gripping my arms and belt and forcing me toward the offstage exit while the music raged on. Something didn't feel right and I fought against them. The onslaught of noise buried my shouts and curses, and the violence of the audience masked my struggles. The next thing I knew, I was stumbling off the dance floor into the rear exit corridor. In the split second before they pounced on me I saw that it was empty of anybody that could help as I was shoved out the back door and into the dark alley beyond it.

CHAPTER TWENTY-FIVE

I landed on the wet pavement outside, where it took me a moment to figure out it was raining. The club's back door slammed open and a car pulled up, its front tire stopping inches from my head. The sound of car doors opening as I struggled to stand, then a glimpse of the two men from inside behind me. Both wearing black, their faces hardly visible in the dank alley light before they threw me into the back seat of the car. Then I heard what sounded like ripping fabric and felt a cold steel gun barrel jammed under my chin as duct tape was slapped over my eyes and wound around my wrists. Four doors thumped shut. The tires skidded briefly on the wet pavement, and my body was pressed back into the seat as we took off.

"Sit still," someone warned. "Unless you think I can miss with this gun right under your chin."

I decided to take the man's advice. The back seat was cramped, with three of us squeezed in. I was in the middle. No room to maneuver. I kept still, trying to concentrate on what I heard and on the turns we were making. I could only hope to learn something by what these men eventually said or did to me and pray to get out of this in one piece. I wondered who they were and how they'd found me. In my mind I saw the bartender on the phone, looking away from me when our eyes met. Had he called these guys after overhearing my conversation?

Nobody said a word during the ride, which lasted less than fifteen minutes. I could feel us stop several times and round a few corners. The two men that boxed me in were quite bulky; I could sense that from their weight against me. I also knew from when all four doors had shut in the alley that there were two more people up front. The driver opened his window a crack, only to shut it again a second later. After that it was just the light rain swishing under the tires, and the occasional movements of the men in the car.

Then the jolt of a driveway and a slow cruise until we came to a stop. The doors opened and I was pushed into a heavy mist scented with salt air and decay. They marched me out of the weather into what seemed like a large enclosure. Our footsteps echoed remotely on a concrete floor; a metal door slammed shut behind us. An abandoned warehouse, I thought, judging from the airy coolness inside, near the docks from the salty tang I'd perceived outside.

Dim light filtered around the edges of the duct tape as we walked further into the building. The iron grip of a fist bit into each of my arms. We stopped and I heard someone mount a set of metal stairs then make his way over a platform or catwalk to a point just above my head. A steel chain rattled, its loops clinking together, then ran over metal—a bar or railing—before dropping onto my shoulder. One guy raised my arms, still bound, over my head while another looped the chain tightly around my wrists, his hot breath in my face, as he clicked a padlock home. Pockets turned inside out, I was relieved of my wallet, the motel key and the map. I heard footsteps on the metal staircase, and a ring sliding on the handrail as he came down. They left without a word, their steps receding into silence.

Nothing now except the sound of my own labored breathing, beads of sweat beginning to pop out on my face and neck. Hanging from that chain, trying but unable to catch my breath. No way could I stand here all night like this.

"Okay boys, when's this party gonna start?" My voice resounded in the far corners of the building, and I could hear the nervous quaver behind the bravado.

No reply, just the intensifying rain pelting the metal roof high overhead.

"Hello? Anybody there?"

The rain continued all by itself.

"Shit!" I muttered under my breath. The seconds stretched into minutes. Straining to pick up the sound of any movement, it was my sense of smell that first caught a change. Just a whiff at first, then it sharpened. Acidic. No, citrus. I sniffed again. Oranges. Someone was peeling an orange not ten feet away from me, and just as I identified it, the voice came.

"Mr. Ryder," he said, chewing, the scent of orange getting stronger.

His nonchalance pissed me off. "It's not polite to speak with your mouth full."

"You'd prefer I finish first?"

Good point, I thought. The sooner this was over, the better. My chest was beginning to ache. "No need," I answered.

"I apologize for our lack of manners tonight. This shouldn't take too long." Another whiff of citrus. "If you're cooperative."

"I can hardly breathe."

"Somebody lower his arms," he instructed his men. "Wouldn't want you to faint on us."

One of them came up from behind and disengaged the padlock, undid a few of the loops to extend the length of the chain, then reclasped the padlock. My hands were now about face level.

"That better, Mr. Ryder?"

"You bet."

"Good. You can thank me by answering all my questions."

"Go ahead."

"First, I should tell you about one of my friends here with us tonight. Star baseball player in college. Used to hit 'em a mile."

I heard something whip by just in front of my face, felt a short burst of air.

"That's a fungo bat," the man continued. "Normally used–"

"I know what they are," I interrupted.

"Great. But I bet you've never been hit by one. One shot to the abdomen in the wrong spot, and you'll never shit right again." He paused to let it sink in, chewing on another piece of orange. "You don't want to carry a bag of shit around with you for the rest of your life, do you Mr. Ryder?"

He was talking about a colostomy bag, which is what you got when your insides were screwed up. I shook my head slowly.

"So I won't have to ask you anything twice, will I? Because I hate repeating myself."

"I'll be straight with you."

"Excellent." I could feel him approach. "Batting practice starts the first time you try bullshitting me."

"Fine. Can we get on with it?"

"No problem." He paused, stepped back. "Number one. Why are you asking around about that boy?"

I took a deep breath. "Somebody got killed in front of my house earlier this week. I'm just trying to find out who the victim was."

"Why?"

I thought it strange that he didn't ask for further information about the crime, but answered the question anyway. "Because whoever did it got my wife next."

A moment of silence. How much did they already know about this? I didn't have time to finish the thought before I heard something whip through the air, then a white-hot pain exploded in my belly. I saw red, and my gut was on fire. My legs collapsed beneath me and the chain bit into my wrists, where all my weight was now hanging. I twisted back and forth, unable to move my legs to find support. The pain was excruciating. But eventually, very slowly, it dwindled to a steady burning sensation. A smoldering fire rather than a full-on conflagration. My feet found the floor again and I steadied myself, trying not to breathe too deeply because of the pain, thinking the worst had passed.

Then I threw up. Agony, much worse than the initial blow because it went on until my stomach emptied. Wave after wave of half-digested food and throat-burning bile. It plopped wetly on the concrete while my gut screamed with exertion. I felt it splash my shoes and pants, and when I was done, a rope of mucus and saliva hung from my lip. I shivered in pain, hawked out a thick gob of spit and vomit. Chunks of food lodged in my nostrils. I gagged one last time, panting and whimpering like a gut-shot dog.

"Jesus, that's disgusting," the man said. "Go and find a mop or something."

"Me, sir?" came the less than enthusiastic reply.

"Who am I looking at? Just do it! Before it makes me sick."

I heard the unlucky one muttering under his breath as he went in search of the cleaning supplies, and got a tiny measure of satisfaction from that. I still didn't know why they'd hit me though.

Then the warning. "A few inches lower, Mr. Ryder, and we're talking permanent damage."

I swallowed a few times, trying to clear my throat. I could have used a glass of water but decided not to ask. "What's the problem?" I got out hoarsely. "I told you what happened."

"I don't buy it."

"It's the truth, I swear it."

"You're lying. You'd be looking for the killer, not the victim."

"It was all I had. I was hoping the victim would lead me to the killer." He wanted more, so I told him about the possible drug connection.

"Where did that come from?" he asked skeptically.

"There's been a lot of drug activity out my way recently," I explained, warming to the story. Let him lap it up, I thought, even if I wasn't sure about it myself. "Meth labs in the desert blowing up, escalating drug arrests. There's talk of a shakeout going down in the trade. Maybe the victim was involved somehow."

We were interrupted by the sound of a bucket being rolled across the floor toward us. It stopped right next to me. The water sloshed around inside, then the wet slap of the mop on the floor at my feet. It took him several swipes to get it all up, huffing and puffing angrily, with the sounds of rinsing and the mechanical wringer in between. My guess was that if he'd had to squeeze the dirty mop out by hand, there would have been a mutiny. Just before finishing, he tripped me up with the mop handle, then slammed it back into the bucket with a loud splash. Still fuming, the man rolled the bucket away.

"That's better," the leader remarked with the putrid smell gone, then continued. "Your story doesn't make sense, Ryder. How did you know to come to New York?"

"The dead guy was wearing a concert T-shirt when he was killed." A painful cough. "I found the band on the Web and came out here to talk to them. See if they knew the victim."

Somebody humphed in disbelief. "You flew clear across country on a hunch?"

"I was desperate. My wife was killed." A spasm of pain down below, but less severe this time. "Flying out here was nothing. I'm gonna find that killer."

"I like a man with self-confidence. Really, I do. But that bat still has a few swings left in it, if you know what I mean. So tell me the rest of it."

"There's nothing else. We didn't know shit. Me or my wife."

"Gimme the fuckin' bat. I'm gonna whack him myself."

"I'm telling you, that's it!" I yelled, and it came out high and weak, tinged with panic. Gasping in desperation, I threw him a bone. "We had a theory, but it was probably horseshit."

"I'm listening."

"There was a guy I ratted out. Years ago."

"Name?"

"Turret. Glenn Turret."

"Turret," he repeated slowly. A few seconds of thoughtful silence. "Why does that name sound familiar?"

"Antiwar activist in the early seventies. Except he had his own agenda. I got mixed up with him."

"That's right, the bank job. I remember it, it happened before the SLA robbery with Patty Hearst," he recounted. "Trial was all over the news. I remember thinking what a loser you were." Someone laughed. "All you hippies thought you were gonna save the world."

I didn't reply.

"What does he have to do with this?"

"He just got out of prison."

"So?"

"So we thought maybe it was more than just coincidence." A pause. I wished I could see his reaction to my answers.

"What, he held a grudge all these years? And now he's getting back at you?"

"I told you it was bullshit."

But he seemed interested. "Where was he released from?"

"I don't know. I didn't ask. Turns out he was still inside at the time of the first murder."

"Well then why the fuck are you wasting my time with it?"

"You wanted everything."

"Who told you all this? The police?"

"Yeah."

He chuckled at first, then broke into a hearty laugh, the others joining in. Really amused, like they couldn't believe anyone could be so stupid. Finally, they were done. "Nope," he said, still not fully recovered. "Never known cops to lie before."

Why hadn't that occurred to me? The police definitely wanted to keep me out of the case, and saying Turret wasn't out in time should have done it. "What's all this to you, anyway?" I asked.

"Where's Turret now?" Like I hadn't even spoken.

"I knew that, you think I would have come all the way out here on a fishing expedition?"

This time I didn't hear the whiplash movement of air before the blow came. A stinging, red-hot slash just below the ribs that knocked the wind out of me, paralyzing my diaphragm and making it impossible to draw even one molecule of oxygen. My knees buckling again, I jerked downwards, still held by the chain around my wrists. The pain radiated outward like an exploding star. My vision went snowy black. No sound except the muffled rush of blood in my ears, as if I were deep underwater, sinking, with the pressure increasing toward blackout.

Which, for all I knew, could have happened for a few seconds, before my chest abruptly moved, suddenly awakened. I gulped in air like a drowning man. Deep, ragged breaths that brought me back into the room, the ambient light once again visible around the edges of the blindfold, the sound of my own wheezing lungs and what I gradually discerned as raindrops plunking on the metal roof. And the pain eating my stomach away like a cancer.

"That was for being a smartass." His voice, low and threatening in my ear. "And to make sure you're not leaving anything out. And if you puke again, I'm gonna make you lick it up."

With nothing left in my stomach, throwing up wasn't a problem. Getting enough air to breathe, let alone speak, was. "There's nothing else," I croaked. "Swear to God."

"Because if I have to do that again, you'll end up in the hospital. Do we understand each other?"

All I could do was nod.

"Take him down."

They clicked open the padlock and unlooped the chain. I dropped heavily to my knees. Slowly lowered myself to the floor, where I curled up in a fetal position trying to ease the pain.

They didn't remove the duct tape from my eyes or wrists. "I suggest you pull yourself together and get on a plane back to Palm

Springs, Mr. Ryder. Then make like one of those lizards out there and crawl under a rock." He dropped what sounded like my wallet on the floor next to me. Nobody said a word as they walked away. The lights went off and I felt a puff of air from the open door, then stillness. I was alone.

CHAPTER TWENTY-SIX

It took a while to work my hands loose, then I ripped off the blind-fold and found myself in an empty warehouse, as I'd suspected. Its echoey darkness suggested far-off corners and unseen spaces. A dark cavern of drifting gray light. Above me, a solitary, smudged window grudgingly admitted only a fraction of the night. I fixed on that window and stayed curled up on the cold concrete floor for I don't know how long, waiting for the burning in my stomach to subside, listening to the sky open up outside. I squirmed like a slug on a sidewalk, trying to find a position that minimized the agony down below.

Practically delirious from fatigue and pain, my thoughts wandered. I caught the scent of oranges still in the air and pictured the early Palm Springs pioneers sitting on their porches after church on Sunday. They'd sip fresh squeezed lemonade in front of acres of sun-drenched citrus groves. The image was so unexpected, so far removed in time and distance and circumstance, that I could only laugh to myself.

Except laughing hurt like hell. Rain drummed in thundering waves on the sheet metal roofing high overhead. Rats scurried and squeaked somewhere nearby. I forced myself to move, gingerly testing my injuries, unfolding my body one part at a time until I was standing upright. I looked down and saw my wallet lying on the floor. It seemed very far away, staring up at me as if to ask how badly I wanted it. At that point, I wasn't sure if it was worth the effort. But I held my breath and bent over, found that the pain wasn't as bad as I'd expected. A quick check of the wallet's contents told me nothing was missing. I put it back in my pocket, my abdominal muscles twitching sorely, but not unbearably with the effort. Maybe the sit-ups I'd been doing since prison had protected me from serious injury.

The chain I'd been secured with hung limp and lifeless in front of my face, suspended from a catwalk that led to an office, where I'd seen the one window. An idea flashed through my head but I quickly dismissed it. My captors wouldn't have left the place open to my inspection if anything in here could tie the warehouse to them. I could make out a razor-thin outline of light around the door they'd used and made my way closer to it. The knob was cold and hard and turned without a sound. The door opened outward into drifting rain. Steady and cool, now diminished to a sibilant hush. In the distance, city lights shimmered between the raindrops and twinkled like stars, as the river, black and shiny as oil, gave motion to the light reflected from its surface. Jersey over the Hudson, I guessed. The stark skeletons of dockside cranes rose into the sky, black spider legs against the smoke-gray clouds.

The salty air followed me away from the docks. Rain streamed down my face and plastered my hair to my skull. In a few minutes I was drenched. Shoes squeaking wetly with every step. Shirt glued to my body like a second skin. But the cleansing downpour felt good, washing away the rankness I'd deposited on myself earlier. I stopped and turned my face upward, eyes closed, until my mouth filled with water and my tongue no longer felt like a thick piece of leather against my palate. I went by more warehouses sheathed in rusting sheet metal. Around listing stacks of wooden pallets and hulking metal cargo containers big as mobile homes. My shadow was invisible on the wet pavement, which reflected only the meager, waterlogged glow of the occasional security lamp. The whole place seemed disused and forgotten, perhaps awaiting a wrecking ball to transform it into another pricey piece of waterfront real estate. I wondered if there was a security guard somewhere nearby, huddled in a tiny guard shack with a portable heater and a miniature TV. Or making the rounds in a slowly creeping automobile with windows shut tight against the weather. If there was, I didn't see one. Nothing moved except the rain. And the puddles as I stepped through them, breaking into random shards of reflected light.

I kept the river to my back, looking for a way out. Eventually I came upon the guard shack I'd envisioned earlier, between two red and white striped wooden gates. Both were snapped off and lying in splinters on the ground. The shack's windows were broken out, the door hanging halfway open on its one remaining hinge. If I blew on it, it would probably fall over. I peeked inside, knowing full well there wouldn't be a working phone, and kicked myself for not thinking to look for one in the warehouse office. It likely wouldn't have mattered though; here, on the wall beside the doorway was an empty phone bracket, with a hole spilling tangled wires. On the opposite wall, an empty clipboard hung on a nail. Broken glass littered the floor and desk. A wooden stool had toppled over, its round cushion ripped open and exposing rotted foam. A half-formed face appeared in the decomposed material as I turned away.

Leaving the yard behind, I continued into the city and found myself on 49th Street, in what looked like a working-class residential neighborhood. Everything had been washed clean by the downpour and the cars parked along the curb glistened under the streetlights. Above them I could see the midtown skyscrapers puncturing the cloud cover. Tendrils of drifting mist reached between them like fingers. The rain was lightening, falling in random flurries, and I could feel the heaviness in the air subside.

My watch said it was close to 2 a.m. Hardly any traffic. I walked by a parked car with the dome light on and two people inside, talking. The window was cracked and I could smell cigarette smoke. The driver closed up quickly when he saw me. Couldn't say I blamed him. My stomach muscles felt each step. I wasn't sure how much further I could go without sleep. I stumbled over my own feet. Small animals darted across my peripheral vision, disappearing when I tried to focus on them. I hadn't seen a cab yet, and wondered if I'd have the strength to flag one down.

A slow-moving vehicle crept up behind me in the street, engine idling, the thump of rap music getting louder as it approached. I kept my eyes forward and my pace steady. When the car pulled even with me I looked over: a late-seventies Cadillac with rust-spots and no hubcaps. Four young men inside, all of them checking me out behind closed windows beaded with raindrops. The driver had his arm stretched idly over the steering wheel. The guy behind him in the back seat bobbed his head to the beat. They continued on, scoping me out as they passed. We momentarily lost sight of each other behind a large two-axle panel truck parked at the curb, squeezed between all the other vehicles that lined the roadway. Beyond it, the car rolled further up the one-way street. I looked back and saw nothing but empty sidewalk. I was on my own, not able to remember how far back I'd seen those people. Up ahead, about ten car-lengths away, brake lights went on in the middle of the block, a bad sign.

I stopped next to a pile of cardboard and newspaper leaning against a stoop. They edged into a space at the curb, obscured by a van parked behind them. The music momentarily got louder as the doors opened, then shut off. Then they were facing me, dark figures against the glare on the wet sidewalk. They started toward me and I froze, my mind turning over on itself like an animal stuck in the mud.

The newspaper moved beside me, and I looked down and saw an older man digging his way out of it.

"Boy, am I glad it stopped."

"Walt?" I said disbelievingly.

He got up, shedding cardboard. Brushed off his filthy wet clothes.

"Can't stand the rain."

"What are you doing here?"

"Trying to stay dry, of course. Called the cops earlier so I could take my clothes off in front of them, but they never came."

"Why would you—"

"Night in jail's better than this," he said, indicating the weather.

"I haven't seen you since you got out."

I'd forgotten about the young men approaching until he looked over at them. "Why don't you boys move on up the road?"

The one in front stopped and the others followed suit, as if they were unsure how to react. "Sure thing, old man," one finally said. They reluctantly turned around, sauntered back to their car.

"Punks," Walter muttered, bending to pick up a heavy laundry bag. "Now what's that you were saying?"

For the life of me I couldn't remember. "I . . . I'm glad you were here." I smelled alcohol, though not very strongly.

"Man, you look worse than I do, and that's the truth. You get beat up or something?"

"I'm just trying to get back to my hotel."

"Well, you sure as shit won't find a cab around here this time of night." He reached into an inside pocket of his tattered overcoat and pulled out a cell phone. "Why don't I just call you one."

"Where did you get that?"

He dialed three numbers, flexed his fingers for me as he brought the phone up to his ear. "I got quick hands." He listened for a moment, then folded it closed. "This guy shut his service off already." He put it back in his pocket and pulled out another one. "Try this one." This time he got through. Asked for the cab company, and gave them our location. "Be just a few minutes," he told me when he was done. He saw me looking at the phone and handed it to me. "One of those new ones. They're all digital now. Less static but you get cut off more. Probably 'cause of the on-off nature of the technology. I liked the analogs better, except you couldn't do the Web on 'em."

"Shit, I can't believe it. How long have you been out here?"

"Out where?"

"Here. New York." I handed him the phone back.

He gave me a quizzical look as he pocketed it. "How bad did they hurt you, anyway?" His voice seemed scratchier, deeper than I remembered.

Then I realized just how out of it I was. This wasn't Walt. Just another street person who happened to resemble my old friend from prison.

"Sorry. Never mind."

A car drove by, swishing through the puddles in the street. I looked around, wondering how long the cab would take. Got a little dizzy.

"Maybe I shoulda called you an ambulance instead."

I sat down hard on the steps, my abdomen protesting sharply as I did so. "No. No, I'll be okay. Soon as I get some sleep."

"You shouldn't be walking around down here in the middle of the night. No telling what could happen."

"I didn't plan it this way."

"Either way." The man reached into his bag and took out a bottle, placed it carefully on the step below me. Then he rummaged around in his belongings, looking for something and muttering to himself.

A cab pulled up in front of us. The driver rolled down his window and asked if one of us had called. I got up slowly, carefully made my way to the street.

"Take care, man," I said. "And thanks for getting rid of those guys."

"My pleasure. How 'bout a tip?"

"Sure," I said, as the cabbie tapped his horn behind me. I took out my wallet, removed everything but a couple of fives, and handed the cash to him.

He reached out and took it, and seeing the amount, kept his hand extended. "You sure?"

"Keep it," I said. I got in the cab and told the driver the name of the hotel, put my head back and closed my eyes.

CHAPTER TWENTY-SEVEN

"Hey. You." Someone was prodding my arm. It was the cabdriver leaning back over the front seat. His breath smelled of cigarette smoke. "Come on, buddy. Meter's running."

I looked out and saw the hotel. Its vacancy sign dripped down through the raindrops on the window. "How much do I owe you?" I asked.

"Five-fifty."

I took out two fives and handed them to him. Dropped my wallet in a puddle when I opened the door and had to wait until the cab left before I could pick it up. My head was throbbing, swimming through a thick current. It had stopped raining but the streets were still shiny, throwing up soft sprays of water with each passing car. I made it to the hotel door, and remembered those men had taken my room key. The lobby was empty and quiet at this hour. A security guard stood near the stairs and the clerk behind the counter was doing a crossword puzzle. When I excused myself, the desk clerk looked up, making no effort to hide a frown over my bedraggled appearance.

"We're full-up, sir," he told me, despite the vacancy sign.

"I'm a registered guest," I said, as he glanced at the approaching guard, who was smaller than I was but had a gun on his belt.

"We okay here?"

I put my wallet on the counter, opened it to my ID. "I lost my key. Room uh . . . it was on the second floor. 2C I think."

The clerk, in his forties with a paunch under his uniform vest, looked skeptical. He picked up the wallet with his fingertips, squinted at my name, then put it down and wiped his hands on his pants before typing the information into his computer. The guard went back to his post.

"Credit card, please," the clerk said without looking at me. I pulled it out and handed it to him, not letting go until his eyes met mine. He got my point and managed a half-hearted "Thank you." After checking it against his display, he gave me the key.

"Did you see a few men walk through in the last couple of hours? Kinda big, wearing black, maybe?"

He put down the pencil he'd just picked up. "No. Should I have?"

"You sure?"

"Yeah. I think I am." He was annoyed. "It's a small lobby."

I thanked him and turned toward the stairs. When I got there, the rent-a-cop asked if I was expecting somebody.

"Not unless you've seen the guys I just asked him about," I said, gesturing to the desk clerk.

"Is there something wrong?"

"No. Did you see them?"

"I don't know what to think, you come in here looking like that."

I told the guard to forget it and brushed past him up the steps. When I rounded the first landing, he was staring up at me. With my aching abdominal muscles, I took the rest of the stairs slowly, shaking my head over the uncanny parallels this thing kept following; not one week ago in Indio, a motel manager had handed out a spare room key under similar circumstances.

I stood quietly in the hallway on the second floor, peered down the dimly lit corridor to my room three doors down. Everything seemed normal—no doors hanging open or busted inward, the window at the far end closed and all the wall sconces illuminated. I checked the carpet and couldn't see any wet footprints leading to my room. Looked back down the stairs, where my own watery shoe-prints, but no others, had followed me. I went cautiously down the hall to 2C, and after a final look around, slid the key into the old lock. It turned without resistance, like it was unlocked. I pushed open the door and stepped back out of sight around the threshold, holding my breath for the gunshots I half expected to ring out.

Nothing happened. A quick peek around the doorway gave me a flash of the bed, which I hadn't used. It was undone and disheveled. I thought I'd left the bedside lamp on, but it was now dark. Other than that the room looked safe and empty. Stepping inside, I noticed the nightstands and their open drawers, then my overnight bag on the chair by the window, unzipped but intact. It was clear they had searched the place without being messy or destructive about it.

I closed the door and switched on the light. In the warm glow from the lamp the room looked homey and lived-in, not at all violated, more like someone had just gotten a good night's sleep snuggled under the covers. Thinking that, it hit me again how wiped out I was, though I wondered if I could sleep with so much on my mind. I checked my bag and saw there was nothing missing or damaged. The room key they'd left on the chair next to it. Considerate. After peeling off my soaked clothing, I fell on the bed and closed my eyes. Thought about how it had gone in that dank warehouse, whether it dictated what my next move should be.

I now had two people to consider as the victim on my lawn: the band manager wannabe and his friend. Of course they could both still be alive and well. But that seemed unlikely, given what had just happened to me. Those men were interested in all this for a reason, and had taken a considerable risk to find out what I knew. Which brought up another point. How had they known where to find me? My earlier suspicion that the bartender had alerted them now seemed off the mark. I wondered if somebody watched me get on the plane in Palm Springs, and one or more of them picked me up at JFK. Wouldn't have been hard to follow me in all the crowds. Maybe that's what I'd felt on the walk over here after the subway. Not just a huge rendering of a clothing model, but someone actually tailing me.

Should I stick around and try to find out who the two friends were? If I could track down the band again, there was a chance one of them would remember a name. But the men who assaulted me probably already had a name, and they seemed as clueless as I was. So I couldn't see wasting the time. And contacting the police here about what happened was completely out of the question if I didn't want to spend hours explaining everything and possibly end up in the can again.

There was something more important anyway. I needed to get back to California to bury my wife.

CHAPTER TWENTY-EIGHT

I woke the next morning with sunlight streaming through the window, and was afraid I'd slept most of the day away. It was still early, though, plenty of time to catch a morning flight home. I showered and dressed as quickly as I could given my injuries. Deposited the clothes I had worn last night, moist and smelly, in the trash.

At the airport, I was able to get a departure before noon, and settled down in the waiting area with a cup of coffee and a Danish. The morning newspaper was on the chair next to me. I riffled through it, skimming over an article about the drug task force being assigned to Washington Square Park. Beyond the coincidence of last night, nothing stood out for me. Negotiations to avert a trash strike were ongoing, and there was an article on the closeness of the fight for a state senate nomination. Soon, my fatigue overtook me and I dozed lightly until the PA announced my flight. I dropped off again once I buckled in.

The time difference between coasts gave me a few hours. It was not yet afternoon when we landed. In the terminal I took a pay phone and called Tidwell's number at the police station. Someone else picked up.

"Detective Rickman," came a gruff voice.

"Detective Tidwell, please."

"He's out. Can I help you?"

"Is Branson there?" I asked, hoping for a progress report on the case.

"You mean *Detective* Branson?"

"Ahh, yeah."

"No, he's not. Who am I speaking to?"

"Where are they?" I blurted out anxiously.

"Sir. They're out. But I'm sure I can take care of whatever it is you need."

I told him who I was and asked about Deirdre.

"Oh. Yeah, I think they're done with her." He gave me a name and number in the coroner's office to call to arrange picking up her body. I fumed at his callous attitude.

"Thanks for your sensitivity," I said when he was done. "*Detective.*"

I hung up before he could reply. Closed my eyes and squeezed the bridge of my nose, wondering how to get through this. Then I picked up the phone again and dialed the funeral home from their ad in the Yellow Pages. They gave me an afternoon appointment and told me to bring the clothing and jewelry I wanted Deirdre to be buried in. They'd arrange to pick up the body from the medical examiner's office.

I drove home on autopilot, dreading the prospect of going through Deirdre's things so soon.

I forced myself to do it though. Picked out her favorite green dress, and added her jade bracelet, a gold necklace and the emerald earrings I'd given her on our last anniversary. I turned the earrings over in my hand, watching them capture the light and hold it inside as if they were alive.

The freeway into Beaumont was clear, and I was there in twenty minutes. Desert Cemetery was a place Deirdre and I had seen many times before, driving by on the freeway. We liked the simplicity and openheartedness of their slogan, "Serving All Faiths," and the way the green grass rolled away from the highway.

They showed me around and I picked out a gravesite, a marker and a coffin, then finalized everything in the office. The service would be on Saturday.

By the time I got back on the freeway for home, I was completely numb. All the little details seemed to trivialize Deirdre's death. I drove like a zombie until the dinosaurs at Cabazon caught my eye. The exit took me to the Wheel Inn, a truckstop-style café that had been here long before the Indian casino and the collection of gas stations and chain restaurants had sprouted up around it.

I ate slowly. The cars on the highway sped by and the giant concrete dinosaurs in the parking lot stared down at me through the window. Years ago, Deirdre and I had visited this place. Climbed up into one of those huge animals and looked through its porthole eye at the cars driving by. I wondered how many of them passed here every day without ever stopping. I watched the windfarm windmills in the area slowly rotate. They sprang from the hills like mushrooms, their shiny propeller blades catching the light as they spun.

At home, I called Allie from the spare bedroom.

"Where have you been?" she said anxiously when she came on.

"I couldn't stay here. Why?"

"So you haven't heard?"

"Heard what? I just got back."

"They know who the dead youth was."

I sat down, my mind stuck in neutral. "Tell me."

"His name was John Clayton." Where did I just hear that name? "His father's running for state senate in New York."

The newspaper at the airport. "When did this happen?"

"It was just on TV. They broke in with it."

I picked up the remote and flipped through the channels, not seeing anything. "Go on."

"The father reported him missing, I guess. Had no idea he was out here."

"Is there a suspect?"

"If there is, the police aren't saying."

"My God," I said, trying to think. I wondered why that cop I'd spoken to earlier hadn't said anything. Suddenly, everything was moving too fast.

"The name doesn't help at all, does it?" Allie said suddenly. "They're not going to find who did it."

"Don't say that, Allie."

"It's just that–" Her voice hitched in her throat. "Goddamnit, I hate this. I haven't been to work since Deirdre. If this can happen to her...I almost scored the other day, Tim. I mean, what's the point?"

"What stopped you?"

"My ATM card." I heard a wet laugh, then a sniffle. "The fuckin' picture on it. Deirdre always liked it. I was all set to get the cash."

"A big part of her is still with you," I told her, hating how hollow it sounded.

"I know." She got herself together. "So why did you call?"

I told her about the funeral, asked if she could let everyone else at the clinic know. "There's a couple of her clients I was going to call myself. You find Terry's number?"

"Yeah. She wants to give the eulogy. I said okay."

"God, I hadn't even thought about that."

"Get some rest, Tim. You sound on your last legs."

"What was the picture, Allie? On your card."

A pause. "One of those nature shots. A dolphin leaping out of the water."

We said goodbye shortly after that. As soon as I hung up, the phone rang again.

"You never told us where you were the other day," Tidwell said when I answered.

"Must've slipped my mind. I'm here now."

"I guess you've heard?"

"You mean about the boy?"

"Uh-huh."

"Just now."

"Name doesn't ring a bell, does it?"

"Only–" I started, then stopped myself, not sure how much they'd said about him on TV. "No, it doesn't."

"What were you going to say?"

"Only what I got from the TV report."

"I assume Deirdre never mentioned the father before? Being from New York?"

"It's a big city, detective."

"Yeah, okay. But you'll let us know if you think of anything, right?"

"I want to find her killer as much as you do." Still nothing on the TV, except for talk shows, court TV programs and a soap opera.

"You called here earlier, right?" Tidwell asked.

"That's right. The guy I talked to didn't mention all this."

"He wouldn't have volunteered it without consulting me or Detective Branson."

I wanted to ask more about the victim and his father, but I didn't. I was sick of spinning my wheels with questions they wouldn't answer. My trip to New York was on the tip of my tongue, but I kept my mouth shut on that too. I needed time to think.

Tidwell interrupted my thoughts. "That's it for now. We have your wife's client files to see if anything jumps out at us. We'll let you know if we need you."

I called Patrick Reed next, and left the information about the funeral on his girlfriend's voice mail, glad I didn't have to speak with anybody in person. There was too much on my mind. I wasn't so lucky with Michael D'Angelo, the man I'd gone out to see in Banning. He wanted to talk, but I brushed him off, saying we'd talk tomorrow evening.

The last of the phone calls done, I unplugged the phone and collapsed on the living room couch. What I'd learned today shed no light on who could have killed Deirdre, or who those men in New York were. The news had just started, and I waited for the story. It didn't take long. Clayton was answering questions in front of reporters, looking pretty shell-shocked. His son had taken a spring break road trip, and hadn't checked in or answered his cell phone. Clayton thought he'd been with a friend, but couldn't say who it was or where exactly they'd been going. He had no idea why his son could have been killed. I scanned the people around him, a few men in suits, but didn't see anyone resembling the pair who'd taken me from that club. The whole thing was baffling, raising more questions than it answered. None of the other stations had anything substantially different to report.

I turned off the TV, drained, and lay back on the cushions. Unable to shut down, I eventually stopped trying. The night in New York kept coming back. I had to make a decision about what, if anything, to tell the police. The men who beat me up were obviously on the wrong side of the law. But that meant less to me than the fact that they were obviously after the same thing I was. And I had to figure that if they were involved in either crime, I wouldn't have made it back here alive. I didn't give a damn what they were into if it couldn't tell me the identity of the killer. Even if I found out how they were linked to the first victim, that didn't guarantee an answer to the most important question. No, whichever way I looked at it, there was only one conclusion: to leave them alone right now. And by extension, not tell the cops anything yet either; I couldn't do much from jail.

Painful as it was, my interrogation by those men in that dockside warehouse had actually helped. Their apparent dismissal of a possible drug connection, along with their obvious interest in Turret, had pointed me straight back here. If they were interested in Turret, then so was I. And I wanted to find him before they did.

CHAPTER TWENTY-NINE

I slept on and off until late the following day, then had to hurry to get ready in time for the funeral. The drive to the cemetery was one of the longest of my life. I was wearing the suit I'd got married in, maybe for the last time. The late afternoon sun was directly ahead, blinding my eyes the whole way. Halfway there, the wind kicked up, bowing the trees at the roadside rest stop, where a line of eighteen-wheelers had pulled over to avoid being capsized. My car struggled through it for each mile like a swimmer going against a riptide.

Just past Cabazon the wind began to subside, and by the time I reached Beaumont the air was calm. From the freeway, I could see the cemetery lot starting to fill up.

In the back of the chapel, I greeted Deirdre's friend Terry, one of the late arrivals. She looked like she'd been crying. Her husband's name went right past me.

"Terry was always talking about Deirdre. Feel like I knew her pretty good. Don't know why we never met," he said. Terry looked away, embarrassed, and her husband stared at his shoes awkwardly. Funerals were a killer.

"I guess we all get busy sometimes," I said, trying to think of the last time I'd seen Terry. It had been a good while.

"I wish I'd kept in touch better," she said softly, a tear rolling down her cheek. She wiped it away roughly.

"Stop it, Terry. You were her best friend."

"I meant to call last week," she said, her eyes searching mine. "After . . . after the first one."

"That's okay," I said with a smile I didn't feel. "You probably wouldn't have gotten through all the reporters anyway."

She squeezed my hand gratefully and followed her husband to a pew. Patrick came in with his girlfriend, who looked radiant in her pregnancy despite the solemn occasion. He pulled me aside after introducing us and finding a seat for her.

"I wasn't sure if I should bring this up here," he began hesitantly.

"What?"

"About what you asked me the other day?"

I nodded, waving my hand impatiently.

"It's nothing really. I talked to a few of my buddies–people I used to hang out with–"

"You mean drug buddies," I said, shaking my head. "Deirdre would have killed me."

"It's okay, man. I'm cool. They just told me they haven't heard jack. Nothing about any drug violence going down lately. As far as this thing goes."

That jibed with the feeling I'd gotten in New York. "All right. I appreciate it. But don't worry about what I need anymore, okay? You have your own things to deal with."

"I just . . . I had to do something. I owe it to Deirdre."

Not like I do.

The service started a few minutes later, a quiet and simple one. Terry gave the eulogy. She talked about her stay at Triumph Outreach, the work camp near Yucca Valley, drying out with Deirdre. The hotter it got up there, the more determined Deirdre became not to let anything beat her, ever again. I was proud to see so many of Deirdre's clients in the congregation nodding at the memory. Afterwards I sat in the empty chapel long after the others filed out, hardly aware of their kind words as they left. Eventually the funeral director put a hand on my shoulder and led me out into the oncoming dusk.

I trudged through the well-tended lawn to the large oak tree overhanging the gravesite. The hole was a perfectly proportioned rectangle, the mound next to it covered by a grass-green tarp. I took my place in front, acknowledging a few people I recognized. A white hearse with blacked-out windows slowly pulled away from the back of the chapel. Nobody spoke as it approached, engine idling softly, gravel popping under the tires. Leaves rustled in the tree above our heads. A solitary acorn dropped to the ground a few feet away with a soft *thunk*. I looked away as the attendants wrestled with the coffin.

The sun was setting behind a low rim of distant purple hills. Sprinklers *snipped* softly in a far corner of the property, throwing lazy arcs of water into the air, the breeze bearing random sprays of mist. Phantom rainbows shimmered in the dying sunlight.

I thought back a few years, to my father's funeral. Standing next to his coffin in an ill-fitting suit, wondering whether Mom would show up. They'd put makeup on Dad's face and groomed his hair perfectly. Hands folded peacefully on his chest. A rosary intertwined in the fingers, which were neatly manicured. He still wore the gold wedding band, hopeful to the end, and I'd fixated on that through most of the service. Then the tap on my shoulder telling me it was time to leave. I remembered being glad that my father's eyes were closed, so I wouldn't have to see the disappointment in them one last time.

The minister's voice brought me back to the present. I tried to listen, but his words all ran together. Behind him, the sun melted like butter on the horizon.

Afterwards, I mingled with Deirdre's coworkers, talking with several of her clients I'd never met before. D'Angelo hadn't made it, and I hoped he was all right. Allie found me and gave me a hug. "I'm so sorry, Tim." She tucked an errant lock of hair behind her ear. "And about yesterday. I didn't mean to burden you with my problems."

I told her I didn't mind.

"We're going to have a thing at the clinic. We got some food and stuff."

I was about to reply when I saw Branson and Tidwell a few yards away. They stood in the shadows of the tree, both dressed in dark suits and wearing sunglasses.

"Maybe I'll see you there," I said, kissing her on the cheek. I approached the two detectives, noticing that the sprinklers in the background had shut off. The last of the sun was a pool of molten gold sinking into the earth.

"What are you guys doing here?" I asked.

Tidwell took off his sunglasses. "We wanted to pay our respects, tell you how sorry we are." He gave Branson an uncomfortable glance, then continued uncertainly. "We know how much good she did for a lot of people," he said, gesturing to the departing guests.

"I appreciate that," I offered, knowing there was something else.

"We also thought we'd see if there was anybody unfamiliar or suspicious hanging around," Branson said. "Killers do that sometimes."

"I thought the official line was that she OD'd."

"It is," Tidwell answered. "We're here on our time." He glanced at the open grave and looked down quickly.

"Any progress on the first murder?"

Tidwell shook his head. "We're coming up zeros on that. Even with the name. Clayton hasn't been able to give us much so far."

I briefly considered coming clean about New York again, but didn't want to risk it. Instead, I asked about something that had been brought up there, tried to put it as mildly as possible. "So where did they release Turret from?"

Tidwell put his sunglasses back on and Branson didn't move. They'd been hiding something. Something important. I tensed, hoping for an answer.

"Why?" Branson asked warily. "You remember what we told you."

Who's kidding who? I wanted to say. "Have you been able to track him down?"

"Not yet."

"I was just curious if he'd ever been transferred out of Lompoc."

They gave each other a quick glance; Branson shrugged. "He ended up at Calipatria. That's where he was released from," he finally admitted.

Right down the road. "You didn't think we needed to know that?" I asked very quietly.

"We didn't want you muckin' around down there," Branson responded.

Is that why you lied to me in the car the other day?

"He was supposed to be getting on a bus for El Paso. Knows some ex-cons who run a church down there," Tidwell explained. "There was no reason for us to believe he didn't do that. Besides, he wasn't released on parole, he did all his time. We have no hold on him."

"So what?"

"So the man deserves his right to privacy, wherever he is," Branson replied. "Unless there was more than just coincidence to link him to a murder. And all that became irrelevant anyway."

"We told you the truth about the mixup on his release," Tidwell insisted.

"Tell me straight. Was he out in time for Deirdre?"

Branson didn't blink. "Barely."

Maybe it didn't matter if they were lying. Maybe, from the start, I'd needed to find Turret for other reasons.

"What the hell was he doing at Calipatria anyway? Why there?"

"He developed some sort of respiratory problem," Tidwell explained. "Almost died from it from what we were told. He needed the desert air to breathe."

"Look, we know you're upset, but we didn't come here to talk about Turret," Branson interjected.

"Fine," I said. "I appreciate you still working on it. But I knew most of the people here, and the ones I didn't were obviously acquainted with Deirdre and the others. No quiet strangers hanging around."

"Okay," Tidwell said. "It was a long shot anyway. We'll continue to do what we can, I promise." He narrowed his eyes. "But I have to warn you again, Mr. Ryder, to stay out of it. No matter how much you think Turret's involved."

"No problem," I lied. "But I want to know the first thing if anything breaks. Deal?"

They both regarded me steadily, and I knew they were about to do some lying of their own. "You have our word," Branson assured me.

We shook hands and walked separately back to the parking lot, the two detectives a few paces ahead. I caught up with Terry and her husband, who were also leaving. Thanked them for coming and turned to Terry, who now ran the Triumph Outreach work camp.

"I was hoping you could help me with something."

"Anything," Terry said.

"I was just told that a possible suspect in all this was headed down to El Paso. To a church started by some ex-cons. You think you could make some inquiries? See if he ever made it there? His name is Glenn Turret."

"Those two cops tell you this?"

"Yeah."

Terry thought a second. "I can make a few calls. You know the name of the church?"

"No. Just that it's in El Paso."

"Okay. I'll see what I can do. They say anything else that could help?"

"This guy was released from Calipatria between the two murders,"

I explained. "Supposedly. He and I have some history. Long story short, I'm looking for him now."

Terry nodded slowly, eyes on mine, squinting into the sunset. She knew not to press further, that I'd tell her the rest when I was ready. After I'd squared things for Deirdre.

"You know about that squatter's camp down there don't you?" she asked me instead.

Seemed familiar, but I couldn't place it. "Not sure that I do."

"Forget what they call it. But it's not too far from the prison. Should be easy to find once you get down there. One of my counselors at Triumph spent some time there after his release. Till he got his shit together."

So if Turret was low on cash . . . I thought. Maybe I'd get lucky.

"Great. That gives me a place to start." I gave her a hug, shook her husband's hand. Thanked Terry for everything and said I'd be in touch. We went to our cars and said goodbye. By this time everyone else had left.

As I drove out of the lot, I noticed a small tractor emerge from a distant outbuilding. It bounced over the cemetery grounds toward the oak tree and the open grave beneath it. I stopped the car and watched the tractor pull up to the mound of dirt beside the grave. The operator got out, pulled the tarp off the freshly turned soil, then jumped back in and used the lowered shovel to push it into the hole. I knew I shouldn't watch this, but I was unable to look away, hypnotized and overwhelmed by the sight. Deirdre was being buried, and she wouldn't, couldn't come back. Very soon, from this distance, there would be no trace of her left. I had a sudden panicky feeling that she was alive down there, screaming soundlessly and gasping for breath, clawing at the coffin lid to get out.

The last pile fell into place and was tamped down by the flat-bottomed tractor shovel–up, down–until the ground was level and even. Then the operator got out one last time, covered the wounded landscape with the tarp, and drove away.

I laid my forehead on the steering wheel and closed my eyes, struggling to hold back the tears. I needed to focus on what lay ahead. The first thing was to try and get some sleep, then be on the road early tomorrow morning. I started the car and headed home.

Just past Cabazon, the freeway elevated and curved to the right, toward the steep rise of Mount San Jacinto. At the apex of the curve, a giant Marlboro billboard rose beside the freeway. In the foreshortened perspective against the inert face of the mountain, the cowboy it depicted seemed to bear down on the car, advancing with great speed and purpose. Then I was out of its path as the highway curved away.

SEA

CHAPTER THIRTY

In low places, consequences collect.

I'd read that somewhere once, and it returned to me now as I descended into the lower southern outskirts of the Coachella Valley. I wondered what sort of reckoning I was headed for, or whether the mistake I'd made in my youth had finally run its course with Deirdre's death. Maybe the final results of my actions thirty years ago would reveal themselves in the blinding desert sunlight two hundred feet below sea level.

I gave it a little more gas and the car picked up speed. A lone vehicle cutting through the desert and the boiling waves of heat already rising from the concrete. It was early Sunday morning, about eight o'clock, but the sun had long since risen to begin its daily assault. The interstate had veered east a while ago, taking most of the other early-morning travelers with it as it snaked over the Mecca Hills toward Blythe. I'd stayed on 111 and followed it straight down, into the widescreen vastness of Imperial County. Past the Avenue 50 turnoff in Coachella, where my car had been shot up and forced into that field several nights ago. Whether the cops were ready to release the car from impound, I couldn't say. It hadn't even occurred to me to ask yesterday at the cemetery.

So I was using Deirdre's car, which felt right, like part of her was still with me for this lonely trip into the badlands. Despite the heat,

I'd leave the windows up as long as I could so the last of Deirdre's scent wouldn't blow out of the car.

I slowed down for the little town of Thermal. It had only a few small intersections to impede the flow of traffic. Run-down mobile home parks, most no more than parking lots for shabby camper shells, became a common sight, betraying the area's itinerant reputation. This was where the dream ended for some. Tapped-out and done-in, living off government checks or the kindness of neighbors. For others like the migrant farmworkers up from Mexico, maybe a better life. What would I find down here? The end of the line? A new beginning? Or something much worse—more questions than answers?

Lower and lower I went, each passing mile turning up the heat while the sun rose higher. The sky was a white sheet covering the desert, all color scorched away. Up ahead, the haze above the Salton Sea became more apparent, a pall hanging over the water. In the distance, I could just make out clouds of steam being coughed up by the geothermal plants at the south end of the sea.

Soon, the agricultural fields began taking over the landscape. Bright green citrus groves. Thriving crops of alfalfa, melons and onions. Date farms straddled the highway, the tall trees lined up majestically in vaulting cathedral columns, broad rows between them dappled with shadow and sunlight. I imagined myself among those massive trunks, looking up at the heavens peeking through, palm fronds waving like angels' wings.

I cracked the windows and was greeted by the sharp odor of the sea and the pungent scent of the surrounding fields. It got stronger and stronger until I had to close the windows and turn on the air conditioner.

A half hour later, the town of Niland, population 1400, appeared. "Downtown" was one dust-strewn block baking under the mid-morning sun. On the right, an unkempt strip of mostly abandoned storefronts, although the Pond Bar and Grill seemed to be a hangout, with several Harleys parked in front. A laundromat next door, no one inside. Across the street, the Jailhouse Cafe and the I.V. Restaurant, whose initials no doubt stood for Imperial Valley but to me implied something else entirely. It was closed up, its windows dusty and opaque.

Calipatria Prison, where Turret had finished out his sentence, was a few short miles away. The squatters' camp, which I'd actually found on a map last night, was just outside town.

I pulled into a gas station mini-mart, proceeded to the dirt parking lot behind it. A young woman had connected a water hose to a spigot at the rear of the building. She was filling up a big steel oil drum in the back of her Jeep. She said hi to me as I got out and went around to the front.

Inside, which was cooled by a rattling window air conditioner, I found a pay phone against the wall. Terry answered on the second ring.

"Hi, it's Tim. Down here in Niland, just about to visit that place you told me about."

"Good. I'm glad you found it. What's it like down there?"

"Quiet. Hot. Reminds me of one of those dying Old West towns you see in the movies."

"Prison's the only thing keeping that area alive, seems like," Terry said. "Anyway, I was able to talk with someone in El Paso. Pastor for the church down there. Not much to tell you, I'm afraid."

"What did he say?"

"Turret's not there. You probably already figured that. This guy wouldn't tell me anything else, but I got the impression he's still expecting him. Does that help you at all?"

"A little. Least I know I have a shot of finding him here."

Terry wished me good luck, said to call her if I needed anything else. I hung up the phone. Bought a Coke and inquired where Beale Street was.

"Slab City, huh?" the clerk asked. He was grizzled and sunburnt.

Mid-forties with a short gray beard. Cramped at a small counter displaying candy and tobacco. Behind him were racks of cigarettes and porno magazines. A tiny portable TV played at low volume on a shelf.

"Yeah. How did you know?"

He shrugged. "Only place the street goes."

I took my change and asked, "So which way?"

"Couple blocks that way," he answered, pointing back the way I'd come. "Make a right."

I thanked him and turned around to leave, then I stopped. I'd wanted to concentrate my inquiries on the outlying areas off the beaten track, figuring the cops had already struck out with the usual places like gas stations and restaurants. If they were even looking anymore. But it couldn't hurt to ask.

"Noticed anybody new in town? Middle-aged man, alone?"

"You mean someone like you?" He smiled.

I shook my head. "Not just passing through. Maybe he's come in here a few times. Just in the past few weeks or so."

"Can't think of anybody. Just travelers like yourself. And truckers hauling loads of produce." He shrugged again. "People I know from town."

"Thanks anyway," I said, not surprised at the answer.

Out back, I sat in the car, drinking my Coke. The girl with the hose finished up and turned off the faucet, unscrewed the hose and methodically coiled it before tossing it next to the oil drum. The Jeep's back end sagged with the weight of all that water inside. Just before she got in she flashed me a quick smile. White teeth, clean blond hair, nice skin. Not the image I'd had in mind of the people who lived down here–the clerk inside was closer to what I'd expected. But you never really knew.

The girl drove off and I watched her leave, wondering what the barrel of water was for. An old lady came shuffling up the street, stooped in the heat. She stopped behind me in the parking lot, looked around like she'd forgotten what she'd come for. After a few moments she sat down heavily in front of one of the rooms at the dilapidated old motel behind the gas station. It reminded me of the Blue Bird in Indio, a short strip of rooms badly in need of paint. This one had a wooden walkway along the front of the rooms, covered by an extended roof to keep it in the shade. The lady was perched on the edge of the walkway half in and half out of the sun, seemingly content to sit still and catch her breath. That would take a while today.

I got out of the car and approached her. She looked up at me expectantly, her blue eyes laser sharp under wrinkled lids. But I could see she was a lot younger than I'd first thought. Probably even younger than me, maybe early forties. Dressed in greasy, dark gray sweats cut off at the knees and elbows. Dark, leathery skin. Broad face under a mop of oily salt and pepper hair that resembled dirty straw.

"Thirsty?" I asked hesitantly.

"Hell yeah." Her voice was thick with phlegm, and she cleared her throat wetly before continuing. The words came slowly, more like a speech impediment than intoxication. "Got a smoke too? Goes good with a beer."

"Not on me. What brand?"

"Doesn't matter," she said, then thought better of it as I turned back toward the mini-mart. "Lucky Strikes," she called out after me. "No filter."

A few seconds later I was back with a cold Miller forty-ouncer, a pack of Lucky Strikes and matches. She took the bottle and put it against her face. Closed her eyes to the chilled glass, then twisted the cap off using her shirt as a grip. Her first gulp drained nearly a third of it. Deep, thirsty swallows with her face turned upward and her throat moving up and down.

"Thanks, mister," she said, as I gave her the cigarettes and matches. She put the beer down carefully beside her in the dirt and took the pack, tapped it on her knee to tighten the tobacco inside. After lighting one up she coughed once and took another drag.

"The hard stuff," I said with a grin.

She showed me a gap-toothed smile. "Helps deaden the tickle in my throat."

I sat down next to her and drank some Coke. "You live around here?"

"Yep," she replied between gulps of beer, then gestured behind us with her head. "Got me a little trailer out at the base."

"Isn't that the place they call Slab City?"

"That's what they call it. Not sure why."

"Need a ride there?"

"Sure, why not?" She blew out some smoke, eyeing me shrewdly. "What's in it for you, though?"

I looked away. The small parking lot was empty except for my car. No traffic on the highway out front. The faucet at the back of the mini-mart dripped the very last of its water. "I'm looking for someone."

"Who?"

"Somebody I used to know."

She scratched her scalp hard, smelled her fingertips afterwards. "Why do you need to find him?"

"I think he may have killed somebody."

She raised one eyebrow skeptically, but I could tell she believed me. She'd probably heard a lot worse. I finished my soda and hurled the empty plastic bottle toward the dumpster a few feet from the car. It went end over end and hit the wall of the building, bounced off and landed in the trashcan.

"I'll help you find him, then," she promised, still struggling with her words. "Does he live out there too?"

"I don't know for sure. But he just got out of Calipatria. He might still be in the area."

"The prison."

"You know anybody that was in there?"

She nodded vigorously and my heart skipped a beat. "Uh-huh. He was my boyfriend. For a while. But he left. Stole my money and disappeared."

"When was this?"

She swallowed some beer and frowned, thinking hard on it. "Few months ago. Last year I guess."

"The guy I'm looking for got out less than a month ago."

"Sorry. Joe was the only one I know of." A deep drag on the cigarette. I could hear the tobacco crackling as it burned. "But we can talk to my neighbors," she said. "You think they'll know your friend?"

"I hope so. But he isn't my friend."

Her face wrinkled up like she was about to cry, and my heart went out to her. "Sorry," she spluttered. "I forget things sometimes." Then she turned away, hitting herself in the head with the palm of her hand. "Stupid, stupid, stupid!"

I wondered if she was okay. Didn't know what to say, so I got up. "Wanna get going? My car's right here."

"Okay," she agreed, standing up slowly. "Here I come." She stood in the hot sun and finished the beer. Walked over and tossed it in the dumpster. "Maybe I should get a beer for the road? Don't worry, I don't get pissy drunk."

"No problem. Wait here."

I came back with the beer and we got into the car. "By the way, I'm Tim," I said, offering my hand.

She put the beer between her knees and took my hand. "Nice to know you. People call me Cat."

"Is that a nickname?"

"No, that's my name."

Chuckling, I started the car, glad I'd come upon her. We got back on the highway and drove slowly up the block. I was looking for Beale but didn't see it. I wondered how I could have missed it in this tiny town. But Cat directed me to turn right at Main Street and I followed her lead.

The neighborhood homes looked around fifty years old, with faded stucco weathered by wind and sun. Patchy, dried-out lawns like threadbare carpet behind sagging chain-link fences. Boxy swamp coolers perched on many of the rooftops. Nobody was about, but we saw lots of rusted-out cars, some of them up on blocks, in driveways and backyards. On the right, a large adobe building looked as if it might once have been a city hall, with broken windows and tumbling roof tiles like missing teeth. A little blond girl, maybe ten years old, drifted by on a bike, wearing a dingy blue dress and tennis shoes. She didn't look at us as we passed.

Two blocks later the houses stopped. The last one had a big backyard, densely overgrown with weeds. It looked like a scrap yard. Huge spools of rusting metal cable. Old tractor parts. Beat-up appliances like stoves and refrigerators and washing machines. Tires and wheels. Numerous items I couldn't identify, though the refrigerators looked like what my grandparents had used.

"That's Larry's place," Cat told me. "He's a scrapper."

"Looks like it."

She lit another Lucky Strike. "Goes up into the shooting range and finds a lotta that shit. Takes whatever he can haul out. Explosives too."

"You mean the gunnery range?" She must have been referring to the Chocolate Mountain Impact Area, where the army did live bombing. "Isn't it kind of dangerous up there?"

"Well, yeah," Cat confirmed. "Larry almost got his foot blown off once." There was live ordnance all over the place, I'd heard. "But you can make a pretty penny off that stuff. If you know the right people."

You could also get blown to kingdom come, it seemed to me.

Or disappear into an old mine shaft or well and never be heard from again.

"Larry knows all the roads and old Indian trails through there," Cat continued, and shrugged. "He's not the only one that does it."

Then she got quiet as we bumped over the railroad tracks outside town. The road turned into Beale Street at that point, heading straight for the bombing range. On the left was a small electrical station, with big transformers and power generators. The road turned to loose gravel, a thin ribbon of white winding through the brown desert scrub. My eyes followed it a mile or so into the distance. I squinted at what I saw. Part of a small hill up there was splashed with bright colors, and it didn't look like a trick of the light.

Cat was pensive beside me. Suddenly she spoke up. "I wasn't always like this, you know."

"What do you mean?"

"Just ... I was regular people, like you. Before I got hurt." She stopped and flicked some cigarette ash out the window, and I waited for her to continue. "Had a job in a bank, my own car, everything."

We hit a pothole and jolted over it, making me watch the road more closely.

"How did you get hurt?"

"Somebody hit me in the back of the head. Right here," she said, leaning forward to put her finger on the spot. The burning cigarette was right next to her hair, its ashy tip emitting a thin line of smoke. "Knocked me flat on the ground. Never knew what hit me."

"Who did it?"

"Beats me. Somebody in a car, driving by. I was jogging down the street. Heard it coming up behind me, then nothing."

"So they never caught them?"

"Nope." Cat looked down at the beer bottle in her lap and started peeling the label. It came off in small pieces. "I was never the same after that." Another gulp of the beer and a last drag on the cigarette. She dropped the butt outside, her face turned away. Fiddled with the control for the window. It went up and down with a motorized whine. "Couldn't remember things. Mixed up numbers at the bank all the time, till they had to let me go. I guess I can't blame 'em. Other people's money and all."

What a world. One second she's a bright young woman with a good future, the next, an alcoholic with a mental impairment. And the worst part of it was that she remembered the way she used to be, that she could never go back. I looked over and saw Cat's second forty-ouncer mostly gone. Sometimes it was better to forget.

"I'm okay now, I guess. I have good days and bad days. Sometimes I get real mad at myself though, like when I lose my Social Security checks." She shook her head and swallowed some beer. "That happened last month. I still haven't found it."

"You like it out here?"

"Yeah, I do. Got used to the heat a long time ago. And I can do whatever I want, because there's nobody telling you what's what. I sleep a lot, walk around, talk with my friends. Listen to my music." She turned to me. "You like Pink Floyd?"

"Definitely."

That seemed to make her day. She was beaming as she spoke. "*Dark Side of the Moon* is my favorite. And the other one. What's that one about the animals?"

"*Animals*," I replied, smiling. "I like that one too."

"Yeah, it's good. Those sheep scare me sometimes though."

I nodded, recalling the eerie sound effects on that album.

"Biggest thing I need all the time is batteries for the tape player. They're always going out. Half my checks probably go for that. But I listen to that stuff over and over."

We were now approaching Slab City, and I slowed down a little. I'd found a short online article about it at the *Desert Sun* Web site last night. Every winter the "snow birds" would gather here, scores of retirees parking their RVs for a few months to escape cold weather. Slab City was literally that–a scattered collection of concrete slabs, foundations left over from the former Marine Corps base that had long since disappeared like a traveling road show blowing town. There were a few official structures that remained, I noticed, like a solitary quonset hut that resembled a half-pipe cylinder of corrugated metal. Here and there, squat brick boxes with viewing ports for observing bomb tests. They looked like carnival ticket-booths. The first one I saw, right at the roadside, was painted a festive purple. As we drove past it, I read *Welcome to Slab City* in colorful letters. A Xeroxed flyer taped to the wall urged people to sign up for Medicare benefits.

The population here could swell into the thousands when the snow birds came to town. But it was apparent now that most of them had left, probably weeks ago. All that remained were the die-hard year-round residents. They lived in a motley collection of scattered trailers, camper shells, and defunct old buses with foil in the windows and no wheels. Not more than a few hundred people, I guessed.

The reason for all that color I'd seen a few minutes ago was coming up on the right.

CHAPTER THIRTY-ONE

"Salvation Mountain," Cat murmured, giving me the feeling that it made the same impression on her, one of quiet wonder, each time she passed by.

It was a thing to behold, a colorful man-made creation sculpted on the side of a mesa. A multitude of religious messages and pictures were painted on the hardened adobe, all beneath a large cross that spread its arms against the eggshell whiteness of the sky. A huge pink heart upturned to the heavens proclaimed, "God is Love." Biblical quotations crowded for position on the flat face of the hillside. JESUS I'M A SINNER PLEASE COME INTO MY BODY AND INTO MY HEART in raised white letters. Doves and fishes and flowers adorned the smaller spaces between the quotations. Another read, FOR GOD SO LOVED THE WORLD HE GAVE HIS ONLY BEGOTTEN SON. Closer to the road, an old abandoned flatbed truck, its hood yawning open in the heat like a panting dog. It was splashed with the same pastel shades as the mountain, with more doves and flowers and trees and hearts. The whole scene was fanciful and surreal, a heat-stroke hallucination in the middle of nowhere.

We'd slowed to a stop at the sight of it, and I took the opportunity to ask where her place was.

"Up ahead there," Cat answered vaguely, pointing through the windshield, still preoccupied with the colorful outdoor shrine.

A rattletrap pickup truck with an odd assortment of pipes and plumbing equipment sticking out the back chugged by in the opposite direction.

A little further into the settlement we came upon a man in a wheelchair inching up the road. He crunched laboriously through the hardpacked gravel. Dirt-clods crumbled under his wheels, which were dusted with a fine white powder. We drew even with him, but he didn't look up, grimly focused on getting wherever he was going. He wore a black baseball cap, also layered with dust, and a T-shirt with the sleeves cut off. There was some sort of emblem on it, and a word ending with RA that I couldn't make out from this angle. His powerful upper arms churned over the wheels like the transmission on an old locomotive.

Cat leaned out the window, greeted him with a good-natured chuckle. "Hey Leonard, where you going like a bat outta hell?"

Leonard looked up like he'd just noticed us and continued rolling. "There's a concrete bunker up yonder. You can follow me if you want."

Cat glanced back at me, grinning like she was used to this, then addressed Leonard. "Haven't you heard? They cleared out. Couldn't stand the heat."

"Shit, this heat ain't nothin' for the Delta," he argued, but stopped his wheelchair anyway. Looked up at Cat as if he wanted to believe her. I stopped with him. "You tryin' to get me killed or something?" he said.

"Well I was just in town and they're nowhere in sight," she said. "But don't let me stop you."

At that, Leonard started up again, pumping furiously, panting hard in the dry, dusty air. He had a beat-up canteen in his lap covered with dents and scratches, and I could see that both legs ended in knobby stumps at his knees. I took my foot off the brake and shadowed him.

"Hey Leonard," Cat continued, but got no response except a tired grunt. That didn't stop her. "You heard of anybody new around here?"

Leonard kept his eyes on the road, no doubt imagining something far different than what was actually in front of him.

Then he spoke up, apparently back in the present time, at least momentarily. "Nah. They all been gone for what? Month, at least. All them old folks in their big buses."

"This guy would be alone," I clarified over Cat's shoulder. "Probably about your age."

"Nope," came the terse reply, ending the conservation. He didn't even look up to see who I was.

"Thanks, Lenny," Cat said. Then, as I accelerated: "Come by and see me tonight on your way back. I got a bottle around somewhere."

Lenny kept quiet, back in his own head. It was a Sierra Club T-shirt, I saw in the rearview mirror.

Cat relaxed inside the car again. "That's my friend Leonard."

We drove by another old camper shell sitting in the dust, where I noticed the girl I'd seen at the mini-mart. She had her little Jeep backed up to a small garden, and was carefully watering the spindly plants from the drum she'd filled up. I wondered how long they'd last in this environment.

Just past that Cat pointed out where she lived. A tiny Airstream trailer with no wheels squatting resolutely next to a skeletal, dried-out smoke tree that provided precious little shelter. The trailer looked like some sort of hump-backed animal that had curled up beneath the tree to die.

I pulled up next to it as Cat murmured, "He told me once about his legs."

I turned off the engine and the car shuddered once.

"His Jeep got blown off the road in the middle of the jungle. When he came to," she continued calmly, without a trace of her stutter, "both his legs were crushed underneath it. Dug himself out and crawled back up to the road where someone could find him."

Then her eyes got wide. "He was there for two days. Can you believe that?"

Cat seemed to be looking through me, and I couldn't hold her gaze. Others had fought and died over there, while I'd been slacking my way through college, going through the countercultural motions. Attending rallies between drunken make-out parties and getting stoned. And finally, throwing it all away in one blaze of stupidity. I thought about that warehouse in New York, lying on the cold floor writhing in pain. Couple of hours, at most, with all my limbs intact.

"Let's go talk to your neighbors," I suggested, as we got out of the car. I surveyed the surrounding area with my hand over my eyes, squinting under the pulsating sun. The brilliant surface of the desert glared white hot in the clear air. Nothing to disturb the awful clarity other than the occasional clouds of dust being kicked up by the roaming winds. They quickly departed though, scattered by those same winds, leaving only the unrelenting heat and blinding sunlight. It burned away all nuance and pretension like a shower of X-rays laying bare the desert and everything in it. I felt Cat watching me from behind, and the heat radiating up from the ground, through my shoes and into my bones.

A bead of sweat dripped into my eye, stinging, and I wiped it away before turning back to Cat. "You still want to help me out right?"

"Yeah, no problem. I gotta do something first though." She disappeared into her trailer, behind a door squeaking on rusty hinges. I heard her rummaging around in there, talking to herself as she shuffled around. The unbalanced trailer rocked with her movements.

She eventually came out with a jar of peanut butter in one hand and a big smile on her face. "I found it," she announced, waving an envelope in the air before stuffing it in her pocket.

"Found what?"

"My government money. I knew if I looked hard enough it would turn up."

"And you're celebrating with a jar of peanut butter?" I kidded her.

Cat looked down at it, frowning. "No. I just like it."

I hadn't meant to make fun of her. I quickly changed the subject. "So who are we talking to?"

"Whoever you want." She stuck her finger in the jar, scooped out a thick gob and licked it off, smacking her lips as she did so. "I know a lot of people here."

"Okay. Why don't we start over there." I pointed to a dusty group of camper shells and trailers ringed together like an Old West wagon train. Camouflage netting covered the open area inside, providing spotted shade underneath. Two mangy-looking dogs sprawled in the meager shade beneath a wooden table. They watched us, ears raised and alert, tongues hanging out. The table was covered with an assortment of items: water- and sun-damaged paperback books, their pages splayed outward stiffly; rusty old kitchen utensils; several cracked Pez dispensers; a pair of headphones with rotted earpads; and a black plastic rotary-dial phone. Third world flea market stuff.

The first door we knocked on brought only a gruff, "Go away." Cat shrugged and led me to the next one, banged on the window as she passed the trailer.

"Hey, Einstein," she said, reaching for the door handle. She struggled with it briefly before the door opened, then looked inside. "Nobody home," she said, pushing the door closed with her shoulder.

"Einstein?"

"He can do all this math in his head. We get along pretty good."

A middle-aged woman appeared near one of the camper shells, stooped over as she walked under the forward bed. She held a little boy's hand. They both wore sandals and shorts, the woman with a loose tank top and the youngster, maybe four, shirtless. He stuck his thumb in his mouth when he saw us.

"How many times I gotta tell you?" his mother said, grabbing his wrist and taking the thumb out.

"Hey, Bernie," Cat said. "Where is everybody?"

"The cave, I guess. Kris got some gas." She gestured over to the table we'd walked by earlier. "See anything you like?"

"I was thinking about those headphones. But the plug thing is too big."

"You read, mister? I got books."

"No thank you," I said, looking at Cat. She asked Bernie if she knew of any strangers passing through recently.

Bernie shook her head no. Picked up the kid and brushed his hair back with her hand. It fell right back down on his forehead. He was staring hungrily at Cat's jar of peanut butter. "But you know how I keep to myself. So don't go by me."

Cat told her to take it easy, and we moved on.

"What's the cave?" I asked, following her out of the circle.

"I'll show you," she replied, wiping smears of peanut butter on her shirt. "But first I gotta get this stuff off my hands."

We came to small ravine just outside the settlement. Below, some hygiene-minded resident had placed an ancient claw-footed bathtub next to a small hot spring bubbling up from the ground. A man sat in the bathtub, poured water over his head from an old cooking pot.

"There she is," he said happily when he saw Cat, and stood up without a trace of embarrassment. "You coming with me tonight, honey? I'll introduce you to Mr. Bob Hope. Play your cards right, maybe I can get you an autograph."

Cat laughed, stepped down and dipped her hands into a small puddle. "No thanks," she said, wringing them dry. "Got a date with Leonard." The man couldn't help us with Turret, but asked me how much I'd pay for that autograph.

We went on, trudging from campsite to campsite. Slab City was a post-apocalyptic vision to me. Something out of a Mel Gibson movie in which all the players were forced to scrape and scramble for every bit of sustenance, but did so gladly in return for the freedom it offered. People like my new friend Cat, who'd drifted from place to place when the money ran out and the landlord called. Addicts and alkies who'd met kindred spirits and weren't looked down upon for their afflictions. A few had been kicked out of mental hospitals during the Reagan years for not being quite far gone enough. Others had woken up and found themselves here by accident, like sediment that ends up in the lowest place, far below sea level in a forgotten land. A land though, with crystal clear air and no restrictions, bright days and star-filled nights. I could appreciate how one could get used to this. Out here, you could breathe deep, let the vastness and serenity of the desert fill up the empty spaces inside.

Late morning, we met two teenagers who used the slabs as a base of operations for running illegals up from the border near Calexico. They offered us cold Coronas they'd swiped off one of the freight trains going through Niland. Cat was tired, and thirsty from all that peanut butter, so we followed them to their trailer. The bottles were swimming in a cooler of melted ice.

"They call us *coyotes*," the taller one said proudly, twisting the top off his beer and shaking his long hair back as he drank. Both kids were thin and wiry, with ropelike muscles showing on their arms. They wore dusty jeans low on their hips, and tennis shoes with the laces untied. Neither could have been more than fifteen. "Mikey here got interviewed by some magazine. Took his picture and everything."

I sipped my beer. It was surprisingly cold. Cat was nursing hers, making it last.

"Got a meal out of it too," Mikey said.

I said nothing, not wanting to stay too long; they hadn't seen

any newcomers either. Above their heads were several small cup-
boards. No door fronts on them. Boxes of cereal, canned food, and
Sterno. A condom wrapper sat next to the pillow on the bed.

"You guys had lunch yet?" Cat asked hopefully.

"I ain't hungry," Mikey said, not getting the hint. His friend gulped
Corona.

"See," the friend said after wiping his lips, "most people don't
know what's involved in our work. Border Patrol has all kind of
high-tech stuff. Magnetic motion sensors. Night vision scopes.
Shit, I got buzzed by a prop plane the other day, and I wasn't doing
nothing. And those four-wheelers they got prowl all the way up to
the interstate. Never know where they're gonna be."

"Gotta know the territory," Mikey agreed. "Lotta things can happen when you're out there. If the van breaks down, or throws an
axle or something, you're screwed. Take your chances in the open
desert. Lost one guy that way. Or they get picked up and hauled
back across." He shook his head. "Ain't no picnic, lemme tell you."

"Pretty dangerous, huh?" Cat said.

"So's a lotta things," longhair said, turning to Mikey. "Remember
that hitchhiker the other day?"

"What hitchhiker?" I asked, leaning forward.

Mikey's beer stopped midway. "You're right," he told me.
"Coulda been the guy you said."

"Where? Near the prison?"

"Down that way."

"You pick him up?"

"No," Mikey's friend answered. "That's what I was saying. Felt
some bad mojo at the last second."

"Enrique woulda killed us if we got his van jacked," Mikey
explained.

"How old was this guy?" I asked.

Longhair shrugged. "I don't know. At least your age. Couple
years older maybe."

"What else you remember about him?"

"Not much. He was carrying a toolbox–"

"It wasn't a toolbox," Mikey interrupted. "It was a tackle box. You know. For fishing. And he had a rod with him. One of those telescoping ones. Woulda been nice to have, but we didn't stop."

Something hit me then, and I knew exactly what my next destination would be if nothing panned out here. They couldn't tell us anything else, so I cut things short and spent the next hour with Cat hunting for more information, without result.

The last place we visited, the "cave" I'd heard about earlier, was actually a concrete bunker. A collection of desert-modified vehicles sat outside. Three-wheelers with big tires. A '70s-era Land Rover that had its roof cut off. A few motorbikes and what looked like an old mail truck missing the sliding door. Next to us, a souped up, tricked-out dune buggy rested in the sun like a coiled beast. A pair of legs stuck out from underneath, a set of wrenches and screwdrivers spread in the dirt.

"Hey, Kris," Cat said over the noise of a gas-powered generator rattling a few feet away. A frayed, heavy duty extension cord ran from it into the bunker. "Whatcha doin'?"

"Shock needs adjusting," he called out.

"Can we talk to you for a sec?"

Kris poked his head out and looked at me. "Who are you?"

"That's my friend Jim," Cat answered. I didn't correct her.

"Soon as I'm done," the man said, and continued working.

"Kris's been here a long time," Cat told me.

"Why wouldn't I be?" Kris asked from his place on the ground. "Got everything I need here–*shit*," he reached for another tool, "–and nothing I don't." He tossed the wrench out and stood up, dusting himself off. "No government, no rules, no taxes, no fees. Just this wide-open desert and anything I can scrounge from it," Kris explained, wiping his hands on a greasy rag. "See that line over there?" he said, pointing over my shoulder. "Up against the mountains?"

I nodded, spotting a concrete wash cutting through the desert. "That's the Coachella Canal. On the other side? Well, that's the promised land. There's gold in them hills, falling from the skies," he said, Cat laughing merrily. "And right behind me is my living room. I'll show you."

We followed the cables inside. The size of the place surprised me. Some sort of underground storage area much larger than a bunker. The first thing I saw was a TV, which ten or so people were watching, some lying back on a stained sectional sofa, several others in chairs and on the floor. A refrigerator hummed in the corner. It must have been twenty degrees cooler than outside. Dim and comfortable. A window air conditioner sat on a table near the entrance, blowing cold air. I wondered if Turret had ever been down here.

"What do you think?" Kris asked.

"I'm looking for somebody," I said. "Maybe you've seen him."

Kris glanced at Cat, then addressed me with a grin. "Everybody's looking for something. We all found it by accident."

But only when you let it all go, Deirdre said in my memory. "His name's Glenn Turret. Late fifties. If he was here, it would have been sometime in the last couple of weeks."

Kris shook his head. "Can't help you. Only strangers I run acrosst lately are you and all those retired folks."

I nodded, disappointed once again. The TV was playing some old mystery on a beat-up VCR. I walked over to it and hit "stop." "Anybody here know a Glenn Turret?" I asked over the protests and the snow on the screen.

"Who do you think you are?"

"Turn the damn TV back on."

"I need to find him," I continued. Kris got a beer from the refrigerator, shaking his head, while Cat went over and stood in front of the air conditioner, billowing her shirt to cool off. "White guy. Middle-aged, alone. I'll turn the movie right back on."

Nothing but a few hostile, impatient looks. I hit "play," apologizing as I did so. Outside, I heard Kris speak to Cat. "Your friend could be a little more—"

A fighter jet streaked overhead, cutting the silence of the desert with a thunderous scream. Seconds later, a rapid series of explosions echoed within the gunnery range as the plane strafed the area. Kris dropped his beer, scrambled to his dune buggy and fired it up. The others rushed outside in a mad dash to their own range-runners, and sped for the hills. They'd fight over the smoking rubble, looking for the diamonds in the rough before the next tracers came whistling in. Cat and I were left with nothing but smoke and dust in our faces as they all roared off.

It was close to noon by that time, and the sun was at its apex. Overheated and talked out, Cat and I returned to her trailer, where I thanked her for her help.

"You should let those whiskers grow out," she suggested as we shook hands. "I always liked a man with a beard."

For just a second, I saw the young woman she used to be. Almost gave her a hug before I left, but I didn't.

CHAPTER THIRTY-TWO

Minutes later I was on the main highway back in Niland. From there, I took one of the two-lane access roads cutting through the farmland that spread outward from the southern shores of the Salton Sea. I tried not to be discouraged about not finding Turret in Slab City. After all, the visit was based on nothing more than Terry's hunch. I was still playing hunches.

As I headed for the water, the landscape suddenly changed from a lifeless brown-gray to a verdant, agricultural green. It seemed much cooler now, an illusion provided by the sprinkler systems spraying water into the air and the blue irrigation canals crossing under the road every few miles. The road looked freshly laid. A shiny black strip bisecting the green on either side, on which trucks laden with produce rolled by. The pungent scent of onions hovered in the air, but as I approached the shoreline, the sulfurous, rotten-egg odor of the geothermal plants took over. Thick white steam billowed from stout smokestacks. A profusion of massive, rusty pipes led to and from inert pools of brackish water in dirt pits. The entire area was a study in contrasts: clouds of pillowy cotton floating tranquilly above rusting metal buildings; foul, muddied soil surrounded by fertile green cropland on one side and a blue mirror on the other. And if you looked beyond that, the blistered brown desert spread far and wide.

After passing the polluted New River, which emptied into the Salton Sea, I made a few turns to get around its southern tip, then proceeded north along the western shore. The town I was looking for was about two-thirds of the way up, a place Turret had described to me many years before.

It was just after noon. I took out the sandwich I'd packed for the day. To my left the Superstition Hills, scene of yet more military training activity as well as recreational off-road vehicle use, rose from the desert in stunted humps, a few shades darker than the surrounding flatlands. More irrigated farmland stretched away to my right, much of it going right up to the water. A few miles farther, I was waved uninterestedly through a Border Patrol check station. The people in the lane next to me weren't so lucky. A couple of brown-skinned men wearing cowboy hats in an old Buick sedan. As I watched in the rearview mirror, they got out of the car with their wallets out. Moments later the trunk flipped up, and was surrounded by two or three inquisitive Border Patrol officers.

Eventually the farmland gave way to flat, graded desert. This area had once been known as the Salton Riviera, with hundreds of subdivided lots squared off from the shoreline. Now it was a checkerboard pattern of desolation and abandonment. Cracked, weed-infested roads being rubbed from existence by drifting, windblown sand. Landscaped palm trees succumbing to the heat and neglect, their fronds collapsed and down-turned like rotting haystacks. Street signs that pointed nowhere, with designations such as Seabreeze Drive and Pelican Way—resort names that evoked sparkling waters, cool breezes and fresh air but now only emphasized all that had been lost. Or truthfully, had never been here in the first place.

In the 1950s, the start of the post-war California land boom, optimistic developers had envisioned the Salton Sea as the ultimate desert resort. A haven for water-skiing, yachting and fishing, blessed by ever-present sunshine and fresh sea breezes. They saw it as a natural extension of the playground for the rich and famous that Palm Springs fifty miles away was becoming. Developers bought huge, ultra-cheap tracts of desert land, subdivided it into lake front property, built a yacht club and golf course, and expected people to come in droves. If they'd looked a little closer they would have seen that it was little more than a mirage built on shifting desert sands. The few buyers that did succumb to the high-pressure sales pitches were somehow able to ignore the hellacious heat and the remoteness and harshness of the region. Their houses stood out few and far between as I approached Salton City. Tiny homesteads defiantly resisting the surrounding emptiness, connected by thin lifelines of utility and telephone wires strung limply over acres of vacant lots and along destitute, pot-holed streets.

The main road into town, Marina Drive, crept from the highway like a brittle snakeskin, looking all the more pitiful for its former glory. The majestic palm trees that used to line the broad four-lane boulevard were now spindly skeletons against the blown-out sky, the once flower-filled median lifeless and colorless and crumbling into dust. The pavement I drove over was fissured and broken, with tumbleweeds parked on its surface and weeds sprouting from the cracks. A peeling, weatherbeaten sign that hadn't seen paint for years rose from the median and whispered "Welcome to Salton City" on the sighing desert winds.

A few hundred yards further up, the defunct Salton Bay Yacht Club hunkered next to the water behind a jagged chain-link fence with a pockmarked notice reading "No Trespassing." The remains of the yacht club sign oversaw it all, still advertising "Cocktails" to the deserted parking lot.

I stopped and got out of the car for a closer look at the place. Off to the right a small two-story inn was falling into ruin, its foundation choked off by weeds and the trash and tumbleweeds that had blown up against it. In front of me, the yacht club and restaurant fared no better. Its big bay windows were broken, with knife-like shards still extending from the frames in various places. The shadowed interior had wires and conduit dangling from the ceiling as if it had been disemboweled. Broken glass littered the floor inside. Patches of rotted carpet clung to it like fungus. The exterior paint was faded and peeling and covered by graffiti, and the broad, curving roofline, once suggesting a seabird in flight, now resembled a broken wing.

I imagined the place in its heyday forty years ago as Turret had described it: the best fishing spot in Southern California, where tilapia and plump corvina were just waiting to be reeled in. He'd come here with his parents to boat and fish, and they'd end the day at the restaurant with a gourmet meal served on cloth-covered tables while seagulls drifted lazily over the water.

It was his vivid description of those trips, on one of which Turret witnessed a near-drowning, that came back to me a few nights ago on the ride down to the Blue Bird. And again when those two coyotes mentioned the hitchhiker with the fishing gear. I wondered if that memory had been trying to get out in the New York warehouse, when I'd referred to my blind trip to the city as a "fishing expedition." I only hoped that Turret and the hitchhiker were one and the same. The age range was right. And if Turret were fishing, that he'd return to a familiar place.

I noticed a girl holding a rod at the water's edge on the other side of the property. She'd probably climbed the chain-link fence to get there. Between us the resort's plaza was scored and broken, a jumble of concrete chunks and dried-out palm fronds. I took a short walk to the left, careful of my footing on the uneven sidewalk, for a view around the side of the building. There the water met a tiny beach. A line of massive boulders had been piled up on the right to prevent erosion of the club's property line. The chain-link fence proved to be only a half-hearted measure against tres-passing. It stopped short of the boulders, allowing access over them to the yacht club grounds–they hadn't bothered to put up a barrier at the shoreline.

I crawled over the big rocks slowly, using my hands often, ig-noring the stink of the dirty bathwater a few feet below. Very little moss on the warm, dry stone, though I did slip once and had to pull my ankle from a narrow gap.

After making it around the restaurant building, which looked no better from this perspective, I climbed up to the patio area. I found a bone dry swimming pool with more dead palm fronds and trash at the bottom, its bleached walls cracked like an egg shell. The girl with the fishing pole noticed me approaching and gave me a quick wave before turning back to the water. Friendly people here, I thought, probably not used to visitors.

I was about to excuse myself and ask for her help, but never got it out.

"How's it going, Glenn?" she said, eyes still on the water. Then she turned around, her hand shading her eyes. "Oh. Sorry. I was ex-pecting somebody else."

"You know Glenn Turret?" A nervous quaver in my voice like the rippled surface of the lake.

The girl had turned back to her task. She nodded without look-ing at me. Her fishing pole extended over the water, its line disap-pearing into the cloudy depths. She hadn't caught anything yet, I could see from her empty pail.

"You a buddy of his?" Her voice was soft, without inflection. When she faced me again her features were blank as a sand dune. Probably coasting on some chemical high, reminding me of the half-baked girls I knew in college.

"Yeah," I lied. "We were going to cast a few today."

She regarded me a moment longer, as if my words were traveling from a great distance. I wondered, in her apparent haze, whether she'd be any help to me. "That's cool." She wiggled her line a little bit, hoping for a bite. Nothing happened.

"You seen him around lately?"

"Not today. We fished together once or twice before though."

I wanted to shake her like a rag doll, shout into her face, *where the hell is he?* but somehow restrained myself. The girl was in her mid-twenties. Skin stained dark by the sun. Barefoot and wearing shabby cutoff jeans and a loose tank top that fluttered in the breeze. Her long brown hair hung limply to her shoulders, oily and dull in the sunlight.

I moved a little closer. "You don't know where he's staying, do you?"

"Don't know him very well," she admitted after a long pause. "I only met him last week. How do you know him?"

I ignored the question, responded with one of my own. "Where did you two do your fishing? Maybe I could find him there now."

"Right where we're standing, mister. One time from that jetty over there." She pointed to a rock-lined extension jutting into the water, beyond the little beach I'd been standing on earlier. There was no one on the narrow pier except a lone gull, still as a statue, perched on its very tip.

"Hope you find him," the girl offered. "Tell him I said hi if you do."

She didn't think to tell me her name and I didn't bother asking. Just made my way back around the ruined building, over the rocks and onto the gritty sand. I scanned the area for any sign of a lone fisherman or a boat, but saw not one living soul. Even the girl I'd just talked to had disappeared behind the yacht club buildings.

Surrounded by stagnation and decay, I felt myself losing hope. At my feet, the sluggish, oily tide licked the beach in a manner that was somehow obscene. Dead fish in various stages of decomposition littered the shoreline, desiccated and eyeless, scales flaked off, bones disintegrating. There were piles of them still submerged too, fins swaying lifelessly with the torpid movement of the tide. The water itself looked like root beer, a caramel color with a touch of fizziness caused by God knew what. I wondered how the sand could be so white until I realized it was composed primarily of fish bones ground together and crushed up into tiny pebbles. I crunched my way through it to the rock jetty, hoping to get a more complete view of the shoreline from its tip. When I got there the seagull launched itself into the air and drifted off lethargically, leaving me alone out on the water.

The sun beat down and I squinted against it. The girl had found a new fishing spot on the other side of the marina and was casting her line from shore. I doubted she'd have any better luck there. To my left, I could make out another small beach shining white in the distance with what appeared to be two solitary sunbathers stretched out side by side on the sand. Other than that, there was no sign of anyone anywhere. I resigned myself to knocking on doors in order to find Turret.

I turned back toward shore. A man was standing there watching me, unmoving, holding a rod in one hand and a tackle box in the other. My eyes went tunnel vision from the end of the jetty. My feet somehow found their way smoothly on the rocky pier. It was as if I were walking on water, gliding over the surface as I approached him. A few moments later, I was on shore.

"Been a long time," Turret said quietly, eyes riveted on mine.

CHAPTER THIRTY-THREE

Before I knew it he was on the ground, a thin ribbon of blood trickling from his lip. Turret struggled against the fishing line I'd wrapped around his throat. He'd gotten his hands up in time to prevent the nylon thread from slicing his Adam's apple, though I could see a razor strip of blood cutting across his palms where it bit into them.

"I didn't . . . kill . . . your wife," he gasped, his pale blue eyes fixed on mine, as direct and unflinching as I remembered but without the murderous intensity I'd recognized too late thirty years ago. He probably saw it in my eyes now as I tightened the makeshift garrote.

"You can't . . . do this," Turret croaked weakly with the last of his strength. His face was beet-red, eyes wide with fear, and when I understood the real meaning of his words, the rage drained out of me and evaporated in the super-heated air.

I got off him, panting hard, head reeling under the hot sun. Put my hands to my temples and let out a primal roar that had no echo from the mirror-flat sea. Behind me I could hear Turret writhing on the ground, taking deep, ragged breaths. When I turned around he was unwrapping himself from the fishing line with trembling hands. The tackle box was upended a few feet away, spilling hooks, line and lures. A shiny fillet knife glinted menacingly in the dirt.

I offered him a tentative hand up and he eyed me appraisingly before grabbing it. With part of the fishing line still draped over his shoulder, the rod came up with him, like some sort of skeletal twin. He disentangled it from his collar and let it drop. Leaned over with his hands on his knees and breathed deeply, catching his breath as the sweat dripped off his face into the dust at our feet. For a second I was tempted to walk away, afraid of what I'd just done, but I knew in the end there was too much between us to let it go at that.

When Turret was done dusting himself off, he squatted next to the tackle box to clean up the mess, methodically ordering the items in their separate trays, muttering agitatedly. The knife he didn't give a second glance to, just tossed it in the main box under the trays. Maybe I'd left it in the dirt for him as a test.

I watched Turret quietly, all words having left me. I wondered what he would say, if anything. Finished with the toolbox, he snapped it shut smartly, picked up a rock and hurled it as far as he could into the water.

"What the hell am I doing here?" Turret asked himself, voice raised to a hoarse shout. "Look at this place!" He spun around, sweeping his arms to take in the area. Behind him a dust devil swirled up, then petered out.

When he turned back to me I spoke, voice tight with emotion. "You ruined my life. And took Deirdre's too, even if you didn't kill her yourself."

Turret didn't respond that nobody had held a gun to my head thirty years ago, or that I'd made my own decision back then. He just nodded quietly, rubbing his injured neck, and followed a bird flying over the water. It glided our way, its shadow darting over us before it disappeared into the glare. "I've come to peace with my past," he finally said, the words coming out as a challenge to me.

"Really?" I spat out, stepping toward him. "Water under the bridge, huh?"

His eyes held mine calmly.

"My wife is dead. And the gladness in your fucking heart won't bring her back. I hope you choke on the peace you found. You don't deserve it." The tears squeezed out of my eyes as I turned to walk away, trying to swallow the lump in my throat.

"I can help you," he said after me, bruised voice cracking.

I whirled around angrily. "You? You can help me?"

"Maybe."

We ended up at the Clarkson's Landing Café, a flimsy, white-washed shoebox of a structure off Marina Drive next door to a small RV park. It was hot inside, and we were the only customers in the place. The tables were small and the booths had seats of ancient, cracked vinyl patched with duct tape. We took one next to a window looking out on the empty parking lot. Dead flies were scattered over the windowsill, baking in the sun.

Turret ordered a grilled cheese sandwich and fries. I was in no mood to eat and just got a glass of water.

I got right to it after the waitress left. "You said you could help." He gave me a cool gaze and I continued. "You know something the cops don't?"

He seemed smaller than I remembered, less arrogant and intimidating. Calmer. His hair had grayed. Cut short and combed forward carelessly. He wore a long-sleeved cotton workshirt, cutoff blue-jean shorts and sandals, with no watch or jewelry. I hated him.

"I only know what I read in the newspaper," he said.

"And?"

"If there's some sort of illegal activity behind what's happened I can probably talk to a few people."

"Who?"

"The early speculation in the news was about a possible drug connection. Is that what you think?"

I shrugged. I'd been over it so many times in my own mind and

I still wasn't sure. But it was the only thing I had if I trusted my gut about Turret. "I suppose I thought that. Until I got beat up by some people that were just as interested in the murder as I was." I watched his eyes. "I really got their attention when I mentioned you." Nothing, not even a flicker.

"Who were they?"

"No idea. It was in New York City. The boy who got himself shot on our front lawn was wearing a concert T-shirt. I tracked the band down to a club in New York, hoping they'd know him. They did, but not well enough. Then I ran into those other guys. Actually, they ran into me. I got rousted from the club and taken to an abandoned warehouse on the docks, where they asked me a few questions. Not too politely." I took a long sip of water. "They seemed real eager to find the killer, and their interest in you pointed me straight back here."

No response.

"What I'd like to know," I continued slowly, "is why they were so intrigued by you?"

At that moment his sandwich came. Our eye contact was broken, so I couldn't gauge his reaction to my question. It didn't seem to faze him though. "Sounds like they were as anxious for answers as you were. You gave them something they hadn't heard yet so they wanted to know more."

That was plausible, but I didn't want to let him off the hook yet. "One thing more. I got into it with somebody else too. In Indio."

"The motel?"

"Yeah. How did you know?"

"That was in the paper too." He took a bite of his sandwich, and I couldn't believe I'd sat down for a meal with him. "It didn't say why you'd gone out there though."

I told him about the matchbook I'd found in the street outside my house, then tried to surprise him. "The guy I fought with gave me your regards."

Turret put his sandwich down and wiped his mouth with the napkin. "I told you, I had nothing to do with this. You either believe me or you don't."

For some reason, I did believe him, though my stomach turned at the thought of trusting him. I sat back and puffed air out of my mouth. Stared at the creaky ceiling fan rotating drunkenly up above, wondering how everything could have gone so wrong.

"I'd say those people in New York are your best shot," Turret said. "That guy at the motel. Did he have a New York accent?"

"Not that I heard. But he only said the one thing."

"Your wife didn't know the first victim, did she?"

"No. And if you ask whether she was mixed up in anything illegal like drugs, I'll shove the rest of that sandwich down your throat."

"What if one of her clients told her something he shouldn't have?" Turret persisted. "Get somebody talking, opening up, it's easy to maybe say too much."

I'd had the same thought. And the other day in the car Deirdre had seemed like she wanted to get something off her chest. I remembered the haunted look in her eyes. Why hadn't I asked what was on her mind?

"So what can you do about it?" I asked sullenly.

"Talk to a few people."

"People you know from prison?"

"Yeah. One guy in particular. Irish guy. Used to be in the construction rackets in New York City. I'll ask him to make some inquiries with the people he knows on the east coast. See if anybody's dealing with a problem right now in this area."

"You'll forgive me if I don't fall all over myself to thank you," I said, getting up to leave, about to suggest we meet again tomorrow.

"I'm not doing this for you."

That stopped me. I sat back down. "What's that mean?"

"I'm doing it for me."

"Trying to polish up your karma?"

"For me in the sense that I know it's the right thing to do." He patted his chest. "Right here."

"And you think doing this will square it with me?"

"No," he disagreed, shaking his head patiently. "And that's the point. I can never repay the people I hurt. There's more than I can count, many I've never even met or heard of. The stuff I've done..." He shook his head. "It's like a rock dropped into the water. The ripples spread outward forever, even if we can't see them. The best I can do is take each opportunity that comes my way to do the right thing. Regardless of what came before."

"You're still a damn smooth talker. Just like when I first met you. I gotta wonder if you're going to screw me all over again."

"You know I'm not. Or else you would have choked the life out of me right outside. Next to that sewer of a lake. And you definitely wouldn't be sitting here with me now."

"What did you mean out there?"

"What?"

"What you said before. About this place."

"Just that it's nowhere to come back to." Turret put his sandwich down and finished chewing. "You know the history of this area?"

"It's a failed resort," I said, shrugging.

He shook his head. "No. Before that."

"I guess I don't."

"They call that thing an accidental lake," Turret began, gesturing outside with his chin. "It's not even supposed to be there."

"What are you talking about?"

"I read up on it when I came down here. Not much else to do when you're locked up." He called the waitress over and ordered an iced tea. When she came back with it, she refilled my water.

"The Indians knew it as Lake Cahuilla, way back when. I'm talking ancient history here. They irrigated their crops from it, trapped fish. You can still see the waterline in some places, like a bathtub ring. Anyway, it had been dry for centuries when the pioneers started coming through in the 1800s. But they saw the crops the Indians grew along the Colorado, and got an idea in their head. All this land, why not turn it into farmland? So they built a bunch of canals and reservoirs for irrigation. Tapped them right off the river. The reclamation of the desert, they said, as if it was the natural order of things. Religious types referred to it as *redemption*, even. Got the government and the taxpayers to pick up the tab."

"So?" I asked, impatiently.

"In 1905, one of the dams broke. The river flooded everything in its path. They couldn't stop it for two years. Two whole years. The result is what you see around you." Turret finished his sandwich, picked some melted cheese off the plate with his fingernail. "I never dreamed how bad it had gotten until I saw it. I mean, who'd want to live here? That lake is dying. Untreated sewage from Mexico, industrial chemicals. Supposedly, there was an accident recently where a truck ended up in the New River, and when they pulled it out, all the paint was stripped off."

I nodded. Heard some other stories myself.

"Not to mention all the pesticides from the agricultural fields," Turret continued. "Birds dying at that wildlife refuge, fish floating belly up–"

"What's your point?"

"My point. My point is that there's always a price to pay. Sure, they got what they wanted. The Imperial Valley is one of the most productive agricultural regions in the world. But look what happened further upstream. Nothing's for free."

Of course, he was right. I knew that better than anyone. What I'd been seeking, Deirdre had paid for. But I didn't want to think about that. I retreated to the past again, like I always did.

"Why did you choose us? Me and my friends."

"You don't really want to talk about that, do you?"

I wouldn't let him look away.

"I took opportunities where I saw them. And I could use that war, big time. Find the right people, tell them what they wanted to hear. I always knew which buttons to push to get what I wanted." He paused, looking inward. "Maybe I got it from my father, I don't know. He was a salesman. The best. Could talk anybody into buying most anything, by making them talk *themselves* into it. It was like he'd wind them up and watch them go. Could have headed sales and marketing departments for every company he worked for. But he didn't, because he wanted that touch with the customer, the thrill of each individual sale. Of defeating that person's better instincts or common sense or frugality. And I guess I was the same in some way. Except I had a different agenda." He paused again, and I took a sip of my water, accidentally swallowing one of the ice cubes. I could feel its burning coldness all the way down and shivered in the hot restaurant.

"Ellen had such a passion about her; it was contagious. Thought I'd get the rest of you pretty easy."

"Greg."

"Surprised me," Turret answered, nodding. "The fact that I misjudged him used to bug me almost as much as getting caught."

"What about me?"

Turret hesitated. Picked up his napkin and wiped his hands with it.

"What about me?"

"You were the easiest in some ways. You'd go whichever way the wind blew. As the old song said."

It had been so obvious, even to a stranger.

"I don't get that impression anymore, if it makes any difference."

"It doesn't."

"Most of us change sooner or later. But it took me a long time in prison to realize how wrong I'd been. In the end I was no different than anybody else facing their own mortality. Death-row inmates with last minute conversions. People who suddenly see the light on their hospital deathbeds. I'm no better than any of them, and turning myself around was no saintly act, believe me." He shook his head. "If my lungs hadn't clogged up and almost killed me I would have taken that first parole and gone right back to what I knew best. Preying on people. Chewing them up and spitting them out."

I flashed on the dream I'd had the other night in the Palm Springs lockup. It was Turret in the boat with me, throwing a dead fish back in the water. Then I thought of what Tidwell had told me about Turret serving his whole term. "Is that why you didn't take parole? Some sort of penance?"

"Not really. I just wasn't ready yet. Maybe I sensed that I'd fall back into my old ways if I got out too soon. Then I had another attack and they transferred me out here. The desert air helped clear out my lungs."

"The cops thought you'd gone to El Paso," I told him.

Turret nodded. "That was my plan. I know some people that run a church there. Ex-cons like me. But I got off the bus in Niland. I guess the pull of this place was too strong. You remember the stories I told you." I nodded, surprised that he did. "You used to fish, didn't you?"

"Whitewater. My father took me when I was a kid."

"Memories of childhood innocence. Maybe I wanted to get back to that for a while." Turret snorted derisively. "Look at it now."

He was right. From a distance the water sparkled blue under the sun. But that was an illusion, a facade that hid the cancer beneath. How well did that describe Turret in his own youth? Or me?

"I'll be on that bus to El Paso come Saturday," Turret announced, and shrugged. "I guess the old saying is true. You can't go back." Except in your own mind, I thought. And that was probably a lie too; memories could be deceiving.

It was time to go. I looked at my watch and said, "We'll meet back here tomorrow afternoon. Late, maybe six. That okay with you?"

"Gimme a few extra hours. Say eight."

"Eight o'clock." As I got up Turret offered his hand, eyes on mine. I stared at it for a second, extended in peace, with a line of dried blood on the palm from the fishing line. Looked back up at his eyes. They didn't blink, just held mine.

I spoke slowly, making sure he understood. "Just because I'm accepting your help doesn't change anything between us. We're not partners and we're not friends, and I'll never have anything but contempt for you. Even if you hand me Deirdre's killer on a silver platter. Because as far as I'm concerned, this world would have been a better place without you. And the fact that doing this for me may help you sleep better at night makes me want to puke. God may have forgiven you, but I don't. When all this is over I hope you rot in hell."

I didn't wait for a response. Just walked out of the café into the pounding sunlight, feeling somehow diminished after my outburst. As if Turret, who'd apparently come to terms with his past, now pitied me. And worse, that I deserved that pity.

I stopped in the gravel parking lot, disoriented by the heat and my own impotent rage. Deirdre's car still sat in front of the ruined yacht club, waves of heat boiling from the hot metal. Across the way, closer to the RV park, was a small motel. A trim building of freshly painted clapboard with neatly pruned bougainvillea vines wandering over the fence in front. It looked like it had dropped out of the sky, curiously immune from the wasting disease all around it. Two stories, with a covered veranda wrapped around the upper level.

I checked in without asking how much the room was, then found a small laundry area off the lobby. Upstairs, I peeled off my sweat-soaked clothing. Wrapped in a bedsheet, I brought everything downstairs to wash. Back and forth in that white sheet, like a ghost drifting through the quiet building.

Later, after a shower and a greasy meal at the café, I took a seat outside on the upstairs gallery overlooking the water. The surface of the lake was gray and opaque in the deepening twilight, giving back none of the light from the emerging stars. Nothing moved or spoke. The only sound was the faint, unearthly hum of the desert as it settled down for the night.

What was Turret doing right now? Had he been able to contact his friend in prison? Did he now have information that would lead me to Deirdre's killer? I knew questions like those would keep me up half the night, which was why I was out here instead of in my room. I'd needed the open air of the desert to relax my mind. I pictured the empty panorama in front of me as a vast refuge for the uncertainties spinning in my head. The slowing pulse of the evening had a calming effect.

But I couldn't shut down completely. Something caught my eye in the east. Yellow slashes against the indigo sky. I realized what they were: fighter jets streaking over the Chocolates, tracers shooting earthward like diving birds of prey. The fireworks went on for a while, making me wonder about all the scrap lying out there waiting to be blown to bits—the old Jeeps and tanks the army dragged onto the range as targets. Some of that stuff was probably Vietnam era, and the thought brought me back to the crippled veteran in the wheelchair I'd met this morning, then my own sad association with that war. It was amazing the way the past kept reaching into the present. I imagined the explosions hidden deep within the mountains right now blowing away all those memories. Down to the right, between the disintegrating yacht club building and its crumbling hotel, beyond the broken concrete that looked like a choppy sea in the moonlight, was the spot next to the water where that girl had mistaken me for Turret.

How different had we really been back then at the height of the war? Maybe that's why I still hated Turret so much; I saw a different version of myself in him. Dishonesty and selfishness were our common bond. Turret had harnessed those qualities for his own criminal pursuits. I'd allowed those same qualities to be exploited by someone like Turret, and in me they were profound weaknesses. If I'd been able to admit to myself the real reasons I had for joining Turret, none of it ever would have happened.

My mind flew forward a few years, to my prison sentence. I remembered the way it had hardened and changed me, not only for my own survival inside but in deeper ways as well. At first I'd accepted that I deserved to be there and derived a certain peace from that. But as the months went by, things changed. Other than the brief periods of time with Walt in the prison shop, anger, mostly at myself, became a constant companion which only occasionally found release in violent disagreements with other prisoners. Once I was out that anger exhibited itself in more subtle though just as destructive ways. The other night in jail, when I'd thrown my cellmate off the one bench just to be nasty, was something I would have done in prison. But after my prison release I couldn't get away with stuff like that without landing right back inside. My bitterness found its way to the surface in more personal and hurtful ways. Determined never to be taken advantage of again, I used others instead, never giving an inch if it meant compromising my own desires. The way I'd acted toward my last girlfriend before moving out to the desert was typical. I remembered the look on her face in the car outside the abortion clinic, when she'd pleaded with me to reconsider my ultimatum and instead I'd just repeated it: the baby or me. Her face collapsed inward, tears streaming down her face as she got out of the car and told me that I could at least come in with her. But I'd handed over the cash for the procedure and said I'd be back in an hour, then drove off without looking back, heart hard as stone.

It was the last time I ever saw her. When I returned a few hours later after getting drunk in a bar, she wasn't on the sidewalk out front or in the waiting room inside. I asked the nurse about her and was curtly informed she'd left. Confidentiality prevented the nurse from divulging anything else, but the contempt in her eyes told me everything I needed to know. The procedure had been done, and the staff knew all about me.

I'd never told anyone about the incident, not even Deirdre.

I thought about Turret again. I'd tracked him down here without much trouble. He obviously hadn't been hiding. Which meant he wasn't involved in what had happened, or, for some reason, wanted to be found. His rap about seeing the so-called light bothered me. Sounded a little over the top. But then again, a lot of people with religious conviction came off that way. Was Turret trying to do the right thing now? Or did he have something more sinister in mind?

Prison conversions were a dime a dozen. Turret pretty much admitted that himself. Twelve-step programs all through the system. Give yourself to a higher power, make amends to the people you've hurt. Etc. I'd seen it more than a few times with fellow inmates, especially as they neared their release dates. Helped them deal with the outside. So Turret was either being sincere, which made him a walking cliché, or trying to manipulate me again to his own twisted ends.

There was only one way to find out: let whatever he was doing play itself out.

CHAPTER THIRTY-FOUR

The following day I slept through early afternoon, and woke up shivering under the covers. With the air conditioner on all night, the room was freezing. Condensation dripped down the window.

I turned the a/c off, showered, and made a pot of coffee on the in-room maker to settle in for the long wait. The hours dragged by, a succession of court shows and soap operas doing little to divert my attention. I checked my watch countless times, finally left around four for a hamburger across the street. Back in my room afterwards, I watched the shadows lengthen outside, the desert light fading from white to gold. If I'd been a smoker, I would have run out a long time ago. I paced the room back and forth, practically wearing a track through the carpet in front of the window.

A phone call came. Turret.

"How did you know I was here?" I asked.

"Saw you walk over there from the café," Turret replied.

Of course, I thought, embarrassed at my paranoia. "So did you find anything?"

"Nothing specific yet. But something is going on. One of the guys at Calipatria I talked to? Real gabber in prison, knows everybody, always has a story to tell. Well, this afternoon he couldn't wait to end the conversation. Seemed nervous talking to me, said he hadn't heard anything. Which I don't believe." A pause. "There's a couple other people I want to talk to. They're in a different cell block, so I gotta wait till after the hour. But we'll meet like we planned at about eight. That cool?"

"Who was the nervous guy?"

"The one I told you about. Did some work in New York a while back."

New York. I wondered if it could be a coincidence. Didn't think so. If Turret hit another dead end, I'd have to go to the cops, come clean about my trip there and tell them everything I'd learned. I'd see what Turret had to say when we met.

At five minutes to eight, I went down to the café. As usual, the place was empty. I just got a glass of water. The waitress gave me a dirty look, but I didn't care. Dead flies were still on the windowsill, a few more now than yesterday. The surface of the lake glinted silver, a frozen pool of mercury. Even the gulls seemed tired out, standing motionless on the shore.

Ten minutes passed. The headache I'd had since morning felt like it was getting worse. I massaged my temples, trying to calm the pounding in my skull, and rubbed my eyes. When I opened them again, the shadows outside were gone, another five minutes with them. A phone rang back in the kitchen. A few moments later, the waitress came by and dropped a piece of paper on the table.

"Why don't you order something?" she said, annoyed, before walking away.

Rod & Reel Restaurant, Salton Sea Beach was written on the paper she'd dropped. I left immediately, the twilight heat hanging in the air. A few minutes later, I pulled off the highway at Brawley Avenue, near a sign advertising the restaurant. It had a tall-masted ship riding blue waves over the word "Seafood." I crept by an abandoned motel on the way in, a painted brick structure resembling one of those restroom complexes you see in public parks. A block or so further, the restaurant sat in a dirt parking lot. A dusty satellite dish out front along with two cars. Across the street, next to the motel, a snarled clutter of deserted mobile homes, most of them barely standing. Some had entire sections of siding missing, as if they were slowly being dismantled for scrap wood. They leaned at odd angles to each other, reminding me of a movie studio backlot as I got out of the car and went into the restaurant.

It took a few seconds for my eyes to adapt. I was in a dark lounge area. Four or five booths with dark red vinyl seats arranged around several tables, with the bar at the far end. Two men sat on stools there, watching a baseball game playing on the TV behind the bartender. Turret was nowhere to be seen.

"Anywhere's fine," the bartender called out. I walked over to him and asked about Turret, describing him as I did so.

"Yeah, I know him. But he hasn't been here today." He wore a collared golf shirt and an expensive watch. Hair combed back in a casual pompadour.

"Know where I might find him?" I asked, sensing it start to slip away.

"You a friend of his?" one of the customers asked me around a toothpick in his mouth. His face was sunburned, except for around the eyes and a line going back to each ear.

"I was supposed to meet him here. It's important."

"He rented a trailer right down the road," the bartender said. "Little one with the green awning. Tell him I got a steak waiting for him after."

I thanked him and left, stopped outside the door to check out the street. A block over was a tiny trailer park behind a wood fence, a trellis curving over the center opening. I walked toward it, going by the ruined mobile homes I'd seen earlier, wondering if the car parked in the street behind me had been there before.

The green awning was the first one in. A round metal pod up on blocks, with no lights burning inside. I rapped on the door: no answer. Looked around. The place seemed pretty empty, except for the insects swirling around a porchlight a few trailers away.

"Hey. You in there? It's Ryder." Another knock, more silence. I put my foot on one of the metal steps and turned the knob. Jerked the flimsy door open, then stepped inside, having to duck my head a little bit.

It was even dimmer than the restaurant had been. I saw a faint human shape lounging on a couch to my right.

"You awake?" I said, reaching for the wall-light next to the door.

The trailer rocked, then someone pushed me into a small dinette table, where I knocked a plate of spaghetti to the floor. It landed with a wet plop, spraying sauce.

"How's it going?" the first one said. Another man squeezed in behind him. Turret still didn't move. Neither did I, with their guns pointed at me. "New York was fun, huh?" He looked over at Turret and asked, "Why did you shoot him?"

Turret was staring straight at me, unblinking, a dark red stain on his stomach. Suddenly I could smell the rusty scent of blood.

"You followed me out here?" I saw the back of a third man's head outside, keeping watch. His hair was red.

The guy closest to me shook his head. "Your friend oughtta know to keep his business to himself in the joint."

The prison grapevine. Turret must have let something slip about his stopover here. No wonder Turret's friend had acted all squirrely with him earlier. He'd given up Turret's location. Guys like these probably had connections all over the place.

"You going to kill me now?"

"No, Turret did that. He surprised you with this," he said, pulling out Turret's fillet knife.

"Why?"

"Your wife didn't tell you?"

There was nothing in this tiny space I could use as a weapon. "I didn't say that."

They looked at each other, and I launched myself toward the door. Two gunshots before I went through it, taking one of them with me and crashing into red-hair outside. Still on the ground, I grabbed his arm and pointed it toward the doorway, where the third man was about to shoot, and pressed his trigger finger. The man ducked back inside, bullets *thunking* into the metal, the talkative one trying to get his foot out from between the steps where it was caught. His gun was lying in the dust a few feet away. I slammed my elbow into red-hair's face and took off, gunshots cracking behind me. There was no way I'd make it back to the restaurant. I veered left into the mobile home graveyard, splinters exploding from the walls. I dove under one of them and scrambled through the dust, noticing for the first time the blood on my forearm. They were coming, footsteps crunching in the dirt. I got up, found a passageway between two trailers and squeezed through it.

"That way," I heard, and looked under another trailer. One pair of feet to my right, on the other side. I ripped off a loose piece of wood and swung it just as he came around the corner. The nail punched into his chest, and he went down with the gun. I grabbed it and heard one of his partners call for him just before I took his knee out. One bullet at close range. He let out a blood-curdling scream.

"Is that you, Don?" Nervous. "Fuck!"

"I called the cops," somebody yelled from the restaurant.

I went that way and saw the guy who'd tumbled out of the trailer with me limping toward their car, dragging his ankle. He turned toward me, raised his weapon. I pointed mine with two hands, but he fell flat on his back on the pavement before I got a shot off. He looked at me fearfully, pointing his gun in the air and telling me not to shoot.

"Don't fucking move," I yelled, inching forward. "Throw the gun away."

He tossed it a few feet, starting at another tortured cry from the man I'd shot in the knee. Red-hair dashed into the street thirty yards to my left, going for the car. I went after him, hoping to shoot out a tire or something. He reached the door, whirled around and fired. Then I had it coming from both sides. The man behind me was struggling to stand on his bad ankle, shooting wildly on unsteady legs. One shot hit red-hair in the shoulder, spraying blood and taking out the window as the bullet went through him. Glass rained down on the street and he staggered backwards, falling into the door before recovering. He pulled the door open, shooting my way without looking, got behind the wheel and roared off. Bad-ankle had emptied his gun, but he wasn't the one I wanted.

I gave it some gas when I hit the highway. A pair of taillights a few hundred yards up, weaving over the center divider. There were headlights coming on quickly, and he overcompensated, veering onto the shoulder, spewing dust before dropping out of sight. Pulling up moments later, I saw he'd plowed into a dirt channel at the side of the road. Horn blaring, steam billowing from the front where it crumpled into the dirt. The airbag had blown, a large dark circle visible on it. More blood ran down the seat onto the door-jamb. Touching what I thought was the wound on my forearm, I found that it was only tomato sauce.

Blood trailed into the brush, the drops glistening at my feet. Eventually, I lost them in the darkness. I wondered how far he could have gotten with the amount of blood he'd lost, but I kept going anyway, gun waving in my hand, the only sound the scratch of my feet in the dirt and the breath wheezing in and out of my lungs. The soil started getting more sandy, like the dunes further south where the recreational vehicles tore up the desert. I stopped and looked around. The unfiltered moonlight gave everything a ghostly cast that was otherworldly and gaunt. Hardy desert brush dotted my vision like febrile hallucinations. The highway noise had faded a while ago; I'd gone much farther than I planned.

It was time to go back. He'd probably already collapsed somewhere, and the cops would find him tomorrow morning. I went down into a shallow wash, where the going was easier, and started following it back toward the road. Suddenly, a quick rush of footsteps from the top of the embankment. A shadow darkened the starry sky as he hurtled downward and landed on me with a bone-jarring thud. He rolled off with a painful grunt, reaching for the gun that had flown out of my hand. I grabbed his ankle, pulled myself toward him and turned him over, throwing sand into his eyes. The next handful I ground into his nose and mouth, forgetting completely about the gun. The intimacy of this violent physical contact was exhilarating. He gagged and spat, head shaking from side to side, and the silver moonlight turned to red as I stuffed fistful after fistful of sand into his open mouth and nostrils.

Then I stopped. Cleared all the dirt away, caked with spittle and mucous. Stood up with the gun and listened to him gasping for air. He turned his head sideways and retched mud onto the ground.

"Hey," I said, kicking his leg. He didn't even open his eyes. I leaned over and squeezed his shoulder, hard. His scream pierced the warm night, and he sprang up halfway before easing back down.

"Tell me everything," I said, cocking the gun.

"You won't do it," he finally said. His hand went to his bloody shoulder. It still hadn't stopped.

"Maybe not. Maybe I'll just stand here and watch you bleed."

He looked at his hand, put it back on the wound. "It was your wife's son."

I almost dropped the gun. "What?"

"I set up the adoption. She used the money to get clean, start over."

The night pitched around me, like the deck of a ship. Dizzy, I staggered back a step before it all snapped into place. "Clayton?"

"I work for him," he said, nodding tiredly. "I used to be Deirdre's dealer way back when."

I squatted next to him. The moon was an unblinking eye high above. "Why did you kill the boy?"

He shook his head. "It was an accident. Wasn't even my gun."

"So what happened?"

"Come on, I'm bleeding to death here, man."

"You better hurry then."

He grimaced in pain, readjusted his hand over the bullet hole. "Clayton sent me out here to stop John from meeting his real mother. If the illegal adoption got out the election would be over. So I flew out, waited for him to show up–"

"You couldn't stop him before that?"

"We didn't know where he was, only that he was driving here with a friend. No credit card records of a flight or hotels. Maybe he did that on purpose so there'd be no trace of the trip. Maybe he just didn't have the money. His friend had a car, so . . ."

"How did he find Deirdre?"

"One of John's cousins spilled the beans about him being adopted. Bound to come out sooner or later. This cousin called Clayton after John left and apologized. It was the first we'd heard of it. Then we found Clayton's files had been gone through. John broke into them and found his original birth certificate with your wife's name on it."

"That information was from years ago. Where would–"

"Probably spent forty bucks on an Internet search, just like we did. Can find almost anybody nowadays."

I wondered why John hadn't called Deirdre first. Probably afraid she wouldn't want to meet him. Harder to shut the door face to face.

"What about the illegal adoption? Why not just go through an agency?"

"Clayton and his wife got tired of waiting. It could take years for a white baby. Plus, they'd been burned a couple times by women who changed their minds after giving birth. When I heard Deirdre was pregnant I thought we could make something work. Everything would have been fine if Clayton had shredded that birth certificate like I told him to."

"Why would he keep it?"

"I don't know, man. Because he's an arrogant bastard who thinks he's smarter than everyone. You'll have to ask him."

"Get back to that night."

"I tried to convince John not to go through with it. There was a lot he didn't know. Come back to New York and have it out with his dad, but don't do something rash now. I was trying to push him back to the car. His friend comes up and says to leave him alone. I tell him to mind his own business. He goes to the car and comes back with a piece. Little .22 popgun, probably shoots tin cans with it or some shit. Has the balls to point it at me. Sideways, like those gansta idiots in the movies—"

"Spare me the commentary, all right? Why didn't you just walk away?"

"Some punk threatens me with a gun, my first inclination is to teach him a little respect. Called me a goddamn Mick too." He lifted his bloody hand, checked his shoulder. Bleeding seemed to have slowed. "Anyway, we fight over it, John gets into the act and the gun goes off." He shook his head. "Twenty-two up top is bad. Bullet pinballs around in there because it ain't powerful enough to go straight through. I checked John's pulse, shook him a few times, but I knew he was dead. His friend took off like the punk he was."

"And you took everything from John so he wouldn't be identified. Including his motel key."

"I was trying to buy some time till we could figure out what to do. I looked around, expecting somebody to start yelling, but no

STEPHEN SANTOGROSSI

one did. And that kid didn't report anything either. Probably because it was his gun."

"But you were looking for him anyway."

"Couldn't risk him going to the cops. Kept on thinking he would, that he'd be on the news any minute, but it never happened."

"Why'd you wait almost two days to go to the Blue Bird?"

"That key didn't have the name of the place on it, just the room number." I nodded, remembering what I'd observed in the motel lobby. "But it was an actual key, not one of those credit card deals, so I knew it wasn't one of the chains. Kid probably high-tailed it already, but I had to make sure. I drove all over the place, checking out every two-bit dump I could find. Couldn't call ahead because I didn't want some nosy manager involved. So it took some time."

"And you were busy doing other things," I said. "Like getting those weapons you couldn't bring on the plane with you."

The man nodded, looking up at me.

"And scoring the dope you put into my wife."

He closed his eyes, like he was expecting a blow. Or a bullet. Somehow I restrained myself. My thoughts were racing, crashing into each other. Deirdre couldn't have known the boy was her son. But if he was identified–from New York, and the right age–it was only a matter of time.

"Deirdre was your idea. You knew about her past. That you could get away with it."

I didn't get an answer. The shot was impossibly loud, echoing among the foothills. The bullet flung sand into his face. He flinched, then looked back up at me, eyes shining with the moon's cold light. Somewhere a coyote howled, its cry plaintive and lonely in the hot night.

"I didn't want to."

"So why did you?"

"Clayton's backers . . . ," he started, shaking his head.

I put the gun to his head. "They're not here. I am."

"They'd spent a lot of money under the table on the campaign. We didn't have much of a choice. We didn't do things their way, they'd expose the black market adoption themselves. And make things bad with John's death."

"Who are they?"

"They're connected. I make it a point not to know exactly. I did my own bullshit stuff back in the day, but not on the same level as these guys. They're into a lot of things, have some powerful people in their back pockets." An ironic chuckle. "Thought I could go legit when Clayton hired me. But he had a few longtime acquaintants, you know? People that did favors for him early on, and expected to be repaid. With interest, so to speak."

"Really not interested in your problems, pal. How'd they know I was in New York?"

"We knew you had no idea who John was because it would've been all over the news. I was supposed to keep an eye on you, make sure you didn't find out what really happened. Thought I'd blown it when you disappeared after your wife . . ." He looked up at me uncertainly. "After your wife . . ."

I kicked him in the teeth and his head snapped back.

"That help?" I asked.

He spat out some blood, but no teeth, and tried to take it like a man. Continued.

"But then out of the blue, you come back home that night. I followed you to the airport. When you got on a flight for New York the next morning, I made a phone call. They were with you the moment you landed." More blood and spit, a dark silver dollar in the sand. "You got lucky with that story about Turret. Gave them a way to tie it up neatly. Otherwise you wouldn't have made it back here in one piece."

"What, some sort of fatal reckoning? Like we did each other in?"

"That was the idea."

His skin was shiny with sweat, and he shivered briefly. "I'm not doing so good here, man. You gonna leave me?"

"Take your belt off."

"What?"

"You heard me."

He got up to a kneeling position. Undid the buckle with one hand, then pulled it through the loops. Looked up at me expectantly when he was done.

"Stand up." He did, stepping back drunkenly before steadying himself. "Put it back on, loosely. Don't use the loops." I watched him do it. "Slide the buckle around to the back."

When he'd done that, I stuck the gun in my pants and pulled his arms behind him, none too gently. "Fuck!" he said through clenched teeth, as I put his hands together under the belt and tightened as hard as I could. "You got the gun, man."

"Where's yours?"

He shook his head. "In the fuckin' car."

I pushed him forward. "Start walking."

We didn't speak on the way back. All of it was hitting me at once. How mentioning Turret had actually saved my life. Then Deirdre, and the way I'd shut her down the other day after the police interrogation. Maybe she wouldn't be dead if that conversation had run its course. Maybe she would have found the courage to finally tell me about having a baby all those years ago. There was no escaping my own culpability. I was drowning in regret, following Deirdre's killer through the sand that had once been at the bottom of an ancient lake. The gravel crunched under our feet, and I thought of the tiny fishbones being ground into dust on the shoreline of the Salton Sea.

Up ahead, the stars twinkled above the highway and the lake I couldn't see, and the lights of the towns next to it glowed faintly in the eastern sky. I wondered how long those marks of civilization—streetlamps and store signs and house lights—would continue to shine, as the allure of the sea that had once supported them steadily diminished. Then the white light became pulsing flashes of blue and red, and I knew the police had found our cars.

WHITE WATER

CHAPTER THIRTY-FIVE

Friday afternoon, four days after it ended, I woke up in a blazing shaft of sunlight. The bedroom window was open and the heat of the silent desert invaded the room. I turned over, groggy with too much sleep and unsure of how I would make it through another day. The last few had been a haze of loneliness and depression.

I got out of bed, stumbled to the shower and turned the water on all the way cold. The phone rang in the bedroom just before I stepped under the spray. For some reason I decided to answer this time, not bothering to turn the water off.

"Is this . . . is this Tim Ryder?" the caller asked.

Soft, hesitant. I knew exactly who it was. "You're John's friend."

For a moment I thought he'd hang up. "I just . . . I don't know why I called. I guess I wanted to say I'm sorry."

"For what?"

"Everything that happened. Your wife." His breath hitched in his throat. "I'm the one that started it all."

"What do you mean?"

"I convinced John to come out here. Never knew my own parents, so I know what it's like, wondering. John wouldn't admit it, but I could tell why he wanted to drive. So he'd have plenty of time to change his mind. But he didn't. And then, that night . . ."

I sat down on the edge of the bed, listened.

"I shoulda left the gun in the car. But that guy, Anderson, wouldn't leave John alone."

"You knew him?"

"I'd seen him before, around John's parents' place. John told me his dad would be pissed if he knew what he was doing. So it didn't really surprise me to see Anderson there. I just wanted to get rid of him. Didn't think he'd grab the gun."

"Was it yours?"

"I found it in an alley behind where I used to live. I just . . . liked it. Always kinda kept it nearby. I guess that's why I brought it. Kept the stupid thing under the seat. John didn't even know I had it."

A long pause. I waited.

"I panicked when the gun went off. Just . . . lost it. Anderson was shaking him, but I knew it was no use."

"Why didn't you report it? Call an ambulance or something?"

"I know. I know. I wasn't thinking straight, afraid I'd go down for it. But I stuck around anyway, trying to make it right somehow. Then your wife–"

"You were in my house that morning," I said, seeing him speed away in that car as I'd run home. "You knew she was dead before I did."

"I finally decided to tell her it was her son, if she didn't know already, and whatever happened after that, I could live with. But they got to her before I did." He stifled a sob, took a deep breath.

"Where are you calling from?"

"I was there the other day. At the funeral."

"You were? At the cemetery? I didn't–"

"Those cops scared me off. But I guess it was too late by then anyway." Another sob.

I wanted to tell him it wasn't his fault, that it had really begun years earlier. But he probably wouldn't believe me. I remembered what Branson told me about his wife's miscarriage, how she'd blamed herself. Guilt could be a tough thing to shake.

"They got everybody," I said. "Even the doctor that signed the fake birth certificate." It occurred to me that Deirdre would probably be in some trouble if she were alive. But I knew she'd done what she thought was best at the time.

"They're probably looking for me."

"Turn yourself in."

Silence. I tried again. "Just tell them what happened. If you don't, this will be hanging over your head for the rest of your life. Believe me, you don't want that."

No response.

"It's up to you," I said, then thought of something. "Do you smoke?"

"Yeah. Why?"

"Never mind. You take care. And think about what I said."

I hung up the phone and got into the shower. The shocking blast of freezing water at first felt burning hot, literally taking my breath away. The world disappeared for a second, then returned brighter than before.

Later, I made some breakfast. Washed the dishes and put them back in the cabinet when I was done. Stepped outside into a blanket of clear sunshine. Everything I looked at seemed new, as if a lens in front of my eyes had been cleaned and focused. The San Jacintos stood out sharply against the porcelain sky, and the flowers in my neighbor's yard suffused the air with color and scent.

I got in the car and drove west toward Beaumont, where Deirdre was buried. The freeway kept to the northern edge of the pass, hugging the sides of the San Bernardino foothills as it rose from the valley floor.

It reached its highest point at the Whitewater turnoff and there, without thinking, I exited the freeway and pulled up to the stop sign overlooking the interstate. If I turned right, the two-laned road would take me past a concrete company, then into the San

Gorgonio wilderness. Eventually it would end at the Whitewater Dam, where I'd fished as a kid. On the other side, the road descended to the desert floor, traversed the sandy bottom of the pass and crossed over the Southern Pacific tracks before meeting Highway 111 into Palm Springs.

I made the left, parked at the side of the road a few hundred feet below the highway, and got out. A hot, dusty wind whistled through the pass and gave motion to the massive wind farm windmills rotating silently in the heat. One hadn't started up. Its three blades were frozen in place, conjuring a '60s peace symbol from the memories of my past.

I looked away, to the Whitewater riverbed below me. Sometimes, driving by on the highway, you'd see swimmers who'd ignored the fence and the warning sign wading in the cool water that flowed briskly over the rocks toward Palm Springs. But the river was dry right now, with rocks and large boulders strewn along its banks and weeds poking through the cracks in the parched soil. I stepped closer to the fence, trying to read the sign. Some of its lettering had been sandblasted away by the windblown dust.

DANGER!
NO SWIMMING ALLOWED

THIS CHANNEL IS SUBJECT TO SUDDEN FLASH FLOODS AND UNANNOUNCED OUTFLOWS FOR IRRIGATION PURPOSES. CURRENT MAY BE DANGEROUSLY STRONG.

COACHELLA VALLEY WATER DISTRICT

Cars whizzed by on the freeway above. Semis lumbered over the hot concrete, flinging highway grit into the air. The wind gusted stronger now, rattling the fence and the metal sign hanging from it, and blew my hair into my eyes. It pushed at my back and whipped my shirt violently. I looked past the sign and saw the valley spread out in front of me behind the chain-link fence.

I reached up, hooked my fingers through the latticework and pulled myself up. The flimsy fence shook precariously under my weight. Straddling the top, I rested a moment while the twinge in my abdomen subsided, then hoisted my other leg over and jumped down to the opposite side. One of the jagged wires at the top caught the inside of my wrist on the way down and ripped a bloody track in my forearm. I landed and rolled in the dust, scraping the wound painfully against the ground. Got up and brushed the blood-moistened dirt away, ignoring the pain.

I made my way carefully over the rocks lining the riverbed, to the caked and hardened soil below. I started walking away from the freeway with no destination in mind, following the line the water had cut through the desert. The sun beat down harder than ever, reflecting off the banks and the hardpan at my feet, and the wind did little to cool the sweat on my body.

I heard a faint rumbling above the noise of the freeway and the moan of the wind, and wondered if the mountain was speaking, shedding large chunks of itself, or if the earthquake faults in the vicinity were trembling and shaking once again.

When I turned around it was already too late, and I barely had time to steel myself against the onrushing water. It was knee-high, white and foaming as it slid over the rocks faster than lightning, a raging torrent that knocked me down and bore me away, kicking and floundering, while I struggled to keep my head above the surface. I swallowed lungfuls of cold water, the swift current tossing me back and forth.

I felt a jagged rock at the river bottom slice across my ribs and another one cut into my thigh, and prayed for a way to save myself. Up ahead, through the white spray of water, I could make out a sharp bend in the river, a split-second glimpse, before my head went under. Then my weight and momentum shot me up onto the rocks at the side of the river, where I was plastered like a piece of wet laundry on a large boulder, clinging for life as the water roared past.

I choked and gagged violently, expelling the water from my lungs onto the warm stone beneath me–solid, blessed earth–turned my head up to the bright blue sky, and breathed in deeply the hot desert air.

AUTHOR'S NOTE

Astute readers may have noticed several liberties I took in the telling of this story. Calipatria Prison is a state prison, not a federal prison. Also, I slightly modified part of Manhattan for my own purposes and depicted the Palm Springs area of a few years ago, not the vastly expanded and more populated Coachella Valley of today.